DRIVE TO KILL

FBI MYSTERY THRILLER

DEAN BLACKWOOD
BOOK 1

SAM JONES

INTRODUCTION

LAPD has a name for cop killers: Dead Men Walking.

No trial.

No shot at parole.

Zero chance they live to see tomorrow.

So when the case comes across my desk, I know time is running out.

When a cop is killed, all hell breaks loose, and guys like me get called in.

And this case might cost me everything.

I'm what they call a specialist.

Army Rangers training, 6'3", and a photographic memory.

And a special set of skills meant for doing one thing.

But this isn't an ordinary serial killer.

And I'm no ordinary FBI agent.

New mission: Hunt down LA's most notorious cop killer and bring him in -- dead or alive.

PROLOGUE
LONG BEACH, CALIFORNIA

The sirens grew louder.

Red and blue lights flooded in through the windows.

Dean Blackwood, his finger easing down on the trigger of his SIG, glared at the man who murdered his brother.

He deserves to die, he thought.

The bastard that killed Tommy finally ran out of places to hide.

"*Kill him*," the voice in Dean's head whispered. "You've been waiting for this your whole life. What are the chances, laddie? This is fate right here. Just end him and avenge Tommy's death once and for all."

Dean's nostrils flared.

The expressionless murderer caressed the trigger of his Beretta. "Your son is about to die, Blackwood," he said, his left arm hooked around Jeremy Blackwood's neck, his left hand pressing a Beretta against the boy's temple. "And I'm going to make you watch. I can live with being in a cell," his eyes glinted darkly, "but I know you can't live with *this*."

Dean clenched his teeth.

The man who killed his brother smirked.

A single tear rolled down Jeremy's cheek.

"Pally," Dean whispered to his child, "don't look."

His son closed his eyes.

His captor depressed his trigger.

Dean held his breath and did the same.

1

Two weeks earlier...
Salem, Oregon

Kicking some dude's ass out of a bar wasn't how Dean Blackwood thought he would be spending his morning, but when his AA buddy Sheriff Riggins asked for help, saying no wasn't an option.

Twenty minutes after Riggins called, Dean walked into the bar, his boots crunching the beer bottle fragments. He saw the wet trails of beer sliding down the walls, the horrified patrons looking anywhere except at the deranged jackass sitting at the bar who was responsible for the mess.

Dean flicked his eyes toward the bouncer who was holding an ice pack to his cheek. "Bar's closed," the bouncer said. "We're waiting for the cops to get here."

Dean slipped a nicotine toothpick between his teeth the moment he smelled whiskey. The nicotine helped keep the alcoholic cravings at bay, but it did fuck-all in keeping the voice of his subconscious from chiming in.

"One drink won't kill ya, laddie," Woody, the leprechaun voice in Dean's head, beckoned. "You can handle it."

No, Dean told the voice in his head. *Now screw off.*

"Hey, buddy," the bouncer said again. "I said we're closed."

"Sheriff Riggins sent me."

"Where is he?"

"He's outside chowin' down on a chocolate Danish. He should know better. The man's prediabetic."

"*Right,*" the bouncer grunted as he appraised Dean's jeans, T-shirt, and leather jacket. "You don't look like one of his deputies."

"I'm not."

"What are you, then?"

"Just a pal of his." Dean motioned to the bouncer's swollen cheek. "Nice shiner, by the way."

"Dude got a load on and just started swinging at people." The bouncer motioned to the patrons huddled in a corner. "It was fucking wild. I tried kicking him out, but he went apeshit. Pretty sure he's hopped on something else other than a few beers, if ya know what I mean."

Dean sized up the guy at the counter. The dude had a bad knee—*right there with you, bud*—arms like oak logs, and a wild look in his eye like he was ready to start swinging again.

"I'll talk to him."

"Have at it," the bouncer said, "but if he fucks you up, that's on you."

"Noted," Dean replied coolly as he approached the brute seated at the bar and posted up beside him. Conrad Twitty's "Hello Darlin'" trickled softly through the jukebox in the corner as the drunk guy raised his belligerent gaze toward him.

The guy clenched a fist.

The customers shuddered.

Dean propped his elbows on the counter. "So," he said, his eyes probing the destruction around him, "shit night, huh?"

"Get lost, stretch." The guy narrowed his swollen, red, manic eyes. "I'm not in the mood."

"Yeah." Dean's nostrils flared at the chemical scents wafting off the man's tongue. "I can tell." Dean shifted his weight. "Maybe we should take this outside, talk it through, and get some fresh air. What do you think?"

"You a cop?"

"Kind of."

"What the fuck does 'kind of' mean?"

Dean took out his snap-button wallet, opened it, and held the FBI shield nestled inside up to the light.

"FBI," the guy groaned. "That supposed to scare me or something?"

"Usually does."

"Not me." The guy took a swig of his drink. "Now leave me alone." He nodded to the door. "I'm waiting for the sheriff to get here."

"Funny you should mention that."

"What's funny about it?"

"The fact that Riggins sent me here." Dean gestured over his shoulder. "He's out in the parking lot right now."

"What are you?" the guy said. "Joe Concerned Citizen? His fuckin' errand boy?"

Dean opted out of telling the guy he was a fellow Alcoholics Anonymous patron with the sheriff, one recovering addict willing to help out another. "He just had a feeling that you're trying to pull a whole suicide-by-cop bit," he said. "He sent me in here to try to talk you down. I mean," he stepped closer to the drunk guy, "based on your repeated disregard for the law, *Ronald*, I take you for a man who's looking for someone to put him down because he can't do it himself."

The guy—*Ronald*—squinted curiously. "Knowing my name doesn't mean you know anything about me, shithead."

"True," Dean said. "But the quick look I had at your record told me a lot. You were recently terminated from your job at Parr Lumber. You're divorced with one kid, a daughter. I also know you've got ten grand in back taxes, your house is being repossessed, and in the past six months you've been hauled in repeatedly for public intoxication and destruction of property."

The color drained from Ronald's face. "How the hell did you know all of that?"

"I told you. I saw your record."

"When?"

"Two minutes ago."

"And how in Jesus Christ's name," Ronald said, "did you remember all that?"

"I've got a good memory." Dean tapped the side of his head. "If I wanted to, I could recite your whole jacket word-for-word."

"Bullshit."

"Straight fact."

"Friggin' *con man* crap is what that is." Ronald backed away from Dean. "Bunch of parlor tricks or something."

"It's called eidetic memory, actually." Dean snagged his badge from off the counter. "But I'm not here to waste time with you on needless exposition. You're going to walk outside with me and take a ride to the sheriff's station." He pinched a pair of twenties out of his wallet and placed them on the counter. "Don't worry about the bill."

"What's door number two look like?" Ronald took a pull of the whiskey, slammed the bottle down, and took up a fighter's stance. "You kicking my ass with some fancy FBI moves?"

"Army Rangers moves, actually." Dean removed his toothpick and placed it on a napkin. "And they're a lot more nifty than the FBI ones."

"Badass soldier boy, huh?" Ronald puffed his chest. "I could take six of you Army pussies on at the same time."

"I'd like to avoid that, Ronald," Dean said. "I don't like putting my hands on people."

Seconds ticked by as Ronald sized up Dean, his alcohol-drenched mind sifting through his options.

"Kick his arse," Woody suggested to Dean. "Pop him one right across the mouth. Don't think—just do it!"

I've got this, Woody.

Now kindly fuck off.

"Let's make this easy, boss," Dean said to Ronald. "If you walk out with me right now, nothing else happens. I'll even have a cup of coffee with you at the station. You can talk until you're blue in the face. I get it—you're pissed off at life, you went on a bender, and it spiraled out of control. Happens to the best of us."

"You don't know shit," Ronald said, his eyes glossy, his bottom lip trembling. "You don't know what it's like to lose your job and your family."

"Believe me," Dean said. "I do. But I mean it, brother." He held up his hands. "Let's put a stop to this before it goes sideways."

A handful of seconds ticked by.

Ronald's fingers curled into a fist.

Then Dean tapered his eyes, watched Ronald throw a jab toward his face, and caught it one-handed.

Dean applied pressure to Ronald's knuckles, fractured them, and heard a bellow slip out of Ronald's lips as the guy cradled his busted hand.

"*Fuck!*" Ronald screamed as he drew back his fist to take another jab. "I'm gonna rip your—"

Dean planted a fist into Ronald's sternum, watched him double over, hooked his left leg behind right leg, and shoved him to the floor.

"All right," Dean grunted. "You done?"

A howling Ronald shot to his feet and dashed toward Dean like some kind of Looney Tunes character, screaming at the top of his lungs.

Dean stepped around Ronald and spun on his heel. As Ronald did an about-face, Dean grabbed him by the collar and headbutted him. The impact broke the guy's nose. His legs buckled. Then his consciousness faded as his body dropped to the floor like a rock.

Silence settled over the scene.

Dean shook his head and picked up his toothpick.

Then he apologized to the bartender, grabbed a slumbering Ronald by his collar, and dragged his body outside.

"I told you, man," Dean said as he kicked open the door and nodded to the sheriff and his deputies. "I don't like putting my hands on people."

2

"Well," Riggins said as Dean yanked open the door to his F-350, "thanks again, kid. I owe you one."

"I'm keeping score." Dean slid behind the wheel, the chilled breeze blowing through the pines and licking his skin. "Putting a guy to sleep wasn't on my list of things to do today, chief. Count yourself lucky that we're part of the same fraternity."

"Just one AA member looking out for another, yeah?"

"Exactly."

"Horse shit. You're a good guy, Deano. You never leave people hanging." Riggins smirked. "Plus, it *had* to feel good putting that maniac on his ass. Don't tell me it didn't."

Dean turned over the engine, saluted with two fingers to the sheriff, and backed out. Moments later, his truck was cruising up the highway flanked with Douglas fir and cottonwood trees. His radio was tuned to a soft rock station as he drove for close to an hour to Hamilton Mountain before arriving at his cabin in the woods.

Dean put the vehicle in park, stepped out, and surveyed his slice of paradise10 acres of solitude nestled in the forest without a single neighbor in sight. Beyond his cabin was a million-dollar view of the Washougal River that sliced through the terrain, the area blanketed with fog that capped the cedar, maple, and fern trees peppering a range that spanned miles.

Dean breathed in the brisk air and grinned at the thought that in twenty-four hours' time, he'd be with his son Jeremy. It was a reunion long overdue in his mind. At the rate Jeremy was growing, Dean worried that he was missing out on too many milestone moments in his son's life.

But that was on him.

His drinking.

The bad decisions he made that forced him to hit the reset button, sober up, and get his act together so he could be the father—the *man*—he needed to be.

Dean had to thank his ex-wife for that one. Had Claire not insisted that he make a few tough decisions with his life, chances were high he would've been buried in a cemetery beside his mother by now.

"Yo, Deano!" Bazz's gruff voice called out from inside the cabin. "That you?"

Dean approached his home, a rustic one-story cabin once used as a base camp for fish and wildlife hunters before he took it over. After he pushed open the thick wooden door, he saw Willy seated on his rear in the foyer, the blue heeler wagging his tail furiously as he greeted his owner with a yelp. The dim light from an ancient lamp beside him cast long shadows.

"At ease, boy," Dean said as stooped down and scratched the mutt behind his ears. "What have you been up to, huh? You haven't been doing a damn *thing*, have you?"

In the small, traditional kitchen on Dean's left, he spotted Clifford Bazz, his buddy and—more importantly—

AA sponsor who was in the process of stocking the shelves with food.

"Where are you keeping the mustard?" Bazz said. "I'm looking to fire up that grill of yours tomorrow."

Dean patted Willy on the back, stood, and wandered into the kitchen. "If you're trying to throw a house party while I'm gone," he said, "I'll bust that toaster over there upside your head."

The fifty-some-odd-year-old guy built like an offensive line coach belted out a chuckle. "*Try it*, fuckwit." He wiped his palms on his oversized Hawaiian shirt. "I'll break you in half. And it's just gonna be me and Willy here for the next week. Last thing I want is company, unless you count the peace and quiet."

"I hear you." Dean opened the sliding back door in the living room so Willy could dash outside to relieve himself. Dean slipped off his jacket and tossed it on the faded couch.

"You pick up that charcoal?" Bazz said. "Grill's not going to be much good without it."

"It's in the truck."

"You plan on bringing it in or what?"

"You've got legs." Dean opened the fridge and snagged a water bottle. "Use 'em."

"You good?" Bazz asked as he shoved some boxes of cereal in one of the cupboards. "You're acting like you just got kicked in the nuts."

"I'm aces, brother," Dean said. "Sitting on cloud nine."

"Said *no* man who's about to spend the weekend with his ex-wife," Bazz chuckled. "Heck, if I were in your shoes, I'd be pacing the floor like Willy out there."

"I'm good. More excited than anything else. I'm nervous about the whole thing, yeah, but seeing Jeremy," Dean's lips bowed up into a proud smile. "I'm just stoked that I get to spend some time with my boy."

"How long's it been?"

"Eight months."

Bazz whistled. "Long time."

"Yeah." Dean flexed his brow. "Too long. I'm planning on talking to Claire when I get out there about coming back on a permanent basis."

"Think she'll go for it?"

"I hope so." Dean whistled with two fingers at Willy to come inside. "I haven't touched a drink in three years. I just need to talk to Wilson about getting a desk job out there at the LA field office."

"Is that possible?"

"The way he made it out, yeah."

"Outstanding," Bazz said. "As much as I hate the idea of you leaving me behind, I'd be glad that you'd be back on your home turf."

"Come with me."

"Negative." Bazz shook his head. "Not a big fan of LA. Too many weirdos out there, yourself included." He laughed. "You've come a long way, brother. I'm sure Claire will see that too. Just stick to your resolve. And if you run into a problem, if you feel like you're going to take a drink, just call me up. Willy and I will be holding the place down until you get back."

Before Dean could answer, his cell phone buzzed inside his pocket. "Wilson" flashed on the display—his former boss, Special Agent in Charge of the Los Angeles FBI field office, *and* the guy who inspired the name of the mutt that had just dashed back inside the cabin.

Dean tightened his grip on the phone.

Based on the way his stomach was knotting, he *knew* it was a call he didn't want to take.

3

"Deano," Wilson greeted. "How are you, kid?"

"I'm doing all right," Dean said as he stepped out onto the back porch. "You?"

"Hanging in there."

"How's the sunshine?"

"Los Angeles is a dirty city," Wilson said, "but at least the weather makes up for it."

"I'm looking forward to it." Dean took a long hard look at the densely forested area beyond the cabin. "It's nothing like the greenery out here though. Not enough time has passed to take it for granted yet."

"Must be nice," Wilson said. "Being in the concrete jungle out here takes its toll after a while. Maybe we should trade places for a couple of months."

"It's the Bureau's cabin technically." Dean shot a look over his shoulder and saw Bazz hauling in the bag of charcoal he bought,Willy following hot on his heels. "The way I see it, you could probably post up here any time you want to."

"It's *your* place, pal," Wilson said. "You earned it. Make no mistake about it."

Dean recalled Wilson saying the same thing when he showed him the cabin. He was three weeks sober by that point with his arm in a sling and a pair of welts on his chest from where his Kevlar had absorbed a pair of 9mm rounds during his last undercover gig. Dean nearly bought the farm that night in El Paso, a memory he still remembered—like all the others—in vivid, 4K resolution.

"Listen," Dean said. "I'm planning on stopping by to see you after I get settled. I'll be in town for a week, so I've got plenty of time to pop by the office. I was hoping we could talk about me making the transition back to LA."

"That, uh," Wilson huffed. "That's actually what I wanted to talk to you about."

I knew it. Dean shook his head. *There's always a catch.*

"We just caught wind of something in the field out here," Wilson rambled on. "Last night an off-duty member of the LAPD got turned into roadkill on the Pacific Coast Highway near Santa Monica. His name was Mike Vendrell. He was a detective attached to a special investigations unit."

"Why are the Feds looking into a traffic collision?"

"The orders came through the Hoover Building in DC. Straight from the top. They've ordered my office to look into the matter."

Dean furrowed his brow. "What does that have to do with me?"

Wilson took a beat. "They asked me to bring *you* in, Deano. They didn't say why, but they've ordered me to have you take a look at what happened and offer your assessment."

"I don't understand." The gears in Dean's brain turned.

"Why is the brass so concerned about the death of an LAPD officer?"

"I'm not sure. All I know is that they want my office to take the assignment, and they want you to take a look through the scene and provide your insights."

"I don't really work crime scenes, Willy."

"You've got a knack for it. Your instructors at Quantico said so. You come from a long line of cops, so it's no surprise."

"But why me?" Dean shrugged. "The Bureau has plenty of other—"

"Kid," Wilson said, "I'm not sure. We all have our orders here, and yours is to get to LA and offer an assessment of the scene. Just go to the crime scene, flash your badge, ask a few questions, and tell me what you think. It'll go a long way with these transition talks we've been discussing."

The scars covering Dean's body, ones he received during his time with the Bureau, began to sear. "I'll give you a couple of hours," he said. "That's all. Once I'm done, I'm done."

"Fair enough," Wilson said. "I'll forward you the details."

"Copy that." Dean switched the phone to his other ear. Anything else I should know about before I finish packing my bags here?"

"As a matter of fact, yeah. There was an anonymous call made to our field office after Vendrell was killed. Someone phoned in and told us we should look into the matter. They also stated that we cannot and *should* not trust the LAPD."

"Intriguing."

"A little bit," Wilson said. "We're working on trying to trace the call right now. Might take some time. Until then, just get to the scene, take a look at it, and get back to me."

"Will do. Talk soon."

After Dean ended the call, he headed inside, informed Bazz about the new task Wilson had assigned him, and went about snagging his luggage.

"*Grizzly,*" Bazz said. "Dead cop got turned into roadkill on a highway?"

"Whatever it is," Dean said as he placed his bags down in the foyer, "it's a Wilson problem. The guy hooked me up with this cabin and a steady paycheck, so the least I can do is take a look at the scene for him."

"Just a look?"

"Just a look." Dean snapped his fingers, called Willy over, and got down on one knee. "I'm in LA for my kid, not some dead cop." He patted the mutt on his back. "As soon as I take a once-over of the case, I'm out."

"Well," Bazz motioned around the living room, "your guy Wilson did give you a pretty sweet setup here. Then again, you did earn it by dodging a few bullets more than once for the Bureau. The way I see it, you don't owe them a goddamn thing."

"Wilson's good people." Dean scratched Willy behind the ears, the blue heeler looking sad because he knew his owner was leaving. "He's helped me out more than a handful of times."

"He also put you in one high-stakes situation after another where you nearly got your head blown off."

"I made my own choices. Besides, if I'm planning on moving back to LA, looking into this thing for Wilson will help grease the wheels."

"I'm just saying," Bazz held up his hands, "your old life at the Bureau nearly got you killed. Wilson played a big role in that. It just bugs me that the guy thinks he can call you up and ask for favors."

Dean said nothing.

"You were a wreck of a human being when I first met you, brother," Bazz went on. "A lot of that had to do with your old job. I just don't want to see you taking up old habits again, that's all."

"I'm not," Dean said. "I've put in too much work to salvage my relationship with that kid, and I'm not gonna screw it up for anyone. Not Wilson, not the FBI. Hell," he winked, "not even you."

"In that case, safe travels, chief." Bazz slapped his hand into Dean's and clapped him on the shoulder. "Say hi to that kid for me."

Minutes later, Dean was on the road, his thoughts fixated on Jeremy and the memories they would make together that weekend. By the time he was on the flight inbound to Los Angeles, a series of PDFs had been sent to his phone from Wilson—files pertaining to the case of the (late) Mike Vendrell.

The first attachment Dean opened was a picture of the dead cop's body, tattered and mauled and positioned on a metal slab in the coroner's office. Flesh had been ripped clean off the man's torso, arms, and legs. His bones were exposed, and half of his face looked as though it had been peeled off with a cheese grater.

As Dean gazed at the photo, the primal part of his brain screamed that the whole thing was personal. He was certain beyond a shred of a doubt that Wilson's hunch of the whole thing *not* being an accident was right on the money.

4

D ean turned his gaze down to the photo he had viewed on the plane, a snapshot the coroner had taken of the deceased, Detective Mike Vendrell, the night before. Saltwater-laced air teased his nostrils, the crash of the ocean tides off to his left howling like the primal growl of a predator as he gazes at the highway.

A portly detective, his gut hanging over his belt, approached and twisted his lips into a sneer. "You Blackwood?"

"Yep."

"Cosgrove." The detective didn't offer his hand. "Been waiting for five hours for you to show up."

"Sorry for the holdup."

"Yeah? My ass." Cosgrove shook his head. "You Feds really have a knack for dicking up the works, you know that?"

"More often than not." Dean glanced at the detective. "How long have you been on the job?"

"Twenty-two years," Cosgrove said. "And you're the fifth suit I've had to deal with during that time. I'm sure I'll get my ass chewed out for saying it, but I'm sick and tired of you Bureau punks hijacking investigations."

"*Bureau punks*." Dean laughed. "I like that. You make me feel like I'm in a *Dirty Harry* flick when you start talking like that."

"Oh, yeah? You like that?" Cosgrove spit on the pavement. "Get *fucked*, agent man."

"Look, I'm not looking to keep you any longer than I have to, detective." Dean held up his hand. "I just wanna know what happened here last night. A few questions and then I'm out."

After Cosgrove took a breath to calm down, he shrugged. "Pretty straightforward hit and run. Guy who did this probably got a load on, took the turn, and hit the vic before he had a chance to slow down."

"You think?"

"I *know*."

"Okay, walk me through it then."

The groaning detective motioned to the restaurant hugging the highway behind him. "Witnesses said the vic came out of the restaurant around 6:30 p.m. last night," he said. "Vic ran toward his car parked over there." He nodded toward a stretch of the highway a few paces from the front doors of the restaurant. "But then someone in some red beater creamed him before he could fish out his keys."

"What kind of car was he driving?" Dean said. "The vic?"

"Mercedes S class."

"Fancy." Dean put his focus on the restaurant behind him: Nobu Malibu, a five-star, ocean-view joint built into the cliffside, the kind of place—according to the menu he pulled up on his phone—a cop on Vendrell's detective salary would only dish out for if he was trying to impress a date.

"Neat place," Dean said. "Cheapest appetizer they got costs around thirty bucks."

"So what? Decs make around 107 a year before taxes." Cosgrove pressed his thumb into his chest. "*I* make that much."

"Guys like you don't really spring for infinity pools on that kind of salary."

"You getting to a point here, Agent Blackwood?" Cosgrove's nostrils flared. "Or are you just being an asshole for the sake of being an asshole?"

"I'm not saying Vendrell couldn't afford to spring for a meal at a place like this," Dean said. "I'm just saying this is the kind of place meant for a date with a wife or girlfriend, and Vendrell was there by himself, not to mention the fact that he rolled up in a Benz."

Cosgrove grunted, waved Dean off, and turned away.

"The car that hit the vic," Dean said, "what did it look like?"

"Red," the detective said. "Older model. Compact. No one got a good look at the thing, but we've got units scrambling all over the area trying to find it."

Dean surveyed the PCH, two cramped lanes. He fixated on the spot where Vendrell had been run over, a tight, hairpin turn. "This stretch of road is pretty narrow," he said. "Any sober driver would be riding his brakes while they're going through it."

"So?"

"Takes some precision driving to run a guy over without running off the road."

"Maybe the guy driving the car was lucky."

"Maybe." Dean eyeballed the front of the restaurant. "Surveillance footage?"

The detective shook his head. "Negative. No cell phone

footage, nothing like that. All we've got is an eye-witness statement from the owner. He was by the entrance when it happened. He's the only one who saw the whole thing go down."

"What's his name?"

"Kristoff."

"First or last name?"

Cosgrove shrugged. "He just goes by Kristoff."

"LA, man," Dean whispered under his breath. "You gotta love it."

Sean made his way toward the restaurant on his left and walked inside. The whole place was cleared out save for a man with a silver ponytail dressed in Gucci clothing who was pacing the floor as he wrung his fingers to relieve the tension.

Dean produced his badge. "You Kristoff?"

"Yes." The wide-eyed restaurant owner spun around and faced Dean. "Yes, this is my restaurant. I'm Kristoff."

"Special Agent Blackwood. Mind if I talk with you for a minute?"

Kristoff gestured to the hallway, rubbing his hands together in a bid to stave off the shakes tremoring through his body. "This isn't right," he said, "keeping me here like this." He tensed his jaw muscles. "I had tickets for the Philharmonic tonight—Yo-Yo Ma, front row orchestra seats."

"That's a shame," Dean said. "One time I got passes for a Stone Temple Pilots concert at the KROQ Weenie Roast, but I got too blitzed to go. I ended up having to eat the 150 bucks I threw down for the passes."

Kristoff flattened his palm across his chest. "Is that supposed to be *humorous*, Agent Blackwood?"

"Nope." Dean stepped closer to the restaurant owner. "And neither is some westside seafood hawker telling me how a dead body threw a kink into his plans for the night. A guy died here last night, a *cop*," he pointed, "and you're the only one who saw it happen, so unless you want this place shut down, pretend like your reputation depends on putting on a brave face here for the next few minutes."

A sheet-white Kristoff swallowed the lump in his throat. "I'll help in any way I can."

"You can start by telling me about the victim," Dean said, "what time he arrived, where he sat, anything you think might be relevant."

Kristoff fastened his eyes to the ceiling. "He came in around 5:30 last night. He was alone." He gestured to a table in the far east corner of the restaurant. "He sat over there. He didn't order anything but a drink, a gin and tonic."

"Was someone supposed to meet him? Did he book the table for just himself?"

"He told the server that someone was meeting him. He made the reservation for two."

Dean squinted. "But no one met him."

"No."

"What time did he leave?"

"Around 6:30," Kristoff said. "He seemed like he was in a rush too. He dropped a $100 bill on the table and left pretty quickly."

"Any idea why he might have left in such a hurry?"

"I'm not sure." Kristoff directed his gaze toward the kitchen. "I was talking to one of my chefs in the back most of the night. We had a problem with our order of lobster that came in this morning."

"First-world problems." Dean snorted. "Did you notice anything strange about the victim? How was he acting while he was here?"

"Other than the fact that he was fiddling with his phone

a lot, there's nothing noteworthy to mention. He simply came in, ordered a drink, stood up after about an hour, and then left."

"He just got up and left?"

"He was on the phone at the time," Kristoff said. "Sounded like he was upset at whoever was calling, the way he was huffing and puffing."

"Okay," Dean said. "So he gets a call, pays his bill, and then heads outside. You saw all this play out according to what you told the detectives."

Kristoff nodded. "I did." He motioned to the table near a window that looked out onto the highway. "I was right there clearing some plates. I saw him leave, walk outside, and then—" his color faded, "I saw the car hit him. It looked like the vehicle sped up before it ran him over. And the noise was," his voice trembled, "was the most terrible thing I've ever heard in my life."

"The car that struck the victim," Dean said. "What did it look like?"

"It was red," Kristoff said. "An older car, the little I saw of it."

Dean threw a glance toward Vendrell's Mercedes parked near the front of the restaurant. "When the car hit the victim," he said, "how close was it to the Mercedes out there?"

"What do you mean?"

"You said a red car approached, sped up, ran over the man, and killed him."

"I did."

"Well," Dean said, "the highway out there is pretty narrow. Your restaurant is seated on a tight turn in the road. I'd imagine more than a few cars have dinged or side-swiped vehicles parked on the road every now and again based on that fact."

Kristoff nodded. "We've seen more than a handful of fender benders here over the years. CHP set up a speed trap a few months back to try to deter drivers. It's been a little safer since then, but it still happens every once in a while."

"But this car," Dean said, "the one that hit the victim—you said it sped *up* before it hit him, correct?"

"Correct," Kristoff said. "I'm pretty sure it did. I could hear the engine throttling right before it happened."

After a few more follow-up questions, Dean threaded his way outside, linked up with Cosgrove, and told him he could cut Kristoff loose.

"Thanks for the green light," Cosgrove replied. "Does that mean I'm free to go too? I mean," he held up his hands, "if it's all right with *you*, Bureau boy."

"Vendrell's body," Dean said. "What was on it when you guys bagged it up?"

"His badge, his wallet, and his cell. Thing was beat to shit. The car rammed into him going at least fifty, from what we gathered, so everything was mangled, his body included." The detective sucked air through his teeth. "Look, this is an internal matter, Agent Blackwood. I don't know why the Feds are stepping on our toes."

"I don't think I need to stress to you," Dean said, "how easy it is for the Bureau to stick its nose into a situation if we feel it's warranted."

"This was an *accident*," Cosgrove said. "Plain and simple. Some asswipe got liquored up, ran over Vendrell, and took off. CHP and Santa Monica PD are still combing the area for the guy. Once they find him, and they *will* find him, he's fucked."

"Did it ever occur to you," Dean took out his toothpick

and slipped it between his lips, "that this whole thing might have been deliberate?"

The detective scoffed. "Based on *what*?"

"A hunch," Dean said. "Sounds like the guy driving this red rig that hit Vendrell knew how to navigate the road pretty well. If he was liquored up, he would have side-swiped that Mercedes, but he did a damn good job at avoiding it."

"He was lucky."

"All right." Dean shifted his toothpick. "If you say so."

Cosgrove, gnashing his teeth, stepped closer to Dean. "This was a hit and run. Don't fool yourself into thinking otherwise. A cop died here last night, and I've been sitting on my hands babysitting the crime scene for you while I could be out there looking for the guy who did this." He backed away. "We're done here. Do me a favor and tell your people to let us handle this."

"Keep me in the loop if you get any updates," Dean said, unfazed by Cosgrove's strong-arm tactics. "I'll be at the Hyatt in Pasadena."

"Yeah." Cosgrove shook his head. "I'll be sure to do that."

"I'm picking up on your sarcasm."

Cosgrove responded by giving the one-fingered salute before he headed out. Dean laughed at the gesture as he pulled out his cell, dialed Wilson's number, and waited for two rings before Wilson answered.

"What do you got?" Wilson said.

"It's fishy," Dean said, "but there's nothing that points to this being anything other than an accident."

"Do *you* think it was?"

"Not at all."

"Why's that?"

Dean shrugged. "Just doesn't make sense. Like you said,

it doesn't feel right, but I don't have much to go on other than circumstantial stuff."

"As in?"

"This Vendrell guy was meeting someone here," Dean said. "Could be a variety of reasons why, but whoever he was waiting there for won't come to light until someone dumps his phone. All we know was that Vendrell got a call, paid in cash for his bill, and left. Then he ran to his car, a vehicle slammed into him, swerved around Vendrell's Mercedes, and took off."

"You didn't mention to the LAPD about the anonymous tip we got," Wilson said, "did you?"

"No," Dean replied. "I thought it'd be better to play our cards close to the chest for the moment."

"Good."

"You working on pinpointing whoever made the call?"

"As we speak."

"Then that being said," Dean made his way to the Prius rental he snagged from LAX parked near Vendrell's Benz, "do you need anything else from me?"

"No," Wilson said. "You're good. Thanks for giving the scene a once-over."

"Happy I could help, boss."

"What're you going to do now?"

"I'm going to head back to the hotel. It's Jeremy's birthday tomorrow."

"Give him a hug for me."

"Will do," Dean replied before he terminated the call, slipped into his rental, and turned over the engine. He idled on the highway for a few moments, his gaze pinned to the rearview mirror and the blood stream fifty yards away.

He squeezed his eyelids shut.

His mind drifted back.

Images played back at high speed through his mind. Dean tensed and clenched his teeth.

He saw his twin brother's body.

The Volvo that ran him over.

Reeled over the fact that whoever was behind the wheel had never been caught.

Heart racing, Dean snapped open his eyes, checked his pulse, and implemented a box-breathing technique to slow the tempo of his breathing. Once his heart rate slowed down, he pushed away memory of Tommy's death, put the rental into drive, and drove away.

Don't think about it, Deano.

Just let it go.

5

Ten minutes had ticked by after Dean checked into his room at the Hyatt in Pasadena when a call came from the front desk. "Mr. Blackwood," the front desk clerk greeted, "your wife is here to see you."

Dean winced. "My wife?"

"Yes, sir. She's waiting for you in the lobby."

Dean had told his ex-wife where he was staying, but the fact that she had popped in to see him at such a late hour, let alone refer to herself as his wife, prompted a four-alarm fire to trigger in his mind.

Someone was playing games.

And he was intrigued just enough to indulge them.

The elevator doors to the lobby slid open. Dean stepped out onto the polished marble floor with his hands stuffed in the pockets of his leather jacket. On his left, he saw a woman seated on one of the couches near the hotel's entrance. A messenger bag was slung over her shoulder, her highly-caffeinated gaze probing the lobby.

"*LA Times*?" Dean said. "*Pasadena Star-News*?"

The woman angled her body around on the couch, her

heart-shaped face, brunette hair, and dazzling good looks momentarily catching Dean off-guard.

"You're a reporter," Dean said as he saw something familiar in the woman's eyes. "Clever ruse, by the way, saying you were my wife to get me to come down here."

"Agent Blackwood—"

"Who told you I was staying here?" Dean said. "I've been in town for about ten minutes."

The woman took a pause, adjusted her messenger bag, and shrugged. "Detective Alan Cosgrove."

"Son of a bitch." Dean shook his head. "I should've known that would come back to bite me in the ass." He furrowed his brow. "This is about Vendrell, the cop that just got smeared across the PCH last night, isn't it?"

"I'm afraid so," she said. "My office—"

"—caught wind of what happened, called the PD to get a comment, and Cosgrove pimped me out, didn't he?"

The woman closed her eyes. "Let me start over," she said, as she offered her hand. "I'm Layla Adrian, *LA Times*."

"And I'm tired," Dean replied as he turned on his heel. "Have a good night, Ms. Adrian."

"Agent Blackwood—"

"No comment."

"I know all about you," Layla said as she shot up from the couch. "You don't remember me, but I spoke to you about six years ago."

Dean terminated his walk, squinted, and pulled a memory out from his mental vault. He was crossing paths with the reporter six years ago outside the FBI's field office in LA where she had rattled off a series of questions about a bust he took part in at the docks over in Long Beach.

"Yeah," Dean said. "Yeah, that's right." He wagged a finger. "You were asking about the shootout I was in."

"I had just started working for the *Times* back then," Layla replied. "My editor sent me down there to get a comment from you about what happened. You told me to get lost, if I remember correctly."

"And I'm saying the same right now." Dean saluted with two fingers. "Drive safe."

"I took a look at your jacket after we first met," Layla said as she tailed after Dean. "You're pretty well-known within the Bureau's ranks. You work in their undercover division."

"*Worked*," Dean said. "Past tense." He checked the time on the G-Shock strapped to his wrist. "And it's *past* my bedtime, Ms. Adrian."

"This is important."

"I'm sure it is."

"I know about Mike Vendrell. I've been following—"

"Let me stop you right there." Dean held up his hand. "I'm in town for personal reasons. I visited the crime scene tonight to give an initial assessment. That's all. I have nothing to say to you, the *Times*, or anyone else for that matter."

A defeated look washed across Layla's face as she reached into her purse, retrieved a business card from her purse, and handed it over. "For future reference," she said. "I have a feeling you might want to talk later down the line."

Dean took a beat, then the card, examined it, and stuffed it in his pocket. "You're as confident as you are tenacious, aren't you?"

Layla bit her lip. "Maybe I can buy you a drink to make up for the trouble."

"I don't drink," Dean said, "but thanks for the offer." With that, he strode back to the elevator and rode it up to his floor, still a little perturbed at being messed with but intrigued nonetheless at Layla's tenacity, as well as the fact that she was, hands-down, one of the more charming reporters he had ever been inconvenienced by.

———

Dean slipped off his jacket and threw it onto the bed. His laptop was open on the nightstand. The email he had drafted detailing his take on the Vendrell crime scene was on the screen, but he was still thinking about Layla, the late Mike Vendrell, and Wilson sending him to check it out.. It prompted him to ring up Bazz who answered the call just a pair of rings in.

"Miss me?" Bazz answered.

"Not at all." Dean made his way out to the balcony. "How's Willy?"

"Licking his rear at the moment. How's things on your end?"

"Interesting." Dean surveyed the line of brick buildings peppering a stretch of Colorado Boulevard. "I just shooed off a reporter who showed up at my hotel."

"Why the hell is a reporter jamming you up at 1:00 in the morning?"

"It was about this traffic collision. I guess word got out about it. The LAPD detective at the scene ratted me out to someone at the *Times*." Dean put the phone on speaker. "That's why I called you, Bazzy. Something's off about this whole thing. The PD is certain it's a hit and run, but I'm not so sure. Between the scene and this reporter at the *Times* showing up, something smells wrong."

"Yeah," Bazz groaned. "I figured Wilson was playing coy about his intentions. You're not gonna keep working on this thing, are you?"

"My part in this is done. Soon as I draft up a report to Wilson, that's it."

"Good." Bazz took a pause. "But there's something else that's bothering you, isn't there?"

Dean closed his eyes. "That crime scene tonight. It reminded me of my brother. It was the same kind of hit-and-run situation that happened with Tommy. It's been a while since I've thought about it." His jaw muscles tensed. "About how they never caught the fucker who did it."

"You need to put it behind you, brother," Bazz said. "You can't control it. You know that."

"I know."

"You're there for your kid. Remember that. And forget about that scene tonight. It's not your problem. Just write the report, send it, and be done with it."

"You're right," Dean said. "And I'm going to start by hanging up this phone."

"Good man."

"You boys have a good night. I'll see you in a week."

Dean ended the call, walked back into the room, and sank down on the bed. His body melted into the mattress as a breeze filtered in from the balcony outside. And then, for the second time that night, he thought about Tommy, about his bloodied body, the car that ran him over, and the guy who killed him who was never brought to justice.

"You could always call room service, you know," Woody whispered. "Order one of those airplane bottles of vodka and an OJ."

Dean squeezed his eyelids shut. "I'm good."

"You sure?"

"Quit asking me."

"You know," Woody sighed, "I don't get you, Deano. I mean,

you *know* that'll take the edge off. You'll stop thinking about stuff. Hell, it'll be fun! We can stay up, crank up some Motown or something." The demon rattled off a smoke-choke cackle. "It's been a hot minute since the two of us kicked back, hombre."

Dean said nothing.

"Don't you miss it?"

Dean turned onto his side.

"Don't you miss *me*?"

Dean drew in a breath.

Held it.

Then he released it.

"Let it go, Blackwood," Dean whispered as he closed his eyes and rested back his head. "*Sleep*."

6

The muscles in Dean's legs tensed as he ran in an all-out sprint, his lungs on fire as he dashed toward the landmark the locals called Suicide Bridge, a stunning piece of vintage architecture with a view of the sprawling San Gabriel Mountains off to his right.

Dean pulled the crisp Southern California morning breeze deep into his lungs. "Start Me Up" blasted through the buds stuffed in his ears. He threw a look toward the blue skies above his head, ripe with billowy clouds, the wind lapping at his sweat-glazed torso as his sneakers pounded the pavement.

Dean checked his watch. He'd been running for three miles. He had two hours to kill before Jeremy's party and three miles left before he completed his six for the day. But the moment the tendons from his old knee injury began to sear, he terminated his stride, cursed under his breath, and braced himself.

"Come on, man," Dean whispered as he massaged his leg. "Don't crap out on me now."

His cell buzzed inside his pocket. Dean puckered his lips

as he pulled the device out, saw Wilson's name on the display, and answered. "You get that report?"

"I did," Wilson said. "That was fast."

"Thank my old high school English teacher. Only subject I was ever good at."

"I'll send her a commendation. I also got an update for you, if you're interested."

"Not really," Dean said. "I thought my end in this was done, boss."

"It is, but I just thought you'd want to know our people dumped Vendrell's call logs."

"That was quick." Dean narrowed his eyes. "How'd you pull that off?"

"We're the FBI," Wilson said. "We're good at what we do. Anyway, I just thought you might find it interesting that the phone found on Vendrell's body was a burner. Looks like he left his regular cell at home. LAPD came across it at his residence when they informed his wife that he died."

"A burner?"

"Yeah."

"Why's a cop got a burner phone on him?"

"That's why I called," Wilson said. "You worked undercover for a long time. Figured maybe you might—"

"*Willy*," Dean cut in. "I don't want any more updates on this case, okay? I did my end, now you've gotta stick to yours. I'm here for my kid. I need to make that clear."

"I understand," Wilson said. "And I appreciate the effort you've put in thus far."

"You got it, chief."

"One more thing."

Dean rolled his eyes. "Shoot."

"There's a reporter from the *Times* that's been sniffing around," Wilson said. "Layla Adrian. A bit persistent, from what I've gathered. You haven't run into her by chance, have you?"

"As a matter of fact, I did," Dean replied. "She cornered me at the hotel a couple of hours after I went to the scene."

"That was quick."

"I thought the same."

"What does that tell you?"

"That I've said my piece on this whole case. Give my condolences to the guy who takes over from here."

"Will do, kid," Wilson said. "Stay sharp."

Dean hung up the phone, stepped off the sidewalk, and prepared to resume his jog—and then a car horn blared from behind him. Dean's heart shot into his throat as he hopped back onto the sidewalk and dashed quickly out of the way of an oncoming sedan.

"*Hey*," Dean shouted. "Watch where you're going, dickhead!"

The driver—in typical LA fashion—honked his horn in reply, the driver sticking his middle finger out the window as the vehicle cruised past and continued ambling its way across the bridge.

Dean pressed two fingers to his neck to check his pulse. His heart was beating at a fever-pitch pace. "Easy," he whispered. "You're good."

A few moments later, Dean continued his run, trying not to think about Wilson, Vendrell, his dead brother, or the reporter asking questions as the muscles in his legs strained from the effort.

7

Dean drummed his fingers on the Prius's steering wheel as he threw a glance toward the seaside residence off to his right. As his heart drummed against his rib cage, he found himself grinning at the fact that being around his ex-wife stirred up more adrenaline than any high-stakes job he had taken up during the course of his undercover career.

Dean peered through the windshield. The house was two blocks away from the beach, a two-story modernist home composed of concrete and glass, the kind of place Dean knew he could never afford. "Nice digs, Claire," he said to himself. "Very slick."

Dean snagged the baseball mitt packaged in blue wrapping off the passenger's seat and stepped out of the Prius. He padded his way toward the open front door and moved inside, his focus on the infinity pool in the backyard, packed to the brim with guests. Kids played in the pool. Adults had gathered off to the side, drinks in hands and smiles brimming from one ear to the other.

"*Dean,*" a voice called out from behind him.

Dean did an about-face and saw his ex-wife, her lips knotted as she extended her arms for what became the most awkward hug Dean had experienced in years.

Claire broke the embrace. "It's good to see you."

Dean nodded toward the pool. "I like your place."

"Thank you."

"You, uh..." Dean motioned to the bob-cut his ex-wife was sporting, "you changed your hair. It's shorter."

Claire tugged on a strand of her auburn hair cut short just above her jawline. "It's new."

"It suits you."

The two shared the silence for a moment—*both* unsure of what to say.

"So, uh," Dean blurted out, "where's Jeremy?"

Claire forked her thumb over her shoulder. "He's inside showing off the Xbox Geoff got for him."

Dean clutched the baseball glove tight, his gift feeling overshadowed by the one Claire's *new* husband had purchased. "And where *is* the fabulous Mr. Shaw?"

"Deano!"

Dean turned and saw Claire's husband approach, a pearl-white set of teeth flashing through the man's manicured beard.

"What's good, Geoff?" Dean said as he offered his hand, gripped onto Geoff's, and applied a little more pressure than he needed to.

"Great to see you, my friend." Geoff clapped Dean on the back. "It's been a minute."

"More than a few." Dean peered at the infinity pool and the scenic view of the beach a half-mile beyond it. "I was just complimenting Claire on the spread you've got here."

"Thank you. I just made partner at the firm."

"Three months ago. They hooked you up with a solid

perk package too." Dean nodded over his shoulder. "Didn't clock that Audi Q7 they gave you in the driveway though."

The smile on Geoff's face dissolved into a wince. "How'd you know about that?"

"My kid's living under your roof, brother." Dean shrugged. "Can't dog a guy for keeping tabs."

"*Dean*," Claire said, her expression pulled taut into a wince. "Seriously?"

"I'm just playing around." Dean swiped his hand through the air. "I mean it though. This is a great place. I'm glad you guys are doing well."

"Thanks, Dean," Geoff said. "Make yourself at home. Let me know if I can get you anything."

"Will do."

Geoff clapped his hands together. "Sorry to cut this short, but I've got to make a quick call to one of my partners. Fire at the home office kind of a thing."

Dean made a finger gun and clicked his tongue. "Hop to it, ace."

Geoff made his way toward the house, greeting a few guests with high energy like he was running for office.

Dean faced Claire as he puttered out a laugh. "Well, he's nice."

Claire cocked her head to the side. "Don't."

"I'm just giving the guy a hard time."

"By running a background check on him?"

"You'd do the same if you were in my position."

Claire said nothing.

Dean furrowed his brow. "I mean it, Claire. Geoff's a good guy." He held his head high and spoke with a sincere tone. "I'm glad things are going well."

"They are," Claire said fondly. "What about you? Everything's good?"

"Big time," Dean replied, feeling like a kid about to present a book report he stayed up all night to work on. "I'm three years clean. Work's low-key. Got that cabin in the woods routine going right now. I can't complain."

"You look good." Claire surveyed Dean from head to toe. "Looks like you've dropped some weight since I last saw you."

"Joggin 9k a day. It's wreaking havoc on my knees." Dean patted his gut. "It's done wonders for the love handles though."

"I'm sure the women in your life are grateful for the effort."

Dean shook his head. "It's just me and the mutt up there in the cabin. I've got a truckload of free time nowadays." He put his gaze on the ground. "That's something I wanted to talk to you about, actually, but first..." He held up the glove in his hand.

Claire beamed. "He's upstairs. I'm sure he'll love you popping in to surprise him. I'll get you something to drink. Anything in particular?"

"Just a soda."

"You got it."

"Thanks, Claire."

"It's good to see you, Dean."

"Good to see you." With that, Dean retreated into the house and climbed the stairway that led to the second floor, strolled down the hall, and passed a series of framed photos on the wall that showcased his son, Claire, and at a variety of different events—the beach, Disneyland, Dodger games, ice skating.

Dean surveyed the gallery for a few moments, his heart weighing heavy at the notion that he was missing out on so many milestone moments of his son's life.

Make a memory with him now, jackass.
Start with today, and go from there.

Dean made his way down the hallway, arrived at a door where a wooden letter "J" had been tacked to the door, and picked up on the muted conversation of two adolescent boys on the other side. The proverbial love of a father welled up inside of him the moment he made out Jeremy's voice.

8

"I heard we've got a birthday boy in the house," Dean called out. "Is that true?"

"*Dad!*"

The door flew open a half-second later. Jeremy dashed out, running into Dean's arms and embracing him as if he were a life raft in the middle of open waters.

"*Pally*," Dean whispered warmly as he lifted him up and made a new memory. "I missed you."

"I missed you too." Jeremy stood back and ran his hand across his father's stubble. "Are you growing a beard?"

"Should I?"

Jeremy nodded. "I like beards. Geoff has one."

"Yeah, I noticed." Dean flexed his brow. "He's a really nifty guy, that Geoff." He placed his boy down on the floor. With every year that passed and every inch the kid grew, he looked more and more like Dean's late brother Tommy.

Same eyes.

Same crooked smile.

Christ, he's the spitting image of T down to his freckles.

"Okay, so," Dean said as he tried not to dwell on his thoughts, what birthday is this? Twenty-one? Twenty-two?"

"I'm eight!"

"Get out of town. You're almost old enough to drive."

"Really?"

"Getting close." Dean ruffled his son's hair. "Are you having a good birthday?"

"Yep!" Jeremy pointed over his shoulder to a boy with blonde hair in board shorts fiddling with an Xbox controller in front of a flat-screen. "This is Andrew. We know each other from school."

Dean saluted. "How's it going, buddy?"

A sheepish Andrew, head cowered, waved and then put his focus back on the flat-screen.

"So," Dean said, "you get a lot of cool stuff today?"

"I did!" Jeremy replied. "Geoff got me an Xbox with a bunch of games. He said I have to make sure all my homework is done and that I read for an hour before I play. Geoff said reading is important."

"Well, Geoff's just *full* of wisdom, isn't he?" Dean held back a sigh. "So, what do you say? Should we get back to the party? I'm pretty sure there's a cake on the way."

"Yeah, let's go! I want to show you to all my friends."

"Let's do it." Dean held up his gift. "But first—"

A wide-eyed Jeremy snatched the gift and tore off the wrapping, his eyes wide as he took out the baseball glove inside. "*Wow*. I don't have a baseball glove!"

"That's an *official* Dodgers glove, Pally," Dean noted. "I'll show you how to break it in."

Jeremy hooked his arms around his father's neck, burrowing his face into Dean as he wrapped his arms around him. "Thanks, Dad. You're the best."

Dean could feel the tears welling up inside of him. "No,"

he said, patting Jeremy's back and wishing that the moment wouldn't end, "*you are.*"

The two embraced.

Dean smirked.

Despite his best intentions, he found himself thinking about Tommy once again.

9

Red and orange hues tinted the skies overhead. Dean, seated in a lawn chair in Claire's backyard, gazed up at them as he heard the last of the guests filing out through the front door. Moments later, Claire returned and began gathering up all the leftover paper plates, cups, and utensils speckled with remnants of birthday cake.

"Are you sure you don't need help?" Dean asked. "I feel like a freeloader sitting here while you clean up."

Claire waved him off. "No, I like it. It's therapeutic. Plus, we gave the housekeeper the week off."

"Where's Geoff?"

"He had to go back to the office for a minute."

"That happen a lot?"

Claire turned her head toward Dean, her tapered eyes signaling to Dean to back away from his line of questioning.

Dean held up his hands. "How's Morgan and Andrews treating you?"

"It's a grind. I've cut down on my hours recently."

"Think you'll stay with them?"

"I've had my fill of corporate law," Claire said. "Geoff and

I have been talking about me maybe making the leap to health law. I've got the degree. Plus, I'll be able to spend more time with Jeremy."

"He seems happy." Dean shot a look over his shoulder toward the second floor. "Looks like he's doing well."

"Yeah," Claire said tenderly. "He's happy."

Dean hung his head, wishing he could give Jeremy a life like the one he had with his mother, with anything and everything he could ever desire. But that wasn't how it worked out.

"What about you?" Claire said as she tied off the trash bag in her hand. "How's cabin life in the woods treating you?"

"Low-key," Dean replied. "Just work, rinse, and repeat. Got a buddy of mine who pops in a few times a week. He's in the program. We go to the meetings twice a week together. He's a solid guy."

"I never would have thought in a million years you would have been able to slow down. I mean—" Claire shook her head and didn't finish the statement.

"What?" Dean said.

"Nothing."

"No," Dean rose from his chair, "tell me."

His ex-wife approached him and rested her hands on the small of her back. "The odds were kind of stacked against you after we split. You were in a tailspin there for a while."

"Yeah," Dean replied as he ran his hand across his shirt, grazing the welts left from a pair of 9mm slugs across his torso. "I was. But that's over now. And I was hoping," he drew a deep breath, "I was wondering if maybe there's a chance I can start coming down here a little more regularly. You asked me to start fresh and get my head screwed on straight. In three years, well, I think I did that."

A contemplative look washed across Claire's face. "I think that's a great idea," she said, "but I'd be lying if I said I didn't have my reservations."

Dean felt like his heart skipped a beat. "What do you mean?"

"I know you, Dean. Three years of marriage was long enough to get well-acquainted with who you are, your life, the way you operate."

"*Operated*," Dean clarified. "Past tense."

Claire shook her head. "You're still the same guy you've always been. You're a door-kicker. It's who you are, and you can't just switch off that way of thinking, that way of *living* with the snap of a finger."

"Claire," Dean said, "I spend my days sifting through clerical work in a cabin in the middle of nowhere. I'm Mister Rogers now. I just don't have those spiffy cardigans to go with it."

"I believe you," Claire said. "I'm sure you're doing every-thing you can to live a different life than you did before." She stepped closer. "But that doesn't change the fact that there's still a slew of people you butted heads with that might come out of the woodwork trying to track you down."

"What do you mean?"

"I'm talking about stuff like that night when we were living in Dallas." The color drained from Claire's face. "The same night you were in El Paso."

The memory was quickly pulled from the files of Dean's mind. The night that a parolee, Darrell Weiss, a guy that Dean put away for armed robbery, showed up at his family's home looking for Dean with vengeance on his mind and a Beretta clutched in his hand. The cops had taken Weiss down after Claire called them, and Dean, posing as a neo-Nazi biker during an undercover sting 600 miles away, the night he took a pair of 9mm rounds to a vest, wasn't there to protect them.

"I can't go through that again," Claire said. "And I can't risk this family's safety in the off chance that something like that might happen again."

Dean paced the lawn. "What do you want me to do, Claire?" he finally said. "What do you want me to say?"

"I just need time," his ex-wife replied. "I need to be sure you're not going to get roped back into your old life."

"I won't."

"What about Wilson?"

"What about him?"

"You were the FBI's golden boy, Dean," Claire said. "After they cut you loose from doing undercover work, they tried for six months to get you to come back. I know your old boss. He's persistent, and I have a feeling he's tried once or twice to get you back in the field."

Between the events of the prior night—Vendrell's crime scene, Wilson's phone calls—Dean suspected that his old handler was jockeying into position to have him dive further into the case, a suspicion he decided to refrain from telling his ex-wife.

"He's not," Dean said. "And I won't. And Wilson said he's going to get me a desk job out here so I can be closer to all you guys." He stepped closer to Claire. "Don't keep my son from me, Claire. I can't keep living my life with him at a distance. I've done everything I'm supposed to do, everything you've asked me to do. I just want to be here for Jeremy. I want to be the father my son needs me to be."

Claire brought her palm to her forehead, her expression tense as she struggled to come up with a reply.

"Listen," Dean said. "I'm still in town for a few days. If it's all right with you, I was hoping to take Jeremy to a Dodgers game on Saturday with my old man. Maybe we can treat the next few days as, I don't know, a trial run or something."

"Yeah," Claire nodded. "Absolutely. We can talk more about it later."

Dean furrowed his brow. "Can I say goodnight to him?"

"Of course."

Dean's lips tightened into a fine line as he turned around, headed inside, and made his way up to Jeremy's bedroom. He nudged the door open to find his son lying on his bed, clocked out and clutching his new baseball glove close to his chest.

Dean sat on the edge of the bed, gently rested his hand on his son's head, and planted a delicate kiss on his forehead. "'Night, Pally," he whispered. "I'll see you soon."

Jeremy turned over. The light from the lamp cast a warm glow on his face, his features so similar to his dearly departed uncle he never met that it triggered Dean to—yet again—think back to the day his twin brother died.

"It's shit like *this*," Woody said, "that you'll never forget, bub."

Don't.

"Have a drink."

Stop.

"*Do it!*"

Dean clenched a fist.

Switched off the lamp.

Then he turned his back on his son, left the room, and closed the door slowly behind him.

He's not Tommy.

He's your son.

Woody's playing tricks on you.

Don't give in to his bullshit.

Minutes later, after Dean bid goodbye to his ex-wife and was led to the door, he was behind the wheel of the Prius, his sights on the lights in Jeremy's bedroom on the second floor.

Dean's heart felt heavy. Memories of his past were playing back at high speed—the guy who came around his house in Dallas, his last undercover job in El Paso, the day Jeremy was born, and the night Claire told him that she wanted a divorce.

I need to show her. I need to show Claire and Jeremy and everyone else that the old ways are behind me. I can do it.

He held his head high.

I have to.

The phone in his pocket buzzed. Dean's train of thought broke as he pulled out the device, saw Wilson's name on the display, and answered.

"What's up?"

"I need you," Wilson said. "North Hollywood."

"Willy," Dean closed his eyes. "I told you—"

"And I'm pulling rank," his boss cut in. "There's another body, another member of the unit Vendrell was in. Same circumstances. Same kind of situation."

"No." Dean shook his head, his mind momentarily fixated on the conversation he just had with his ex-wife and his promise to be done with his old ways. "Write me up for insubordination. Fire me if you have to."

"It's not that simple, Deano," Wilson said. "The body we've got is someone you know, an old friend of yours."

"Who?"

"Cole Harlow. He was in the same unit you were in back in Afghanistan."

Dean, playing back the memory of him gearing up

beside Staff Sergeant Cole Harlow in Kandahar in preparation for Operation Rhino, closed his eyes.

"Dean," Wilson said. "Get down here. Right now. I'm not going to ask again."

Dean snapped open his gaze.

Shot a look toward Jeremy's bedroom.

Then he clenched his jaw, told his boss he was on the way, and peeled away from the curb.

The body of Cole Harlow was sprawled off Vineland Avenue in North Hollywood near the intersection, covered by a white plastic sheet and guarded over by two patrolmen standing tall like Buckingham Palace sentinels. A crowd had gathered, the LAPD doing their best to corral the onlookers.

Dean pulled up and flashed his badge to the officer outside the yellow caution tape. The officer waved Dean through, and once Dean parked his rental near the curb, he threaded his way inside the nearby restaurant. He made a beeline to the patio area where Special Agent In Charge Kent Wilson was waiting with a burly man that had an LAPD detective's shield clipped to his hip. The pair cut a glance Dean's way as he walked in.

"Boss," Dean called out, noting the silver streaks in Wilson's hair that weren't there the last time he saw him.

Wilson was a stoic, dark-skinned man whose eyes always held an inquisitive gaze. "Deano." He shook Dean's hand. "It's good to see you."

"Wish I could say the same." Dean withdrew his hand. "Not like you gave me much of a choice to come down here."

"Dean—"

"We'll talk about it in a minute." Dean slipped a toothpick between his lips. "Just give me the rundown."

The detective next to Wilson, a tall man with the height and lankiness of a basketball player, injected himself into the conversation. "Sandusky," he said. "North Hollywood."

"Special Agent Blackwood." Dean swept his gaze toward the street. "What happened?"

"Witnesses inside the bar here reported a hit and run," Sandusky explained. "When one of my units rolled in and checked it out, they found a badge in the vic's pocket. An interdepartmental memorandum was floating around today that the FBI had been investigating a similar call night before last, so my LT told me to give the heads up to your field office. We're letting you boys take the lead on this."

Wilson gestured like a bellhop toward the corpse in the road. Dean and Sandusky followed after him, the pair crouching down beside the body as the patrolmen positioned by it stepped back.

Dean pinched the corner of the sheet, lifted it up, and did an appraisal of Harlow's corpse. It was mangled, coated with blood, bits of bone and muscle showing. Harlow's right arm was folded back at an unnatural angle behind his neck, his left arm nearly snapped in half, his legs contorted and twisted like a pretzel.

"Cole Harlow," Dean said as he gazed deep into the lifeless eyes of his fellow Army Ranger. "Served two tours with the guy."

"How well did you know him?" Wilson replied. "How close were you?"

"We weren't exactly friends. Harlow was a bit of a

psycho. He liked having an excuse to shoot people for a living. Pretty sure he got away with a few unsanctioned kills during his time in the service. He almost got me killed by friendly fire at one point. The crazed asshole was firing off his weapon at a band of insurgents like he was Scarface or something. Almost got me clipped in the process." He huffed. "*Prick*." He put his eyes on the crowd. "Witnesses?"

"Over there." Wilson flicked his gaze toward a couple standing off to the side of the patio area and a man and woman in their late twenties, the man's arm around the woman as she sobbed into his chest. "They saw the whole thing go down. They also got some details on the vehicle— red, older model, no plates."

"Same description as the rig that took out Vendrell."

"The car came in from the north," Sandusky said, "right here up Vineland. Witnesses on the curb said it plowed into Harlow the second he stepped off the sidewalk, then it hooked a left and booked it down a residential street." He motioned toward the chopper flying in circles above his head. "Units are doing a sweep of the area to see if they can find the car. Nothing so far."

Dean said nothing as he scanned the street. The busy intersection consisted of bars, a comedy club, coffee joints, and a string of shops ranging from weed dispensaries to a slew of poke bowl restaurants. It was a high-traffic area, a very public stage for what he suspected was a deliberate act of murder.

"It's a good spot," Dean said as he pointed toward the freeway on-ramp a half-mile away. "There's a lot of exit points, a lot of escape routes someone can take." He pointed to the traffic cameras near the intersection. "What's the status with NHPD on the footage?"

"We're working on it now," Sandusky replied. "We should have it within the hour."

"Anyone cross paths with Harlow before this went down?"

"Only the witnesses. And the bartender inside said he spoke to Harlow when he came in. It was the only interaction our guy had before he got run over."

Dean stood up. "Show me the bartender."

11

The bartender was a white guy in his thirties with chiseled good looks and a sour attitude. His tight clothing was shrink-wrapped to his vanity muscles, his arms crossed defensively, biceps flexing.

"Special Agent Blackwood," Dean said as he flashed his badge. "You saw the victim, correct?"

"I did," the bartender replied. "And this shitshow going on outside is making us lose money every second that I'm not pouring."

"A dude just died here tonight, hombre."

"That sucks, but this place is expensive to run, and the owners are going to chew out my ass if I'm not serving." The bartender huffed. "I've gotta be up at *five* tomorrow, man. I can't not hit the gym. Not gonna happen." He puffed his chest. "I give 110 percent *every* day."

Dean pinned his unblinking gaze to the meathead. "I work for the FBI."

The bartender shrugged. "*And?*"

"Well," Dean leaned in close, "that means I could smack

you upside the head with impunity if you don't shit-can the
Andrew Tate bullshit."

The bartender closed his mouth.

"The guy that came in here," Dean said, "the one that
was killed. You talked to him, yeah?"

"Yeah."

"Tell me everything that happened."

The bartender uncrossed his arms and braced the sides
of the counter. "He came in maybe an hour and a half ago.
He came up to the bar, ordered a beer, and paid in cash.
Then he went over there." He pointed toward a group of
tables corralled in an alcove area of the bar. "He stood there
for like thirty minutes, maybe. I wasn't really paying attention to him. Then he came up to me and asked if anyone
was asking about him."

Dean's eyebrows met in the middle. "He asked that
specifically?"

The bartender nodded. "Yeah."

"Interesting." Dean spotted the security camera on the
crown molding in the corner behind the bartender. "You
know how to access the security footage here?"

The bartender nodded. "Any idiot can do it."

"Good," Dean said. "Prove it."

He followed the scowling bartender, the pair weaving
their way through the crowd toward the outdoor area in the
back. There were couches, a couple barbecue pits, a tree
jutting up through the concrete, And a little stainless-steel
camper cordoned off with thin yellow rope.

The bartender opened the door to the camper. Inside
was a folding chair. In front of it was a desk with two
monitors on top of it and a series of drives stacked
beside it that displayed live, full-color footage of the inte-
rior of the bar. There were four screens in total. They

reminded Dean of the opening credits to *The Brady Bunch*.

"Play back the footage." Dean said. "Start from the moment our guy walked in."

The bartender sat in the folding chair, fiddled with the keyboard, rewound the footage, and played it back.

Dean, close to the screen, watched Harlow enter the bar. The guy was bulky, built like a powerlifter. He had jeans on. A black shirt. A denim jacket and a pair of Solomon tactical boots. *He's a narc*, Dean figured, leaning closer to the monitor where he saw Harlow approach the counter, order a beer, pay in cash, and linger. He was waiting for someone..

"Fast forward it to the part when he leaves," Dean said. "I wanna see when he walks outside."

The bartender complied. The footage sped up.

Dean watched it and saw Harlow reach into his pocket and pull out his cell.

"There," Dean said. "Play it back."

The bartender clicked the mouse. The footage played back at normal speed, showed Harlow reading a text on his phone, and whatever the text said had triggered him to frown. Seconds later, Harlow pocketed his cell and moved briskly out of the bar. Not long after that, the plateless red vehicle plowed into him near the curb.

Alive one minute, dead as Dillinger the next.

Dean moved outside and found Wilson conversing with the couple who had witnessed the collision. The man and woman were trembling and cowering their heads like a pair of toy dogs being berated by their owner.

"Boss," Dean said, nodding over his shoulder to cue Wilson to talk with him off to the side. "Can I have a word?"

Wilson uttered something to the couple before moving with Dean out of earshot. "What did you find?" Wilson said.

"I watched the security footage," Dean replied. "You need to find Harlow's cell phone. He got a text right before he left the bar. Whatever it said, it made him split as soon as he read it."

"What did the bartender say?"

"He said that Harlow was asking if anyone was looking for him while he was in the bar."

Wilson narrowed his eyes. "Interesting."

"Agent Wilson," a voice called out. Dean turned around to the approaching crime scene tech dressed in a wind-breaker, chinos, and boots. The man was scrawny, his jittery demeanor indicative of a guy on his third or fourth cup of coffee.

Wilson and Dean greeted the tech. The man held out a cell phone wrapped in a plastic evidence bag, the device blotched with bits of blood. The tech gave Wilson and Dean a pair of latex gloves, and the two men slipped them on before Dean took the bag and pulled out the small, black, prepaid phone.

"It's another burner phone," Dean said. "Same as Vendrell."

Wilson looked over the device. "Is it working?"

Dean pressed a few buttons. "Not anymore." He put the phone back in the bag and handed it to Wilson. "You'll have to dump it. But first," he ripped off his gloves, "I want to exercise my God-given right in this moment to give you the what-for."

"Dean—"

"*Shitcan* whatever cue-card rhetoric you're about to throw my way, boss. Between this," Dean nodded toward the corpse in the road, "and the thing the other night, I think you owe me some answers, and some goddamn good ones at that."

Wilson handed the tech the bag, told him to get to work on dumping it, took off his gloves, and slipped his hands in his pockets. "Three months ago," he said, "the DC office opened an investigation into an LAPD unit called SMASH."

"SMASH?"

"It stands for South Central Anti-Gang Special Hitters."

"Shitty acronym." Dean huffed. "What's their mandate?"

"Are you familiar with the Special Investigative Services?"

"My old man had some run-ins with them when he was still on the job. They're a tactical surveillance unit in the LAPD. People refer to them as the Death Squad. They've been around since the 1960s, I think. SIS pretty much has carte blanche to do whatever the hell they want."

"SMASH is an off-shoot of that unit," Wilson said. "It's run by a guy named Eldridge."

Dean furrowed his brow. "*Larry* Eldridge?"

"You know him?"

"He used to play golf with my father. He was a lieutenant back then."

"Well, as far as I can tell," Wilson said, "Eldridge and his boys are real pieces of work. They've got a stellar closure rate with their cases. It's pretty much why they've had the keys to the city for as long as they have. It's probably why LAPD's Internal Affairs Division has turned a blind eye to whatever alleged extracurricular activities they may have going on."

"Vendrell and Harlow were in this unit."

"That they were."

"So someone might be targeting the unit," Dean said. "We've got two dead SIS detectives killed under similar circumstances, so it's safe to entertain that theory."

"Yeah," Wilson said. "That looks to be the case."

Dean paced, logging everything Wilson told him to memory. During the entire course of his career—and life— he never needed a notepad or a recorder. He had jotted down mentally everything he had seen, done, and knew. His mind was a vault of highly detailed recollections.

"When you called me before I got out here," Dean said, "you told me that the Bureau wanted me to look into Vendrell's death. Now they want me to look into Harlow's. My question is why?"

Wilson turned down his gaze. "I wasn't given the scoop until an hour ago. I spoke with the Associate Deputy Director of the Inspection Division, the same guy who ordered me to assign you to look at the Vendrell crime scene. Once he heard about *this*," he motioned to the body in the street, "he gave me the full story. The Bureau opened an investigation into the SMASH unit six months ago. They believe SMASH is corrupt. They wanted my office to look into it, and for you to take point on the investigation. There's been a slew of tips in regard to excessive force, drug-running, and racketeering, but LAPD IAD has always dismissed the charges in the blink of an eye. Reports and tips landed on my desk at the field office a few times, but there was nothing substantial enough to warrant an investigation."

"Until Mike Vendrell and Cole Harlow," Dean said, "got turned into meatloaf on the streets."

"Precisely." Wilson gestured to the cops scattered throughout the scene. "It's clear there is some kind of old-school, Rampart-division era scandal business playing out here, and the cops are going to do what they can to try to keep a lid on it. The Bureau needs someone to infiltrate their ranks to sniff this thing out and find out what the hell is going on."

"Not someone," Dean said. "*Me*." He flared his nostrils. "The brass must've known that Eldridge was the head of SMASH, that he used to work with my old man back when he was in the LAPD. They also knew that I knew Cole Harlow, so all those facts combined made them figure I was the perfect guy for the job, but they knew I wouldn't come out here willingly." He gestured to the SAC. "They needed you to apply a little bit of a squeeze."

"I didn't know, Dean. I wasn't aware that DC was going to make this kind of play, to get you involved in the way they have. That's the truth."

"Because the big wigs over at Hoover knew I wouldn't come on my own accord—again, they needed you to light a fire under my ass to motivate me."

Wilson turned his gaze down to the pavement, smoothed his tie, and said nothing.

"Three years ago," Dean said, "I nearly got my head blown off." He pointed a finger. "For *you*. For the Bureau. I was throwing back two shots of JD for breakfast and polishing off my nights with a pint of it just so I could go to sleep."

"Dean—"

"I spent two years working undercover assignments for you, Willy, and when I left, after I almost got fitted for a toe tag in El Paso, I told you I was never going back."

"You're not going back," Wilson replied. "This isn't an undercover assignment. You know Eldridge. You knew Harlow. Your old man was an LAPD captain. You grew up with these guys. You know how they think, how they operate. You're a shoe-in for this, not to mention the fact that you're one of the best investigators I've ever known."

Dean smirked. "You've got a gift for sweet-talk, Willy."

Wilson huffed. "A pair of ex-wives would say otherwise.

And to be frank with you, kid, the people over in the Hoover Building have stressed that your involvement in this matter is mandatory.

"I guess I shouldn't be surprised. Figured it was only a matter of time before someone tried to get me out in the field again." Dean ran his hand across his stubble. The sea of red and blue emergency lights coating the scene was a sight he was all too familiar with, one he hoped he'd never see again. "I can't get involved in this, boss," he said. "I promised my kid and my ex that I wouldn't do shit like this again."

"You're not doing the same work you did before," Wilson explained. "I'm just asking you to take a look into this from an investigative standpoint—like a detective, not an undercover agent. I need you to find out what the hell is going on. But if you opt out of this, I've got your back. I'm not going to make you do something you don't want to do."

"Not if the people at Hoover have anything to say about it. If I don't do it," Dean sighed, "they'll take away my pension, the cabin." He waved his hand through the air. "All of it."

"If you do this for me," Wilson said, "I'll have you transferred back out here to LA when it's finished. I'll post you up at a desk. You can pick whatever assignments you want to take. You can come back home. You can be closer to your kid."

Dean laughed. "This is all contingent upon me closing out the case though, yeah?"

"No." Wilson shook his head. "Whatever answers you come up with, whatever you find, regardless if it closes the investigation or not, I'll stick to my word. Think about it, kid. You've been wanting to come back to LA for a while now." He clapped Dean on the shoulder. "This is a layup."

He's right. You wanted to come back home. You wanted to be closer to Jeremy. Hell, you could reconnect with Dad while you're at it.

This is how you get back.

Do this thing, close it out, and you've earned your one-way ticket back home.

"If I do this," Dean said, "if at *any* point shit starts to get hairy, I walk."

"Agreed." Wilson nodded. "You're running point on this."

"What I say goes."

"What you say goes."

Dean closed his eyes.

Thought it through.

Then he shot out his hand, slapped it into Wilson's, and shook.

12

The early morning sunlight filtered in through the windows of the technician's office at the FBI's Los Angeles field office. Golden rays glossed the walls and furniture. Dean, standing beside the tech with Wilson at his side, fiddled with a toothpick as he assessed the computer monitor in front of them.

"The burner phones we dumped," the tech said, "don't have much on them. Both Vendrell and Harlow refrained from using the devices to text, save for the pair they both received the night they were killed."

Dean stepped closer to the monitor, the tech motioning at the screen where two text messages had been enlarged for his view.

"This one was on Vendrell's phone," the tech explained. "It said, '*You are compromised. They know. Get out of there now.*'"

"Cryptic," Dean replied. "Sounds like a text Tom Cruise would get in one of the *Mission: Impossible* movies before he breaks out in a sprint." He nodded toward the screen. "What about the text Harlow got last night?"

"Same kind of thing." The tech ran her cursor over the text message she exhumed from Harlow's burner. "His text read, '*Move. Get out. Someone is there to burn you.*'"

Dean cut a glance toward Wilson, his boss shrugging in reply.

"Okay," Dean said. "What about call logs?"

"Still working on that." The tech held up the evidence bag containing Vendrell's burner. "These devices were fairly new. Prepaid cell phones. Both of them are TracFone models. You can get them almost anywhere. Both Harlow and Vendrell's devices only ever made contact with the same number—another burner, it looks like."

"I'm gonna put some people on pinpointing where Vendrell and Harlow's devices were purchased," Wilson said. "Same with the number they were in contact with."

Dean flicked a glance toward the evidence bag containing the burner phone. "What about the LAPD? They're not pissed that you've got their hands on their evidence?"

"Now that we've got the full cooperation from the LAPD, it makes things a lot easier."

"What do you mean?"

"Captain Larry Eldridge," Wilson said. "I got off the phone with him a couple hours ago. He agreed to lend full cooperation to us, and he's pulled the right strings with the rest of the LAPD brass to make sure no one gives us a hard time. The case is ours, Deano." He slapped Dean on the back. "*Yours.*"

"Sweet." Dean tamped down the urge to roll his eyes. "My lucky friggin' day."

Minutes later, Dean was seated in a chair in Wilson's office, his boss sifting through a series of folders with information about the SMASH unit.

"Detective Mike Vendrell," Wilson said, "Detective Cole Harlow, Officer Tyler Adams, Lieutenant Ron Wyler, Detective Sean Mohr, and Captain Larry Eldridge." He rapped his knuckles on the folder. "Those are the guys in the SMASH unit. If we want to think of this in football terms, Eldridge is the head coach. Wyler's the offensive and defensive coordinator. Vendrell and Harlow tag-teamed being the quarterbacks. As for Mohr, Adams, they were the players, the grunts."

"All right." Dean grabbed one of the files, looked it over, and logged the details away to memory. "Tell me more about the unit. Who were they? What was their mandate? Their mission statement?"

"That's where I'm having a difficult time painting a full picture," Wilson said. "It's probably best if you talk to Eldridge to get the rundown on that. When you're done talking to Mike Vendrell's wife, have a chat with Eldridge, but I think it'd be smart if you—"

"Checked out Harlow's place?"

The SAC squinted knowingly. "You already did, didn't you?"

"About an hour ago."

"What did you find?"

"Not a damn thing." Dean shook his head. "Harlow's two-bedroom in Eagle Rock was cleaned out by the time the manager let me in. Everything was gone—the furniture, the clothes in the closet, even the food from the fridge had been dumped. Someone also made it a point to scrub the place down with disinfectant. There wasn't a single trace of anything."

The newsflash triggered a laugh from Wilson. "Who cleared out the apartment?"

Dean raised an eyebrow. "The manager claimed the

place was cleaned out in the middle of the night. He wasn't there, so he didn't see who did it. When I asked the neighbors, only one of them saw something, an old lady in the apartment two doors down from Harlow's." He snickered. "Olivia Baena. She's ninety-one, and her vision is shot to shit, so she only saw, and I quote, '*Dos hombres. Eran grandes.*'"

"Two men," Wilson translated, "and they were big."

"We're not going to find out who cleared out Harlow's apartment, boss," Dean said, "and whoever did wiped it clean and probably did a deep six on whatever evidence may have been inside of it."

"Outstanding." Wilson sighed. "Back to square one."

"What about these allegations that came forth?" Dean tossed the file in his hand on the desk. "When did the Bureau take a proactive interest in these guys?"

"A reporter," Wilson said. "Layla Adrian. She's been writing an exposé on the SMASH unit. She came forward to us several times in the past six months with bits and pieces of information that shed light on the SMASH unit's alleged corruption. She was trying to get the FBI involved, and with what she presented to us, we deemed it appropriate to launch an investigation."

Dean laughed, closed his eyes, and sat back in his chair.

"What did I miss?" Wilson said. "Something amusing there, slick?"

"She came to my hotel," Dean said. "She stopped by the night Mike Vendrell was killed. She was asking questions about what happened. The cop who was babysitting the crime scene on the PCH dimed me out after I got under his skin a little bit."

"No surprise there." Wilson flicked his gaze toward the windows. "Layla Adrian has had her finger on the pulse of this whole thing for a while. She's called this office about a dozen times in the past couple of months. She's tenacious."

"Yeah." Dean clicked his teeth. "I'm curious what's led her to believe that the SMASH guys are corrupt, being that she seems to be your sole source of this information."

"For starters, she interviewed a guy by the name of David Delroy. That's how this started. He was arrested by the SMASH unit. Guy served eight months before he was cut loose. After Delroy got out, he sat down with her at length. He told Layla that he was set up, that the SMASH unit framed him when he wouldn't give them a taste of his monthly take from his heroin peddling. The story sounded legitimate, but before Layla could interview him further, Delroy fell off a balcony at his apartment building."

Dean furrowed his brow. "He fell off a balcony?"

"Convenient timing, right?" Wilson said. "LAPD said that Delroy had three times the legal limit of alcohol in his system when they scraped his body off the pavement. They chalked it up to an accident, though Ms. Adrian felt the need to underscore the fact to us that Delroy wasn't a drinker, and the division who handled his so-called 'accident'—"

"Was the same division," Dean cut in, "that SMASH is a part of."

Wilson nodded. "Correct." He tapped the files in front of him. "Ms. Adrian's got about ten of these stories of the SMASH guys setting people up, and she's got some solid evidence to back it up. I've made digital copies for your consumption that I'll send over immediately."

"Okay." Dean rose from his chair and paced. "We've got a reporter diming out bad cops. She's the source of all this, the person who kicked this thing into motion." He put his gaze on the window that looked out to the city and replayed the night he met Layla Adrian. "And if she's not careful, she might end up tripping over some railing just like our buddy Delroy did."

"Talk with her," Wilson said. "Find out more about what she knows. And you're right. If what she says about SMASH being crooked is true, she might end up caught between someone's crosshairs if she stumbles across something of value."

"Will do."

"So," Wilson crossed his arms, "where do you plan to start with all of this?"

"I want to talk to Vendrell's wife, Sharon." Dean moved to the door. "Vendrell was the only one with any living family members. Harlow was single—no kids, no girlfriend. Same goes for the rest of the guys in the unit." He motioned to the file folders. "Tyler Adams is the only other one in the unit with a partner, a girlfriend. I'll get around to talking to all of them at some point. First, I want to talk with their spouses, at least the one guy who had one."

"Why not talk to the SMASH members first?"

"Because they're cops," Dean said, "and cops tend to hold back, to say only what they need to say or were approved in advance to say. They might bullshit or stonewall me—but Vendrell's wife, Sharon, if someone like her late husband Mike was as corrupt as certain people are making him out to be, she would have benefited from his ill-gotten gains. I want to take a look at Mike's house. Talk to his wife. See what kind of man he really was."

"Sounds good." Wilson held up a finger. "But one more thing before you go."

Dean turned around. "What?"

"What kind of piece are you carrying?"

Dean pulled open his jacket to reveal only his FBI shield.

"You're kidding me," Wilson said. "Why aren't you carrying a weapon?"

"I haven't needed one," Dean replied. "Haven't wanted to either, quite honestly."

"You're an FBI agent."

"No shit."

"Then you should always have a weapon on you." Wilson threw up his hands. "You might be the first former Army guy I know who doesn't want to have a piece on him."

"I'm not Tim Kennedy or Jocko Willink, boss," Dean replied. "There are plenty of guys out there guarding the gates. I used to be one of them." He put his focus on the window. "But that's not who I am. Not anymore."

"What are you going to use if a guy starts shooting at you?" Wilson asked. "Harsh language?"

Dean said nothing.

"All right," Wilson groaned as he closed his files and motioned to the door. "Come with me."

13

The shooting range was in the basement level of the building. It was a small space, not much larger than a two-bedroom apartment, with paper targets lined up in a row in front of five shooting lanes.

Wilson handed Dean safety earmuffs and glasses as they strolled to the end of the range where a husky man with thinning hair and rolled up sleeves with a lockbox in his hand waited.

"When's the last time you went to the range?" Wilson said.

"Nine months," Dean replied, "six days, twelve hours, and forty-two minutes."

"Well, I don't need you walking around sticking your nose into this thing without the proper protection." Wilson pointed to the husky man next to them. "This is Special Agent Dietz. He's going to clear you to carry a weapon today."

Dean slapped his palm into Dietz's. "Blackwood."

Dietz shook it. "Pleasure."

Dean placed on the safety muffs and glasses and came to

the second-to-last lane on the right. He flexed his fingers as Dietz placed the case in front of him, plugged the combination into the lock, and then opened the lid to reveal the SIG P226 inside.

"Have you ever handled one of these before?" Dietz said.

"Yeah." Dean racked back the slide. "Once or twice."

"Good." The instructor motioned to the paper target 50 yards down the range. "I just need you to put a few rounds into the target. You do that, you're cleared for field duty. Easy peasy." Dean slipped on his muffs and glasses. Wilson followed suit as they stood behind Dean and waited.

Dean ran his hand over the gun and tallied how many men in his military and law enforcement career had been taken down by his hand. He counted ten in total.

It was them or me.

Hopefully I won't ever have to add to that count again.

Dean examined the weapon from barrel to grip, grabbed a magazine from inside the box, slapped it into the magazine well, and planted his feet. He raised the gun. Lined up the center mass of the target between the sights. Then he drew a deep breath as he heard the buzz of the all-clear signal ring out behind him.

Dean disengaged the safety switch.

Coiled his finger around the trigger.

Blew out his breath, squeezed the trigger twice, but didn't strike the target.

"Damn it," Dean whispered. "I'm rusty."

Dietz took a step forward. "Hey, if you want—"

"Can you adjust the target?" Dean cut in. "Set it back another 50 yards?"

Dietz nodded, reached forward, and hit the switch on the booth to the right of Dean. The paper target drifted back another 50 yards before it fluttered to a stop.

Dean changed his stance, shook off the tension in his right hand, and narrowed his eyes.

Breathe.

Don't think.

Just shoot.

Dean straightened up, raised the weapon, took aim, and unloaded all fifteen rounds inside the magazine into the paper target until the slide racked back empty with a harsh metallic *click*.

The smoke cleared. Dietz took a step forward and hit the switch. The paper target rolled toward them until it came to a stop.

Wilson smirked.

Dean shook his head.

Dietz motioned to the fifteen holes that had been punched square in the center of the chest.

Tight groupings.

Fatal shots across the board.

"The kid's a natural," Dietz said. "Not bad at all."

"Yeah," Dean replied. "Just like riding a bike."

14

It came as no shock to Dean that victim one, Mike Vendrell, was living in a house that was way above his pay grade. Like most cops, his residence was a safe distance from his normal work route in a wealthy suburban section of Silver Lake. The house was two stories, plantation style with manicured lawns and hedges to match, the kind of house that reflected no less than a million-dollar price tag—and it was only a six-minute drive from where Cole Harlow, his old buddy, had been killed the night before.

Dean put the Prius into park, slipped out, and saw Mike Vendrell's wife, Sharon, seated in a lawn chair. Her face was pale and her eyes glossed over, telltale signs of a woman grieving the loss of her spouse.

Dean unzipped his leather jacket to show his FBI shield, stuffing his hands in his pockets as he craned his neck to catch the woman's eye. "Mrs. Vendrell?"

Sharon shuddered, shooting a glance in Dean's direction as she clapped her hand over her chest. "Yes?"

"I'm Dean Blackwood," Dean said. "We spoke on the phone about an hour ago."

The wife of the late Mike Vendrell breathed a sigh. "Oh, right." She stood and motioned to the front door. "Please, come in."

Sharon led Dean into the home. Once the pair stepped into the foyer, Dean did a scan of the home. Everything from the red Parisian rug to the plush leather sofas and the 50-inch television confirmed that Mike Vendrell had some extra income that wasn't being claimed on his tax returns. Even Mrs. Vendrell's attire looked like it was made from expensive material, but it was the home theater down the hall off to Dean's left, roughly the size of a small gym, that really caught his attention.

Sharon closed the front door, crossing her arms like there was a chill in the air. "Can I get you anything?"

Dean shook his head. "No, thank you." He approached the framed photos on the hand-carved credenza in the living room. There were pictures of Vendrell in his dress blues. His LAPD graduation photo. A couple of snapshots of Vendrell and his wife on their wedding day, and a few more pictures of various family gatherings. Above the photos was an indentation in the wall that looked like it was made by a grown man's fist.

"So," Sharon cleared her throat, "how can I help you, Agent Blackwood?"

"First and foremost," Dean stepped away from the photos, "I'm very sorry for your loss."

"Are you?"

Dean, suppressing a smirk, knew his attempt at sounding sincere sounded anything but.

"To be honest," Sharon said, "I don't understand why the FBI is involved. I figured this would be an internal matter with the LAPD."

"The FBI has deemed it fit to become involved, Mrs.

Vendrell. When they decide to step in and decide that something is going to happen," he reflected back briefly on his reluctance to take part in the case, "no one can say otherwise.

"That's going to cause some headaches."

"Especially after Cole Harlow was killed three nights ago."

A tear slid down Sharon's cheek. "Yeah." She wiped it away. "I heard about it this morning. Actually, when you called to tell me you were coming by, my lawyer said he should be present for whatever questions you had."

"Why isn't he?"

"Because I have nothing to hide." Sharon spread her hands, palms out, in a show of transparency. "The way I see it, the FBI getting involved might help speed up the process of finding who killed Mike. The LAPD hasn't made much headway with the case so far. "

Dean waited a beat before speaking. "I need to ask you a few questions about your husband."

Sharon moved to the couch. Dean noted the bruising on her left wrist that appeared to be made from a hand that had gripped on and dug into her flesh.

Interesting.

He narrowed his eyes.

Very *interesting.*

"Well, ask away," Sharon said flippantly. "You'll forgive me if I'm only able to stomach a few minutes of this, considering the circumstances."

"Can you tell me more about Mike? How was he in the days leading up to the incident?"

"Mike's been," Sharon closed her eyes, "*was* working a lot lately. I only saw him a few times in the past few weeks.

We got into, well," she wrung her fingers, "a little disagree-ment about it."

"How so?"

"I told Mike he was working too much. That maybe he should cut back. That his work with the unit was too much for him to handle."

"And did you know," Dean said, "the kind of work his unit was involved in?"

Sharon shook her head. "Mike never told me the details. I knew they served high-risk warrants, things like that, but we always agreed that the moment Mike walked through the door, he'd leave his work at the office. Still, we had been talking lately about him taking up something a little less stressful within the department. He was stressed out, and it was showing."

"How did those talks go?"

Strain crept into Sharon's tone. "Those conversations never went too far," she said. "Mike was always going to do what Mike was going to do. I loved him." She looked away. "He just had a hard time hitting pause on work when he came home."

"Did he seem off lately?" Dean said. "Anything out of the ordinary?"

"No, not really," Sharon replied. "Doing what he did for a living," she huffed, "he was always a bit on edge, but that was expected."

Press her.

She's giving you standard, bullshit responses.

"So," Dean said, "you probably wouldn't know why he had a burner phone on him, then."

Sharon's eyelids narrowed into slits. "I assume it was work related."

"You sound pretty certain."

"Should I not be?"

"Not necessarily," Dean said. "I guess I'm just inclined to think if I found out that my significant other had a burner phone on them, my mind would assume they were up to something they wouldn't want anyone to know about." He motioned to Sharon. "Their spouse included."

Sharon flexed her jaw muscles. "That's an extreme assumption you're making there, Agent Blackwood."

Dean shrugged. "It's the kind of question I have to ask, Mrs. Vendrell. I need to go through all the scenarios to figure out which one falls in line with the truth."

"Again, Mike could be defined by a lot of words, but *unfaithful* was definitely not one of them."

Dean had logged enough hours in interrogation that he could sniff out when someone was withholding information, when they were saying something or—in this case— *not* saying something. He'd worked with enough clients coached by their attorneys that he knew when answers were rehearsed, and he sensed that Sharon had some preparation with her responses before he even arrived at the house.

"This is a very nice home," Dean said as he gestured to the home theater room down the hall. "Mike had a lot of neat toys."

Sharon furrowed her brow. "And?"

"People on this block are corporate attorneys, studio executives, things like that." Dean motioned to the bay window that looked out toward the street. "The caliber of people who pull six figures or more a year."

"So?"

"So," Dean stepped closer to the couch, "Mike was pulling in a little over $100k a year before taxes, right? Guy like that couldn't afford half the stuff in this home if that were the case."

A scowling Sharon fished a pack of cigarettes out of her pocket, popped one in her mouth, and lit it. "Are you married, Agent Blackwood?"

"I was."

"Well," Sharon took a drag of her cigarette, "hopefully it was long enough that you can empathize with someone losing their spouse."

"I can."

"Then how would you feel if you were in my position and you were being treated like some kind of accessory?"

"Your husband," Dean said, "and one of the members in his unit were killed in the same fashion. That would indicate a pattern, and my job is to find who's responsible for creating that pattern—and why."

"Then explain to me," Sharon said, "how treating me like I'm a suspect instead of a victim assists you with your investigation."

"Because I feel like you know something," Dean replied. "I have a sense that you had a strained relationship with your husband based on the way you're acting and speaking." He pointed to the welts on Sharon's wrist. "You have bruises on your wrists that are probably the result of someone pinning you down. Also," he motioned to the indentation in the wall above the photos on the credenza, "that fist-sized dent right there leads me to believe that you and Mike weren't exactly the Cleavers."

Sharon straightened her back. "You think I'm *lying* to you, Agent Blackwood?"

"The thought crossed my mind."

The widow of Mike Vendrell took one final pull of her cigarette, tossed it in the coffee mug, and stood. "I have to bury my husband this week, Agent Blackwood." She moved to the front door and opened it. "So, please, if you don't mind."

Dean offered a slight nod, produced a business card, and placed it on a console table near the door. "Call me if you change your mind. I'd be thrilled to get a straight answer from you."

"Marcus Haywood," Sharon said.

Dean stepped onto the porch and angled his body around. "Come again?"

"Marcus Haywood," she repeated. "Mike and Cole had a run-in with him when they worked patrol together a few years ago. I'd suggest you look into him."

"Why's that?"

"Just..." Sharon brought a hand to her face. "Just do it, Agent Blackwood."

The grieving widow threw the door shut behind Dean and engaged the locks, muttering a stream of curses as Dean headed to the street, piled into his rental, and then rang up Wilson on his cell.

"How'd it go with Vendrell's wife?" Wilson asked.

"She was giving me static," Dean said as he slipped the key into the ignition. "I'm pretty sure she was holding something back."

"What makes you say that?"

"Everything. The house, the whole battered routine thing she had going on." Dean shook his head. "It's like a bad procedural cop drama, Willy. All signs point to Vendrell being on the take here."

"How hard did you press his wife?"

"Very," Dean said. "If we're trying to smoke these guys out, we need to be stern with these people. Sharon Vendrell was holding something back, and I want her to feel like she needs to fess up now that the Feds are involved before things go bad for her. That's why I started with her. She seems to be the most vulnerable, so I wanted to apply some pressure. Until she starts talking, though, I'll need to take a look at Vendrell's work history. Speaking of which," Dean recalled the name Sharon had given him, "we need to run the name Marcus Haywood through the databases."

"Who is he?"

"Not sure. Sharon said that Vendrell and Harlow had a run-in with him back when they were working a beat." Dean shook his head. "When she said the name, she..." His voice trailed off.

"What is it?" Wilson said.

"I don't know," Dean replied. "It sounded forced, like someone *instructed* her to give me that name. It's just a feeling though. Either way, we should still run the name and cross-reference it to Harlow and Vendrell's jackets."

"We're working on pulling them now. It's taking a little time. I've been playing pin the tail on the warrant with the deputy assistant director over the phone every couple of hours."

"What about Eldridge?" Dean replied. "I told you last night I wanted to roll by his place to talk with him."

"He's agreed to lend full cooperation to the FBI, ironically enough. I told him I'd be sending one of my people to have a chat with him."

"Text me his number. Any luck with the traffic cam footage from last night?"

"We should have it within the hour. I'll connect with you when we've got it. Give me a call after you talk to Eldridge."

Dean hung up his cell. Moments later, the text from Wilson with Eldridge's number arrived. Dean then plugged in the number and dialed, holding the cell to his ear as he glanced to his right at the Vendrell house.

In the window of the living room, Dean spotted Sharon Vendrell glaring at him through the blinds.

I've seen that look before.

Dean pulled away from the curb.

That's a look of warning.

15

Dean parked his rental in front of Captain Eldridge's house and did a scan of the home, a cream-colored Cape Cod with green trim in a residential neighborhood nestled in the hillside.

I've been here before. Dad took us here for a barbecue.

He chuckled.

Tommy and I got in trouble for trying to climb onto the roof.

It was no mystery to Dean why Eldridge had such a lofty place. He had grown up long enough among the elite of the LAPD that he knew the type. Guys like Eldridge were administrators, people with connections, the kind of guys who proudly showed off the framed photos in their den that featured them shaking hands with politicians and celebrities—the influential power-wielders of the city.

Dean always relished that his family couldn't be counted among those ranks. They were a blue-collar tribe who *worked* for a living, people who approached the job like any good nine-to-fiver would, earning a meager paycheck but taking pride in what they did.

Dean slid out from behind the wheel as a man exited the front door of the house. He was tall, well into his sixties with a mustache, wrinkles at the corners of his eyes, and buzz-cut, salt-and-pepper hair.His build was athletic with rock-hard muscles underneath the polo tucked into his khakis, the kind of guy Dean knew if he picked a fight with, he'd still land a few punches despite his age.

Larry Eldridge.

Dean offered the man a wave.

Oh, Captain, my Captain.

Eldridge swaggered toward Dean, full of confidence but with an essence of caution and a bit of self-entitlement. "Dean Blackwood," he said. "It's been a long time, my boy."

Dean shook his hand. "Thanks for taking the time to meet with me, Captain."

"Never thought I'd lay eyes on Donny Blackwood's kid again." Eldridge's smooth voice was akin to that of a seasoned politician. "How's he doing?"

"He's all right," Dean said. "Just riding out his retirement years."

"Don Blackwood was one of the best homicide detectives in the department. And I remember *you*, buddy boy. Summer of '98 you caught a pop fly during the kids' baseball game. It was one of the best plays I've ever seen, no question about it."

He's pretty chipper for a dude that just lost two guys in his unit.

"Mind if we have a few words?" Dean said. "You already spoke to my SAC, but I have a few clarifying questions I need to ask."

"By all means." Eldridge strolled toward the garage. "As I said, I'm happy to offer the Bureau my full cooperation."

"I'm inclined to think the LAPD would find the guy who did it, box him in, and tell everyone he took a spill off a roof by 'accident.' Hell," Dean smirked, "I wouldn't blame you."

Eldridge's smile turned down into a frown. "That's not how I operate. I've made it a point to purge the department of the kind of trash who uses the badge for personal gain. And to be frank with you, it would be foolish of me to not look to the Bureau for an assist here. I lost two of my guys in under twenty-four hours. They were good cops, good men. I want whoever did this to get nailed on a *federal* level."

The two men strolled toward part of the lawn that faced west toward La Cañada Flintridge, a small, affluent township that embodied the "bubble-minded mentality" of Los Angeles. From what Dean remembered, La Cañada prided itself in terms of academics and its deep-pocketed citizens but didn't have much in the way of scruples or a notable high school football team. Even though Dean grew up in Echo Park, he knew a few kids from the area—immoderate folks who, post-college, were gifted a house by their prosperous parents as a wedding gift while they ventured into real estate and resold the same seven-figure properties over and over again.

Those morons never stopped hanging out under the bleachers.

"So," Eldridge said. "Don Blackwood's son joined the Feds, huh?"

Dean nodded. "Indeed, he did."

"I've always liked your family, Dean. And I admired your father for being as diligent as he was after your brother passed away." Eldridge clapped Dean on the shoulder. "And I'm sorry that our people failed to find the guy who did it."

Yeah.

A lot of us are.

"Why do you think this is happening?" Dean asked in a bid to change the subject. "I think we can state with a degree of certainty that Harlow and Vendrell were being targeted. SMASH probably has a long list of enemies, I'd imagine. You guys have taken down some rough characters all around the city. I would think there might be some kind of vendetta against your people as a result."

Eldridge huffed. "*A lot* of people are looking to kill cops in general, Agent Blackwood. It comes with the job."

"Without question," Dean said, "but is there any reason or someone in particular who would want Vendrell and Harlow dead? Or any other members of the squad for that matter?"

"SMASH is an elite unit," Eldridge reasoned. "We tackle big cases all around the city. Kind of causes a ripple effect that trickles down. That was my pitch when I started it. I went to work with this Ivy League brainiac I recruited. We mapped out how organized crime units would topple like dominoes if you shut them down in a certain order. Taking down one guy would start a war or a rivalry with certain crews who already had bad blood. I had the Ivy League whiz break it down to sheer numbers. I essentially got a think tank together to figure out how to approach police work with, well, an algorithm."

"So, SMASH," Dean said, "is pretty much the equivalent of a private military company the CIA uses to cripple regimes. The city doesn't simply have you arresting and busting people. You do it in a methodical way that essentially lets gangs wipe other gangs out, in a lot of ways."

Eldridge nodded. "One could say that. And the results speak for themselves. We've shut down or watched the self-destruction of a litany of crews—Grade A assholes. Crime has gone down, and that, Agent Blackwood, is the endgame."

"But it's no doubt pissed off a significant number of people," Dean noted. "The list of enemies and complaints have to be pretty long."

"Definitely. But SMASH has been so successful maintaining alliances with the right people that the blowback on us from our cases has been significantly low. Sure, there are a few horseshit rumors of misconduct and other allegations floating around, but that's standard. Someone's always lodging a bogus complaint."

"I'm the son of a cop," Dean said. "I know how hard the job is, but, and I hate to say it, there are a few bad eggs here and there. You find them in pretty much every vocation."

"Believe me, I know," Eldridge said. "But like I said before, I can't stomach a rogue cop in my ranks, and the checks-and-balances system I've implemented weeds out people like that. I burned a recruit just last year for merely *entertaining* a conversation with a pimp about being on his payroll, and that moron's pulling traffic duty for the remainder of his career."

Marcus Haywood's name popped into Dean's mind. "Is there anyone that stands out? Anyone who had a beef with Harlow or Vendrell that might have been looking to kill them?"

The captain squinted in thought. A few moments passed. Then he closed his eyes and said, "Marcus Haywood."

Dean felt like his heart skipped a beat.

Don't tell him you talked to Sharon.

Eldridge might flip if he finds out you were questioning the wife of one of his officers.

"Who is he?" Dean said.

"Vendrell and Harlow used to be partners on a beat," Eldridge replied. "I was the one who recruited them into the unit. They had solid arrest records and the commendations to show for it. However, they *were* involved in a police brutality lawsuit by a suspect they arrested in Compton when it was claimed that Vendrell and Harlow split his skull open and partially paralyzed his hand."

"What happened with the lawsuit?"

"It got dropped," Eldridge said. "Haywood was spinning yarns. The DA knew that. After that, Haywood spent six months in San Quentin for possession with intent and assault on a peace officer. Haywood was known for running his mouth while he was locked up. Word got through to me that Haywood was talking about 'getting his' when he got out."

"When was Haywood paroled?"

"About eight weeks ago." Eldridge snapped his fingers. "God almighty. *Marcus Haywood.*" He shook his head. "I should've known this was going to come back to bite me in the ass."

Dean held up a finger. "There's one thing I'm curious about, Captain."

"Speak your mind, son."

"Vendrell and Harlow had burner phones on them when they were killed."

"They were both working with the same confidential informant. They used burner phones to keep in touch with him."

"Why use burner phones? Don't you have to log conversations with CIs?"

"SMASH works a little differently, my boy," Eldridge said. "And it takes time and a bit of improvisation to coerce some of these CIs to work for us. Harlow and Vendrell were using burners to keep in touch with this informant they were working with. The guy was nervous, really spooked, so he didn't want to communicate with them through the regular channels.The burner phones were set up in advance."

"By who?"

"The informant," Eldridge explained. "He left the burners under a bench in Glassell Park about a month ago."

"This guy must be a high-valued CI if you guys were willing to go to those lengths to keep in touch with him."

"He is."

"What does he know?"

"He's got inside knowledge," Eldridge explained, "on a pair of gun-runners we're looking into." He held up his hand. "But it's confidential. I can't really get into too much of the nitty-gritty. The tidbits of information that were given to us by this informant so far ended up panning out, so I gave Harlow and Vendrell the green light to pursue this guy further. Swooning a CI is a process, you see. It's a lot like dating. And Vendrell and Harlow were supposed to meet this informant at the locations where they were killed— that's why they were there."

"So it's possible," Dean said, "that this informant set them up for a hit?"

"That's what I'm inclined to believe."

"Who is he? This confidential informant?"

"We only know his street name, "Eldridge said. "Tookie. He's slick, whoever he is. We haven't been able to find anything in any department with his street name tagged on it. I'm working on trying to get a line on him though. As soon as I do, I'll let you know." He hung his head. "*Christ.*

Now, I'm starting to think Haywood set Vendrell and Harlow up. Maybe he was the CI all along."

Dean furrowed his brow. "Why do you say that?"

Eldridge crossed his arms. "When Haywood filed his complaint, he claimed that he got run over by Vendrell and Harlow with their cruiser the day they took him down. Like I said before, he was running his mouth in the joint about doing the *same* thing to them once he got out."

"Marcus Haywood's name came up again," Dean said to Wilson over speakerphone as he merged the Prius onto the on-ramp. "Eldridge mentioned that this guy had a lawsuit against Vendrell and Harlow a few years back after they ran him over with their cruiser during a drug bust. He lost the suit and ended up doing a stretch in San Quentin not long after. Apparently, Haywood was a little bitter about the whole situation."

"They ran him over with their cruiser?" Wilson said. "Eldridge told you this?"

"He said Haywood's story wasn't up to snuff, so the DA and Internal Affairs cleared Vendrell and Harlow of misconduct."

"And what does your gut tell you?"

"It's possible Haywood is a suspect, but I wouldn't put all our chips into that basket just yet."

"Why's that?"

Dean merged the Prius into the next lane. "I still get the feeling there's more about Vendrell and Harlow that we don't know about. Everyone is vouching for them, but I think maybe there's something we haven't learned yet. Maybe these guys fouled up somehow and it came back to bite them in the ass." His cell buzzed, an incoming call from Eldridge. "Wait one sec," he told Wilson before switching over the line.

"Blackwood," Eldridge said. "I took the liberty of calling up Marcus Haywood's parole officer. I'm forwarding his address to you now—and his PO said he didn't check in this morning."

16

Dean drove east down Moss Avenue, scanning from left to right for signs of Haywood based on the physical description his parole officer was giving him over the phone.

"Five-ten," the parole officer said. "African American. One hundred forty pounds. Has a tattoo of his mother on his inner right forearm."

"Let me guess," Dean pulled to the right and parked, "the tattoo reads 'Mom.'"

"Circle gets the square. Haywood was consistent with his check-ins for the past few weeks, but he missed today's call an hour ago. I tried him again a moment ago, but he didn't answer. I was getting ready to check in on him in person."

"He doesn't have a car, does he?"

"No," the PO said. "It's against the terms of his parole. Also, he's supposed to be looking for a job right now. I had one lined up for him, but there was an influx of parolees we had to square jobs for in the past few weeks, so it's taken a minute."

"Gotcha." Dean fastened his gaze on the house to his

right. "Well, I'm at his residence now. I'm going to knock on the door."

"Let me know. I'll be waiting."

Dean hung up and looked to his right at Haywood's residence—2349 Moss Avenue, dirt-colored, Spanish-style bungalow with barred windows and minimal upkeep on a lawn blotched with dead grass.

"Okay, Deano," he said. "Hop to it."

He nudged open the car door.

Shot a look toward the house. Saw a guy matching Marcus Haywood's description slipping out the front door.

Haywood stopped in his tracks.

He locked eyes with Dean.

Then Dean whispered, "*Shit,*" as Haywood hopped off the porch and took off in an all-out sprint.

17

Dean slipped back into the rental and threw it into drive. He tightened his grip on the steering wheel, his focus fixed on Haywood as the parolee turned right at the end of the block.

Haywood threw a quick glance over his shoulder as he dashed toward the intersection. Traffic was heavy, drivers blaring their horns and cursing out their windows as Haywood zigzagged his way around the vehicles.

Dean's heart rate ticked up as he cranked the wheel hard to the right at the end of the block, his teeth clenched as he then turned left and cruised through the cars, screeching to a stop in the middle of the street.

"God, I hate this car," Dean whispered. "Economy rigs *blow*."

Haywood cleared the next intersection and ran in a straight line, his eyes wide and mouth open as he cut a glance toward Dean's rental that was closing on him hard and fast.

Dean stomped down on the accelerator. Haywood was 20 yards ahead of him, close enough so Dean could make out the sweat on the back of the parolee's neck. He sped up. Crept up on Haywood's right. Then he slammed on the brakes, pushed open the door of the Prius, and put it in park before he continued the pursuit on foot.

Haywood threw a look at Dean over his shoulder, fear brimming in his eyes as he hopped onto the sidewalk.

Dean was 10 yards behind Haywood now, the parolee scampering across the lawn of a house where a woman tending to her garden shrieked at the top of her lungs.

Dean dived into a slide feet-first across the lawn like a ballplayer flying into home base, grass stains slicking his jeans as he collided into Haywood, knocked the parolee onto his back, and heard a gust of air shoot out of Haywood's lungs.

Dean stood up.

Drew out his SIG.

Then he planted his foot into Haywood's back, trained the gun on the guy's neck and winked. "Morning, Marcus," Dean said as he flashed his badge. "Got a minute?"

18

The woman who owned the house where Dean took Haywood down had phoned the cops seconds after Dean tackled Haywood to the ground. Three minutes later they arrived. Dean showed them his badge and explained the situation, and once the dust had settled, Dean spoke to the handcuffed Haywood seated on the hood of his rental.

"Why'd you run, Marcus?" Dean said. "A guy with priors shouldn't be doing that. It's not a good look."

Haywood, sweat clinging to his brow, hung his head. "I didn't do *shit*, man."

"If I had a nickel—"

"*Fuck you*, white boy!" Haywood widened his eyes. "I was just going for a walk when you rolled up on me."

"Where were you going, Marcus? Morning errands or something? I don't take you for a 'I'm gonna hit up a Starbucks' kind of guy."

"What do you care, bitch?"

"Rude."

"For real, bruh." Haywood writhed his body around and nodded toward his cuffs. "Take these things off me."

Dean shook his head. "We're gonna keep them on for a second, brother, at least until I get some answers from you."

"Answers about what?" Haywood said. "I don't know you. You're not my PO."

"Well, I know that you didn't check in with your parole officer this morning." Dean sat beside the parolee and took out a toothpick. "That's grounds enough for your ass to get busted back to a cell. We'll have you fitted for a jumpsuit here within the hour."

"What is this, man? God *damn*, I can't even go outside without getting harassed for taking out my garbage."

Dean inched closer. "Look at me, Marcus."

Haywood slowly turned up his gaze.

"Mike Vendrell and Cole Harlow," Dean said. "You know them. They allegedly split your skull open a few years back."

Haywood chuckled. "*Allegedly*? Vendrell threw my ass on the ground before Harlow ran me over with his cruiser."

"Well, after that happened," Dean said, "you filed a lawsuit against them that dissolved quicker than a sneeze. Then you did six months in SQ. That's the story, right?"

Haywood sneered. "Yeah."

"Well," Dean stood and paced, "did you also know Vendrell and Harlow are dead?"

Haywood's eyes widened.

"Someone ran them over with a car," Dean said, "a red beater that matches a description of the one you used to own."

"I didn't do it." Haywood held up his shackled hands. "I swear on my mother, man."

Dean narrowed his eyes. "Does the name Tookie mean anything to you?"

Haywood shrugged. "Is it supposed to?"

"Vendrell and Harlow were in touch with a confidential informant by that name. This same CI might have set them up the night they were both killed."

"You're saying I'm this guy Tookie?"

"Maybe."

"That's bullshit, man." Haywood shook his head. "I didn't kill those fools. I'm not mad that they're dead though. Those crooked-ass punks had it coming."

"Still," Dean said, "kind of a solid plan to set Vendrell and Harlow up for a hit, don't you think?"

"*Hell no*."

"Why not?"

"Because if I was gonna kill them," Haywood said, "I would have shot those fools *dead*. None of this shit you're talking about. I'd just walk right up to them and smoke 'em."

"Apparently," Dean replied, "you were running your mouth about that in SQ after you got shipped up there. A handful of informants in there, your old cell mate included, said you were talking about smoking Vendrell and Harlow once you got out."

"It was just talk, man."

"Was it?"

"It *was*." Haywood gnashed his teeth. "Those motherfuckers tried to kill me." He gestured to his back. "I still got nerve damage in my hand because of them. So what if I was talking shit about smoking them? Who wouldn't? Look, man, I'm not stupid. As much as I was hoping Vendrell and Harlow would get theirs..." He looked Dean square in his eyes. "You don't mess with SMASH, man. Everyone knows that. They own the city, and trying to go up against them is suicide."

Dean took a moment to assess Haywood's tone and body language.

He's telling the truth.

Plus, he's not all that smart, and whoever killed Vendrell and Harlow is. Haywood didn't do this.

He's just too stupid to have pulled this whole thing off.

"Why didn't you check in with your PO?" Dean asked. "Tell me that much."

"I was busy."

"Busy doing what?"

Haywood hung his head. "Because I had someone over with me. I'm not supposed to be chillin' with people I associated with before. I'd get busted back if my PO found out. Just go back to my house. Ask the girl that's there. Her name's Kara, man. She'll tell you everything."

19

Several minutes later, Dean escorted Marcus through the front door of his house. Sure enough, the woman Marcus had mentioned—Kara—was passed out on the couch—a beach bunny type that Dean felt was way too attractive to be hanging out with a guy like Marcus.

How in the hell did Marcus score a girl like this?

Kara awoke.

She yawned.

Then she saw Dean's FBI badge, the handcuffs on Marcus's wrists, and proceeded to scream as she threw an ashtray at Dean's head.

"Okay," Dean grumbled as he ducked out of the way, the ashtray shattering against the wall behind him. "Everyone chill out."

He flashed his badge. Kara sat down on the couch. Then Dean instructed Marcus to take a seat next to his "girlfriend" as he proceeded to do a walk-through of the home.

He found weed in the bedroom.

A half-empty liquor stash in the kitchen.

Popped a toothpick in when Woody suggested he "take some for the road."

After that, it didn't take long for Dean to piece together that they'd had a two-day long party, passed out, and as a result, Marcus forgot to check in with his parole officer.

"The hell is wrong with you, Marcus?" Dean said. "You get out of the joint, and the first thing you do is get a load on?"

"It was Kara's idea," Marcus said as he pointed to the bleary-eyed woman beside him. "It was *all* this bitch."

"For real?!" Kara screamed as she shot up from her seat. "You're seriously gonna rat me out to a *Fed*, you punk-ass,limp-dick?"

"Keep your inside voice on , bitch!"

"Fuck *you*!"

A screaming match ensued between Kara and Marcus for several moments. As they exchanged a series of insults and curses, Dean pinched the bridge of his nose and sighed. When Kara started slapping Marcus—who proceeded to curl up into the fetal position on the couch—he decided to step in.

"*Enough*," Dean grumbled. "Both of you sit the fuck down."

The pair cursed under their breath, and plopped back down on the couch. Dean's focus was on Kara who trembled as she ogled the FBI shield clipped to his belt.

"You look worried," Dean said.

"You're a *cop*," Kara replied.

"I'm the *FBI*," Dean clarified. "That means I could look up anything and everything about you. If you have an overdue library book, which, by the way, I seriously doubt you read anything beyond TikTok captions, I'll know about it."

"*Fuck. You*," Kara whispered under her breath. "You don't know anything about me."

"I'm betting I can make some reasonable assumptions that'll hold water," Dean said. "I'm betting that Marcus may have paid you to hang out with him here the past few days."

Kara, eyes narrowed, said nothing.

"You see," Dean wagged a finger, "the fact that you didn't clap back at me when I said that told me everything I needed to know." He gestured to Marcus. "Where'd you find her, man? You damn sure didn't pick her up on some street corner. This is a high-class caliber of woman you got here, and she's *way* out of your price range."

"We're friends," Kara said. "That's all."

"Bullshit." Dean propped his booted foot up on the coffee table in front of the couch. "How much did Marcus pay for you, Kara?"

"He didn't."

"But you *are* a working girl, aren't you?"

Kara said nothing.

"Answer me," Dean said, "otherwise I'll have you locked up before the hour is out."

"*Fine!*" Kara threw up her hands. "I am. So what?"

"And I'm supposed to just believe that you're hanging out with Marcus because you dig him?" Dean nodded to the half-empty tequila bottle on the table. "Did you foot the bill for that too? Marcus can't rub two cents together right now, so he sure as shit didn't pay for the ganja and the booze on his own."

"I brought it, okay?" Kara said. "It's mine."

"And what did *you* get in exchange for all of this?" Dean asked. "We both know you're not spending time with Marcus willingly. How much did he pay for this?"

Kara hung her head.

Took a deep breath.

Then she said, "Two grand," pulled out her purse, and showed Dean the twenty $100 bills that backed up her claims.

"Marcus," Dean said as he counted the cash, "this isn't your money, is it?"

Marcus shook his head. "No."

"Where did you get it?"

"Someone *else* paid for it," Kara said. "They said they were a friend of Marcus. They said Marcus got out recently, that they wanted to pay for him to have a good time to celebrate being out on parole."

"Who?"

"I don't know." Kara shrugged. "Some guy."

"You're going to have to be more specific," Dean said. "I can't put out an APB on 'some guy.'"

Kara went on to explain that someone left a voicemail on her phone—she made most of her appointments with clients on that line—and after the call came in, she returned to her apartment to find a box of liquor had been left along with $2,000 and instructions to meet Marcus at his home.

"They left a note with everything," Kara said. "It said 'Show him a good time.' They gave me Marcus's address too."

"That was it?" Dean huffed. "Some guy just walked right into your apartment, left you booze, two grand, and a note?"

"Yeah."

"And I'm supposed to believe that?"

"It's *true*." Kara's eyes widened. "That's exactly how it happened. I swear to God!" She held her head in her hands. "I'm not even supposed to be here. They told me to leave before noon."

Dean tapered his eyes. "Come again?"

"I was supposed to leave at noon today," Kara said. "That's what the note said. I only stayed around because I fell asleep on the couch and forgot."

Why would someone want her to leave at that exact time?

The gears in Dean's brain turned at full speed.

Because they wanted to stick to a timeline.

Whoever paid Kara to do this only wanted her around for a short time, but why?

The more Kara spoke, the more the story, as insane as it sounded, appeared to be genuine to Dean. Nothing in her tone, body language, or demeanor indicated she was being deceptive, and even though the whole story sounded absolutely insane, Dean, to his surprise, believed every word of it.

"The number that called you," Dean said, "do you have it on you?"

"It was a blocked number," Kara explained as she pulled out her cell phone and handed it to Dean so he could verify her claims. "There was no number listed. The cash was good. The liquor was there. It was an easy $2,000. That's the way I saw it. I didn't ask any questions."

Someone set Marcus up, Dean thought as he scrolled through Kara's phone, found the unlisted number and corresponding voicemail from that number, and handed it back. *They knew Marcus was on parole, sent him a call girl, and hoped he would get caught and busted. And he did.* Dean held his head high. *By me.*

But who *exactly set this whole thing up?*

"Get your stuff, Kara," Dean said. "And before you leave, I want you to write down your full name, address, phone number, and Social Security number. You're not in trouble, but I want to know that I'll be able to find you if we need to talk again. Once you leave here, I never want to see you near

Marcus or this house again. I don't want to see you hooking either. If I find out you've gone against that advice, you're going to jail."

The woman jotted down her information for Dean, grabbed her purse, and bid her apologies. Moments later, she was out the door, and as soon as Dean heard the squeal of her car tires peeling up the street, he put his focus back on Marcus, pulled out his cell, called up Marcus's parole officer, and placed the call on speaker.

"Marcus is here," Dean told the PO. "I'm looking right at him."

"Where was he?" the PO replied. "Why the hell didn't he check in?"

Dean took a moment to look Marcus over. He knew that if he told the PO the story about Kara, the booze, and the weed, Marcus would be locked up until the second coming of Christ. The guy was stupid, the textbook definition of a fool, but Dean couldn't find it in himself to watch the guy get locked up for the rest of his life because he made a foolish, victimless mistake.

"Wait one sec," Dean told the PO. "I need to ask him something."

A bleary-eyed Marcus flickered up his gaze as Dean muted the call.

"Marcus," Dean said, "if I cut you loose, if I let you go here today, you're on the straight and narrow?"

"I *swear*, man," Marcus replied, his mouth open and eyes wide with hope. "If you cut me loose—"

"If I cut you loose and find out that you step outside of your bounds one more time," Dean held up a finger, "*one* more time, I'll personally see to it that you rot in prison for the rest of your life. I mean it, brother—you fuck around with this, you fuck around with *me*, you will never, and I repeat *never*, breathe free air again. You're a fool, Marcus, a goddamn dumbass, and I'm giving you one last chance to do the right thing, to get your life in order. Are we clear?"

Marcus trembled and nodded his head repeatedly as Dean unmuted the call and continued speaking with the parole officer.

"It was a misunderstanding," Dean explained to the PO. "Marcus has the flu. He's going to call you in a few minutes to clear the air."

"Fine," the PO said. "But this is his one and only screw-up. Make sure that's clear to him."

After the call ended—and once Dean had dumped and flushed Marcus's liquor and weed stash—he reiterated his deal with Marcus, took the handcuffs off him, and headed out of the house. Once he was back behind the wheel of his rental, he put in a call to Wilson.

"It's not Haywood," Dean said. "He's got nothing to do with this. He was too busy partying with a call girl by the name of Kara Shardlow the whole night."

Dean then told Wilson the same story Kara had told him about the booze, the two grand, and the anonymous caller who paid for the whole thing.

"This guy just broke into this woman's apartment?" Wilson said. "He just left this woman cash and booze and told her to show Marcus a good time?"

"As insane as it sounds," Dean replied, "I think it's true. I'm going to forward you this woman's information. I think we should try to suss out who paid her to hang out with Marcus. My guess is that they were trying to get him busted for smoking weed and sleeping with hookers so he'd get thrown back in prison."

"Who would do that? And why?"
Eldridge?

Could he have set Marcus up?

I mean, he's the one who sent me after him in the first place.

"Let me think on that one for a little bit," Dean said. "All I do know is that Marcus isn't responsible for killing Vendrell or Harlow. The guy can barely keep his own head screwed on straight. Plus, he's got an alibi. He was busy with his little beach bunny the nights that Vendrell and Harlow were killed. I need to keep digging. We also need to have another chat with Ms. Shardlow soon. We need to find out who paid her to hang out with Marcus. I'm forwarding you her details."

"Understood. Where are you headed now?"

Dean did the math and estimated he was about five minutes from his old man's place. "I'm gonna stop by my dad's house." He ran his hand across the steering wheel. "Figured I might borrow his Catalina. This POS ride of mine isn't doing me any favors."

Wilson laughed. "You chase Haywood down in your car or something?"

"Long story," Dean replied. "I'll tell you all about it later. I'm just gonna pop in, say hi to the old man, and then I'll get back to it."

Dean hung up, turned over the Prius's ignition, and cruised down the road toward his father's place.

Within two blocks, he was certain that a minivan was tailing him.

20

D ean clicked his teeth as he twisted the door handle and entered his father's house.

Still keeping all the doors unlocked.

He rolled his eyes.

Nice job, old man.

"Hey, Pop," Dean called out. "You around?"

"I'm in the office," his father replied. "Back here."

Dean came into the living room and looked around. The house was a hodgepodge of furniture purchased second-hand, a bachelor pad setup void of any feminine touches. Posters for *The French Connection* and *The Magnificent Seven* hung above the LCD in the living room, and tacked to the walls were photos, placards, and other mementos of now-retired LAPD Robbery-Homicide Captain Donald Jeffrey Blackwood's career.

Way back when, Dean'sfather was a rockstar, a renowned detective who, in his prime, had participated in some of the most well-known cases the LAPD had ever seen —the Hillside Strangler, the Grim Sleeper, the Night

Stalker. But now he was just a retired old man living out his days watching TV and sipping coffee. That always bothered Dean. Being a cop was Donald's purpose, his reason for living, but now, in his golden years, he was just another old man trying to get from one day to the next.

Dean strolled into the hallway, turned left into the second door, and found his father hunched over his laptop. Dean lingered in the doorway for a moment, his heart weighing heavy as he realized his father looked much older than he did when he last saw him.

"Howdy," Dean greeted. "This a bad time?"

Don held up the "one minute" finger and continued to type.

Dean checked his watch, feeling like he did when he was a kid waiting for the old man to give him permission to speak. He wasn't surprised that his father was acting like Dean had been there for a week, even though it was the first time Dean had seen him in over a year.

The Blackwoods, Dean knew, were not that big on Hallmark-league sentimentalities.

"All right," Don grumbled as he removed his glasses and rubbed the bridge of his nose. "That's enough of that."

Dean squinted at the computer. "What are you working on?"

"Spreadsheets for the Airbnb unit," Don said. "I'm getting ready for tax season."

"You're renting out the cabin?" Dean recalled the two-story cottage on North Lake Tahoe, the one his father had purchased with the life insurance payout he received after the death of his wife, Dean's mother.

"No, I keep that place all to myself. I still go up there when I can." Don shifted his muscular, sixty-six-year-old frame on his seat. "I invested in some property out in Silver Lake last year. My money guy said it'd be good to put some of my pension into real estate. It's working out well so far."

"Sounds like a lucrative enterprise, Pop."

"It's doing all right." Don flicked a glance toward the door. "You want some coffee?"

"Sure."

The two men walked into the kitchen. Don snagged two mugs from the cabinet before he proceeded to pour him and Dean a pair of coffees—no sugar, no cream.

"You wanna borrow the car," Don said as he handed Dean a mug and moved into the living room, "don't you?"

Dean laughed. "How'd you know?"

"You got that look," his father replied as he sat down on his recliner positioned in front of the television. "That whole timid thing you used to put on display when you were a kid."

"Well, can I?"

"Maybe." Don sipped his coffee. "Thing needs an oil change. It's not in my budget right now."

"I'll pay for it, Pop. I'm good for it."

"Just don't take it to Jiffy Lube."

"Why not?"

"They don't put the right oil in."

"That's a load of malarkey." *Now you're talking like the old man, Deano.* "Plus, Jiffy Lube is cheaper."

"No Jiffy Lube," Donald grumbled. "Take it to my guy over in Glassell Park. I'm not asking you—I'm telling you."

"All right, Captain." Dean held his hands up in surrender. "Copy that."

"Keys are in the foyer on the table." Donald gestured toward the front door with his mug. "Just bring it back with a full tank."

"Will do."

"So," Don placed his mug down on the Dodgers coaster beside him. "How've you been?"

"Hanging in there."

"How's Jeremy?"

"He's good." Dean glanced at the coaster under his father's coffee mug. "Trying to take him to a Dodgers game while I'm in town, actually."

"Season starts back up next week."

"You're more than welcome to join us."

Don's lips twitched into a subtle smirk. "That sounds nice. Haven't seen that kid of yours in a while."

"Haven't seen *you* in a while, Pop." Dean took a seat on the couch beside his father's recliner. "You doing okay?"

"Crying out loud," Donald groaned as he waved his hand through the air. "I'm tired of people asking me that."

"Like who?"

"You. The doctors. Everyone."

"*Christ*, Pop," Dean groaned. "Don't tell me you're not going to your appointments."

"Negative."

"Why the hell not?"

"Because I'm old." Donald scooped up the television remote and surged through the channels. "And I don't need to pay some hack to tell me my heart and joints are shit when I *know* they're shit."

"That's real good," Dean replied as he watched his father sift through the channels. "Live out your remaining years malnourished."

"I drink plenty of water."

"There's more to it than that."

"You a nurse now?" his father snapped. "I'm just south of being seventy, kid. I think I know how to take care of myself. Just keep your goddamn comments to yourself, okay?"

Same old Donald, same old bullshit.

If Mom were still here, she'd swipe the remote out of his hand and cram those vitamins down his throat.

A few moments of silence passed as Donald turned on KCAL 9 news, put down his remote, and shook his head at the anchor covering a story about the LAPD dealing with protestors in the middle of shutting down a section of the 134 freeway.

"I swear," Don said, "the fake news never covers anything accurately. It's all about ratings, son. Always has been, always will be."

Dean fixated on the TV. "Have you heard about those cops? The ones that got run over?"

"Damn tragedy. Gibbons called me the other night and told me all about it."

"Lieutenant Gibbons?"

"It's *captain* now. Old bastard should retire, but he's more belligerent than a bull."

Takes one to know one, Dean thought. "You know," he said, "I, uh, came into town early because the Bureau wanted me to take a peek at the crime scenes."

A twinkle glimmered in Don's eyes. "You're kidding me."

"My old handler asked me to come into town a day early to give him an assessment."

"And?"

"Two cops get run over by a car in the span of two days." Dean wrinkled his nose. "It stinks, Pop. That much I do know."

"Who were they?"

"Members of the SMASH unit. I'm sure you've heard of them."

Don turned down his eyes. "SMASH started up after I left the force."

"You know Eldridge, though," Dean said. "He's the captain of the unit."

Don nodded. "We worked together a handful of times when I was still on the job. Haven't seen him in a while. You met him too. We went to a few of his barbecues when you were a kid." His eyes glossed over. "You, Tommy, and your sister."

"Yeah, I remember," Dean said. "You probably don't know much about the two of his guys that got killed then, Vendrell and Harlow."

Donald perched forward in his chair, narrowed his eyes, and fastened them on his son. "You're barking up the wrong tree, Deano. I left the job when they were still forming the SMASH unit. I never met any of those boys. Heck, half the kids in uniform were still your age when I left."

"So you don't know anything about the allegations of misconduct and excessive force that were leveled against SMASH?"

"It's the LAPD, son," Don said. "We've all had run-ins with that sort of thing. I can't even count how many times a perp tried to file some grievance to throw shade on me. It's politics. Nothing more than that."

"Yeah," Dean said. "But something isn't right about all this, Pop. I've only done a little bit of legwork, but there's something off with Vendrell and Harlow. Eldridge is vouching for them, but the whole case just feels...*wrong*."

"You spoke to Eldridge?"

"I did."

"How does he feel about the FBI being involved in this thing?"

"He's offering up his full cooperation," Dean said. "He's looking to take down the guy who did this."

"You got any leads? Anything pointing you in the right direction?"

"Eldridge was inclined to think that a guy named Haywood might have been responsible. Haywood had a bad run-in with Vendrell and Harlow before. I just spoke to him before I got here."

Donald flexed his brow. "*Spoke* to him, huh?" He laughed. "Knowing you, you probably pinned the guy against a wall and choked his answers out of him."

"I don't work like that anymore, Pop," Dean replied. "But yeah, the little prick took off running. Turns out he had an alibi though. Plus, he's too stupid to take out Vendrell and Harlow. He doesn't have it in him."

Don put his coffee mug down and looked at his son with an inquisitive expression. "So, back on the job, then? After, well, everything that happened?"

"It's only this one case," Dean said. "I'm already in town, and my old boss thinks I can offer him a perspective that no one else can."

"You *do* have that magic eye, son."

"Yeah." Dean turned his gaze down to the carpet. "Wilson said the same thing."

"It's true though." His father tapped the side of his head. "You've got a gift for recall, son. Ever since..." His voice trailed off. "Well, you know."

"Yeah." The memory of his twin brother's death flashed through Dean's mind. "I know."

Nothing was said for a moment. Dean was certain that both of them were dwelling on the memory of Tommy.

"I gotta go," Dean said as he stood up from the couch. "Got some stuff I gotta square away."

"Sounds good," Don replied. "Give me a buzz when you can."

"I'll be back, Pop." Dean snagged the keys for the Pontiac Catalina from the tray in the foyer. "We still gotta talk about that Dodgers game."

His father nodded, put his focus back on the television, and said nothing more. He rested back in his recliner as he continued surfing the channels, everything playing on the television an apparent offense to his senses based on the groans and mumbles he made.

Dean lingered by the front door for a moment. He took a long hard look at his old man, his heart swelling with sadness as he watched Don sitting in his recliner with his eyes glued to the television, a task his father had done day in and day out for years ever since his mother had passed.

I miss her too, Pop, Dean bid his father silently. *We all do.*

After Dean slipped out of the house, he padded his way down the stairs, turned left, and pulled open the garage door. Inside was a 1967, raven-colored Pontiac Catalina, the vehicle still in pristine condition after so many years.

Dean ran his hand across the hood, his mind drifting back to the times he had his brother sit behind the wheel and pretend to drive before either of them could even reach the pedals. "Wish you were here, T," he whispered as he approached the driver's side. "The car still looks cherry."

Dean slipped behind the wheel, slipped in the key, and turned over the ignition. He throttled the engine, the throaty rumble of the V8 motor vibrating through the steering wheel.

What's next, Deano?

You got the rig, now you just need a lead.

Dean fished out his cell phone. He planned on calling Wilson to have one of the lackeys down at the field office stop by his father's place, pick up the Prius, and return it to LAX—but when his fingers grazed Layla Adrian's business card, he thought back to the conversation he had with his boss about Layla being the one who kicked the whole investigation into motion.

21

Halfway through his second cup of coffee, Dean looked up and saw Layla walk through the front door of the coffee shop. For a moment, he wasn't thinking about the case, too mesmerized by how beautiful she was.

"Layla," Dean called out.

The reporter waved as she made a beeline toward the table. "I'm surprised you called, Agent Blackwood." She slung her messenger bag on the back of the chair and sat. "After our last meet-up..." She shrugged.

"Water under the bridge." Dean nodded toward her bag. "I assume you're recording this, by the way."

"I'm not," Layla patted her bag, "but feel free to pat it down if you think I'm lying."

"I trust you."

"Talk about a 180."

"Well, I'm starting to think we both might be able to benefit from sharing some information with each other," Dean said. "A lot's happened since our first encounter."

"You're talking about Shane Harlow."

"So you know."

"Of course I know."

"I take it you were there the night he got run over in North Hollywood."

"I was," Layla said. "I saw you, actually. I was hiding in the background so no one would see me. I also know that Wilson made you the lead on the investigation."

"Did you also know I talked to Vendrell's wife?" Dean said. "That I spoke with Marcus Haywood earlier today?"

"Really?" Layla's eyes widened. "What did they have to say?"

"A lot of things. To get right to the point, with what I know and what you know, I think it might be a good idea if we put our heads together on this one."

"I'm not against it." Layla flagged down the server, ordered a latte, and put her focus back on Dean. "What are you thinking?"

Dean held up a finger. "First, I want to make sure we're on the same page before we go any further. I know you're writing an article on SMASH. Wilson told me that you're the source that came forward to the Bureau, that you're the one who got them to open the investigation."

Layla nodded. "I was."

"Then you know the stakes," Dean said. "You know it isn't a game. I'm inclined to trust you because you clearly know things about these guys that might be of interest to me." Dean inched his chair closer to the table. "But we need to have an agreement. I need to know I can confide in you and not have it blow back on me, on either of us."

"You can trust me, Agent Blackwood," Layla said. "I'm not in this for fame or notoriety."

Dean paused. "Why do it?"

"Why do what?"

"The line of work you're in. I've had my fair share of run-ins with reporters. Most of them are blowhards who like writing clickbait pieces."

Layla flashed a wry smirk. "I had a cousin," she said. "We were close. She was..." her complexion paled, "*assaulted* back when I was in high school. The LAPD and the District Attorney dropped the ball on convicting the guy. It never sat well with me, and a big reason was that a certain Detective Mike Vendrell was the one who fouled up the paperwork."

Dean wrinkled his brow curiously. "You're kidding."

Layla shook her head. "I've been working on trying to expose Vendrell ever since. The more time that's gone on, the more I've looked into Vendrell, the more I've learned that he and the rest of those SMASH flunkies are about as dirty as a sixteen-year-old boy's browser history. I don't have the whole picture yet though. There are too many missing pieces of the puzzle that I still need to fit into place. I do what I do to see that guys like Vendrell are booted out of the department, Agent Blackwood, but I'm not going to throw anyone under the bus in the process who doesn't have it coming."

Dean nodded. "I understand. And I'm sorry for what you've had to go through."

"I've been offered enough apologies in my life," Layla replied. "As cliché as it sounds, all I want is justice, plain and simple."

"Well, start by telling me what you know about SMASH. What do you have on them that the Bureau doesn't?"

"You said you spoke with Marcus Haywood."

"I did."

"Then you know all about what happened, that Vendrell and Harlow used their cruiser to run him over."

"Captain Eldridge tipped me off about Haywood," Dean said. "He was inclined to think that Haywood might have been responsible for Vendrell and Harlow's murder. But Haywood had an alibi."

"Eldridge knows more than he's letting on," Layla said. "I think he was hoping to pin this thing on Haywood to sweep the whole thing under the rug as quickly as possible."

"You really think so?"

"Most definitely. Like I said before, there's a slew of allegations that have been leveled against SMASH."

The reporter proceeded to tell Dean a few stories—the drug dealer who took a dive off a balcony after he ratted to her about Vendrell and Harlow trying to shake him down; a pair of sex workers who reported Vendrell for assaulting them only to disappear from the city limits completely; the excessive force complaints that had been reported about the other members of the SMASH unit, the fishy arrests they had made, and the seemingly countless allegations of bribes taken by nearly every member of the unit from people both inside the LAPD's ranks and those on the outside.

"Any complaint that's been lodged against these guys," Layla explained, "has been dismissed or shuffled to the bottom of the pile. Anytime they find themselves in hot water, anytime there's a problem, it goes away," she snapped her fingers, "just like that. It's that age-old story, Agent Blackwood. Dirty cops being protected by their own."

"The question of the hour," Dean replied, "is what Harlow and Vendrell were into that led to them being killed. Eldridge was certain it was Haywood who did it, but I can say for sure that it wasn't." He went on to tell Layla about the informant Eldridge had mentioned, how Vendrell and Harlow were keeping in touch with whoever it was, that Eldridge was inclined to think the informant might have something to do with the two members of SMASH being killed.

"I don't know," Layla replied skeptically. "I think Eldridge is covering up for something. I think Harlow and Vendrell were engaged in something—something big that blew back on them pretty hard."

"Then I'll try to keep pressing Eldridge," Dean said. "He's offered his full cooperation with the Feds. In the meantime, you should keep digging through public records, anything you can get your hands on."

"Maybe you could help with that. The FBI has resources that I don't. You guys have access to all kinds of databases."

"You got it." Dean took out his toothpick and slipped it between his lips. "Let me know what you need, and I'll try to get my hands on it."

Layla motioned to the toothpick. "Former smoker, huh?"

"Good eye." Dean flexed his brow. "How'd you know?"

"Tried those things myself. The gum too. Didn't really work so I just went cold turkey. When did you quit?"

"Few years ago," Dean said. "Smoked my last cigarette in a bar in El Paso. Haven't gone near them since."

"Good for you." Layla tapered her eyes. "The way you said El Paso sounded loaded, by the way."

"Did it?"

"Something happened." The reporter widened her eyes curiously. "I can tell."

"You're resourceful. You've probably read my files, at least the ones that weren't redacted, that is."

"You got me there." Layla held up her hands. "Honestly, I was kind of hoping maybe you'd tell me what happened. You worked undercover for years, but that all stopped after whatever happened that night to you in Texas."

The scars on Dean's chest throbbed as he replayed the memory of that night. "Maybe some other time," he said. "Until then, let's just work together on these murders and find out why they happened." He took out his cell phone and slid it across the table. After Layla plugged in her phone number, she followed Dean outside where he escorted her to her green Honda Civic parked by the curb.

"Do you have a gun?" Dean said.

"God no." Layla winced. "And I don't plan on it."

"Reconsider that. Now that we're going full steam ahead on this thing, it would be wise for you to have some protection."

"I can take care of myself." Layla pulled out the can of pepper spray from her messenger bag. "It's bear mace. The second I douse someone in the eyes with this, they'll go blind for a few days."

"That's cute," Dean said, "but it's not going to stop a bullet." He shot a look over both shoulders. "You need to be careful, Layla. The more we look into this thing with SMASH, the more heads are going to turn because of it. We're going to piss off folks in some top-tier positions, if you know what I mean."

The reporter suppressed her urge to flinch. "I understand." She fished out her car keys, held them up, and moved to the driver's side. "Thanks for looking out for me."

"Thanks for taking the time to meet with me," Dean said. "I'm glad we're—"

"Working together on this?"

"Yeah." Dean laughed. "*That*."

A bit of color returned to Layla's complexion. "I'll call you tonight," she said. "Until then."

Dean waved, cringed at the fact that he did so, and watched as Layla pulled away from the curb. He received a text from Wilson a moment later, informing him to return to the field office. As he made his way toward his father's

Pontiac parked across the street, he could hear the voice of his late twin brother teasing him inside his mind.

"Dean and Layla," Tommy whispered, "sitting in a tree..."

Dean laughed.

Hearing his late brother's voice was far less of a concern than listening to Woody's.

22

The entire drive to the FBI field office, Dean couldn't stop thinking of how charming and intelligent Layla was. It had been a long time since he felt any interest in a member of the opposite sex, but instead of dwelling on it, he whispered to himself, "Now is not the time."

Then it occurred to Dean that a whole day had passed since he last spoke to Jeremy—his whole point for being in LA in the first place—an issue he decided to fix by ringing Claire on his drive to the field office.

"Hey," Claire greeted over the speakerphone.

"Hey back." Dean eased the Pontiac onto the freeway. "Just thought I'd take a shot at saying hi to J."

"He's at soccer practice right now."

"I didn't know he played soccer."

"He's been playing for about a year now. I mean," Claire laughed, "the games are just kids kicking a ball around and scoring them into the wrong goals half the time, but he likes it."

And you haven't been there for a single one of them, Blackwood.

You're missing out on everything.

"Are you guys around later?" Dean asked.

"Later tonight, yeah," Claire replied. "If you want to stop by for dinner—"

"I can't. I've got some work to sort out for Wilson."

"Really?" Claire's tone strained. "What kind?"

"Nothing noteworthy."

"I see." Claire sighed. "Well, let me know when you plan on stopping by. You said something about taking J to a Dodgers game."

"I am." Dean tightened his grip on the steering wheel. "I *will*."

The call ended with Dean giving a rough estimate on when he would call and doubling down on his promise to take Jeremy to a Dodgers game. After he hung up the phone, he cut a glance toward his reflection in the rearview mirror. In the backseat was Woody, the disheveled leprechaun bastard delightedly jumping up and down in his seat.

"Oh, *boy*!" Woody shrieked. "You feel that, D? That *rrrrrush*?"

"Get bent, you celtic shitweasel."

"Oh, grow up." Woody clapped Dean on the back. "You know I'm right. Look at your *eyes*, laddie!"

Dean took a long hard look at himself in the mirror. His eyes shimmered with an electric charge.

"Just like the old days, Blackwood," Woody said. "You *live* for this shit."

"Wrong."

"Then why'd you take the job?"

Dean said nothing.

"*See*?" Woody snickered. "That's what I thought. You *wanted* this gig. You wanted to dip your toes back into that pool. You want to rub shoulders with all of them crazy folk again. You wanna run and shoot and chase down the bad guys. You want it, Deano, just like you want a little *sip* to fuel yourself for the race, if you know what I mean."

Dean dismissed Woody.

Held his head high.

Then he pinned his gaze to the windshield, slipped in a toothpick, and grumbled, "Don't screw this up, dipshit. Remember why you're here."

When Dean arrived at the field office, he headed through security, took the elevator, and arrived on the floor where Wilson's office was. The atmosphere on the floor was intense. Agents filtered in and out of cubicles. Phones rang. Files were exchanged. There was a buzz of people solving crimes and serving justice.

"Blackwood," Wilson called out from his office.

Dean walked into the room and closed the door behind him. His boss, pacing near the windows, held up the paperwork for the toxicology reports for Mike Vendrell.

"Verdict?" Dean asked.

"Vendrell had barbiturates in his system," Wilson said. "Harlow was also on a significant number of antidepressants."

"Poor guy." Dean slipped into the chair behind Wilson's desk. "Guilty conscience, maybe?"

"That's my chair, Deano."

"I know."

"Then why are you sitting in it?"

"Thing's got great lumbar support. Plus it does this." Dean fiddled with the bar underneath the chair and lowered it with a *swish.*

"Try yoga," Wilson said. "Now get out of my seat."

Dean chuckled and moved toward the chair on the other side of the desk as his boss retook his throne.

"I spoke to Eldridge not too long ago," Wilson said. "He's still adamant that Haywood is responsible, but I told him that you checked in on the guy, that he has an alibi. Nevertheless, he's insistent that Haywood has something to do with this."

"He doesn't."

"Then if Haywood's not at fault, where do you plan on looking next?"

Dean explained to his boss how he met up with Layla, how the two of them were going to work together, that the reporter would do a little digging on her end while he did some of his own, starting with interviews with the surviving, still-alive members of the SMASH unit.

"I'm stating the obvious here," Dean said, "but I have a feeling this whole thing is going to get worse before it gets better." He thought of the van that followed him after he left Haywood's place. "I think someone was following me earlier, by the way. It's just a feeling, but my gut rarely steers me in the wrong direction. Point being, something is going on, and certain people aren't fessing up to what that is."

"What do *you* think it is?"

"I think Vendrell and Harlow were probably dirty. Maybe Eldridge knew that, maybe he didn't. After all, the guy does pride himself on being incorruptible."

"You should try talking to the other members of SMASH," Wilson said. "We also need to get our hands on some more records for the unit, maybe talk to other people who've had run-ins with them. Maybe that's where this reporter will come in handy."

"I think she will." Dean replied. "She's a crusader, Willy. She's smart. She'll prove to be a great asset in this whole thing."

"You're glowing a bit there, Deano." Wilson flexed his

brow. "You talk about her like she's, what do the kids call it, a Tinder match or something."

"It's not like that." Dean held his head high. "It's strictly professional."

"*Right.*" Wilson turned his chair and faced the window. "What do you think is going on here, kid? I brought you on because you've got solid instincts. Tell me what you're inclined to think with what you know so far."

"Our suspect is using a car as his weapon of choice," Dean said. "Whoever did this is brazen, looking to grab headlines. He's clearly had a beef with Vendrell and Harlow, and he wants people to know it. He could've just shot them, but he didn't. He's not keen on keeping things quiet."

Wilson nodded. "The Behavioral Analysis Unit is building a profile for us as we speak. Should take a couple of days. Either way, what we know thus far indicates that whoever is doing this is pissed off to the point that we can assume anyone who gets in his way is going to end up like Vendrell and Harlow."

"He's not done, boss," Dean said. "Whoever's doing this is far from finished."

"You think?"

"Big time." Dean put his gaze on the window and looked out to the city. "He's out there somewhere. My guess is that the other members of the SMASH unit are being lined up in his crosshairs as we speak."

23

S hades of dusk streaked the parking garage beside the field office. A blacked-out sedan with signature FBI antennas on the back drove past Dean and Wilson as they made their way toward Dean's Pontiac.

"Any updates with the vehicle that ran over Harlow and Vendrell?" Dean asked.

"I've got four agents running circles around LA trying to track it down," Wilson said. "Junkyards, abandoned lots, and more. LAPD and the Los Angeles County Sheriff's Department put out an APB as well. So far, no one has turned up with anything. It's possible the car's been torched or dismantled by now, but we'll keep working on it."

"What about the traffic camera footage from North Hollywood?"

"We managed to pull a few images. Thing is a real junker. Our people identified it as a 2000 Toyota Corolla. There's a dent on the passenger side."

"Did you get a make of the driver from the footage?"

"Negative." Wilson shook his head. "The driver was

wearing a face mask, gloves, and sunglasses, so we didn't get a make of their physical description."

"This wasn't Haywood." Dean slid a toothpick between his teeth. "He's too intimidated by the SMASH crew to retaliate over that thing he had with Vendrell and Harlow. Also, he's not the brightest bulb in the chandelier, so he doesn't possess the brains or bandwidth to pull off something this elaborate. I feel bad for the guy, actually."

Wilson squinted. "Why's that?"

"He's a victim," Dean said. "This guy gets tuned up and then gets grinded up by the gears of the prison system. They screwed him. Now he's a parolee trying to square away his bullshit."

"He made his choices, it sounds like."

"Him getting strong-armed by the five-oh didn't help. It's not the first time this has happened to a man, and it damn sure won't be the last."

The two arrived at the Pontiac, Dean fishing out his keys and then unlocking the door.

"Where are you going now?" Wilson said.

"I'm thinking I'll talk to the other guys in the SMASH unit. Do you have their info?"

Wilson handed Dean a file. "This is what we've got so far on the unit, a basic rundown. Eldridge's right-hand guy is Lieutenant Ron Wyler, the one I mentioned before. He essentially runs the day-to-day operations of the unit. I'd suggest you start your talks with him."

Dean sifted through the file. "If Wyler is the one who's running point for the unit, maybe he'll have the scoop on what Vendrell and Harlow were getting into."

"He's going to give you static, most likely."

"I'm counting on it."

"How do you plan on getting him to talk then?"

"Because I'm *me*, Willy." Dean clamped down on his toothpick. "And I can be very persuasive when I want to be."

The cell in Wilson's pocket rang, the SAC answering it after a single ring. "Talk to me." His color paled. "Okay," he said. "I understand."

Dean furrowed his brow. "What is it?"

"Well," Wilson pocketed his phone, "I don't think Ron Wyler is going to give you much in the way of answers. He just got run over in front of a bar in West Hollywood."

24

Dean surveyed the twisted and blood-drenched corpse of Ron Wyler, partially covered with a sheet, lying a few feet from the sidewalk. A small group of people had gathered outside a bar behind him, staring at the body with terror-stricken expressions.

"You're right," Dean said to Wilson. "Don't think Wyler's going to be much help."

A muscle-bound, West Hollywood PD Sergeant with the name tag "Kliner" approached, wiped the sweat off his brow, and pinned his eyes on Wilson. "You the FBI?"

Wilson showed his badge. "SAC Wilson." He motioned to Dean. "This is Special Agent Blackwood."

"Worst shit I've seen here," Kliner said as he motioned around the street, a spotless part of West Hollywood that set back most residents three grand a month for a two-bedroom. "The driver just ran this guy over and took off."

Dean puckered his lips and fished out his toothpick. "What happened?"

"Looks like the vic," Kliner explained, "stopped in the bar on the corner here about an hour and a half ago. We checked the footage inside the bar with the bouncer. This guy Wyler came in, had a drink, got a call, and then walked outside. We've got six witnesses we've corralled on the curb here that confirm the same thing. They saw the guy get run over."

Déja vu, Dean thought as he pulled Wilson aside. "What is this?" he said. "The same MO? For all three SMASH members? How did Wyler not get wise and buckle down after two of his teammates got smeared across the pavement?"

"I don't know," Wilson said. "I just don't know."

Tires squealed from around the corner. Seconds later, an unmarked sedan pulled up to the scene. Captain Larry Eldridge slipped out of the passenger side before the vehicle came to a full stop.

Dean could sense the anger in Eldridge's eyes, the SMASH captain tensing his jaw muscles as he hustled over to him. "This is the third of my men who have gotten fitted for a toe tag," Eldridge said as he crooked a finger at Dean. "The *third*." He put his eyes on Kliner. "I want anyone in this bar who even looked at Wyler pulled aside for questioning."

Kliner straightened his posture. "We're working on it, Captain."

"This situation is *unprecedented*," Eldridge snapped as he stared Wilson deep in the eyes. "Someone is targeting my people, and I want answers. I was willing to let you guys take the lead on this because I was under the impression that you could resolve the matter in a swift and timely fashion, but now I'm seeing that's not the case."

"Clearly, there's some kind of hit list going with all the members of the SMASH unit," Dean said. "You need to inform your men that they're in danger."

"I already have," Eldridge replied. "I'm pulling them off

of active duty until I can figure out what the hell is going on." He stepped closer to Dean. "I have three dead bodies on my hands, Agent Blackwood—three separate families I now have to console. I put my faith in you guys to track down the prick who did this, and you've made zero headway." Eldridge threw his hands up. "I also have a hard time believing that Haywood isn't responsible for this. Did you question him?"

"He had an alibi," Dean replied. "He's clean."

"Bullshit." Eldridge pointed to Wyler's corpse. "Did it ever occur to you that he might've hired someone to do this thing for him?"

"With what kind of a bankroll? Haywood is a parolee who can barely feed himself."

"He's got *friends*, Blackwood. He's got connections, people who might've helped him out. Christ, Haywood *said* that when he got out he was going to go after Vendrell and Harlow."

Dean huffed. "Then why would Haywood go after Wyler? He didn't have a vendetta against him. Besides, I'm sure Haywood's PO is all over him like white on rice after I talked to him."

"Well, according to Haywood's PO," Eldridge said, "he disappeared from his residence earlier today. The PO doesn't know where he is, so that means Haywood is, as of this moment, completely in the wind. You didn't know that, did you?"

Dean narrowed his eyes. *Sweet Jesus*, he thought. *What the hell is going on?*

Eldridge waved his hand through the air. "I should have never agreed to let the FBI handle this. You guys royally fucked this up—six ways from Sunday."

"Captain," Wilson chimed in, "let's take a second here to—"

"No." Eldridge shook his head. "I'm done working with you assholes. I'm taking the lead on this. You pricks can pull all the jurisdictional crap you want. I don't care. Take it up with someone else." He pointed to Kliner. "I need to talk with you." He walked away, shoulder-checking Dean as he spoke with the West Hollywood PD Sergeant off to the side.

Dean was fuming. Everything around him was moving at the speed of light.

Three dead cops.

Nothing in the form of a lead.

And now we've got the LAPD's most prized captain ready to start a war.

Wilson pulled Dean aside. "This isn't good."

"No shit."

"Eldridge is going to pull out all of the stops to try and shut us down."

"He doesn't have the pull."

"He might," Wilson said. "He knows a lot of people. He's going to do whatever he can to clog the gears on our end. He'll call in whatever favors he has to. *Think*, my friend. Work the problem."

Dean slowed his breathing, pressed two fingers to his neck, and checked his pulse.

Think, Deano.

Don't let Eldridge or any of this insanity fog your mind.

Work the problem, and find a solution.

He thought back to the first scene, his first night in LA, the stretch of the PCH where Mike Vendrell had been killed.

Someone called that in.

Someone left that anonymous tip.

"Did you get a trace on the call?" Dean said. "The one for the anonymous tip the field office got?"

It took Wilson one call to pinpoint the answer.

Minutes later, Dean, behind the wheel of the Pontiac, was breaking the speed limit to get to a corner in Silver Lake as fast as they could.

25

The Pontiac was parked at the top of a steep paved hill, flanked on all sides by palm trees and residences lit up by the dull glow of street lamps. Dean padded his way toward the intersection, the one spot on the stretch of road that wasn't lit up by street lamps.

"This is it?" Dean said. "This is where the call for the tip originated from?"

Wilson, pacing the street, replied with a nod.

"What time did you receive that call?"

"Thirty minutes after Vendrell's body hit the pavement."

Dean thought it through. "Do you have the rundown of the SMASH crew on you?"

Wilson slapped the file in his hand onto the hood of the Pontiac. Dean rifled through the reports, examining the brief rundowns of the men in SMASH, complete with pictures beside their names.

"What are you looking for?" Wilson asked.

Dean flipped through the pages. "The home addresses for these guys." His eyes widened as he spotted something of interest. "There it is."

"What?"

"Detective Sean Mohr." Dean pressed his finger to the page. "He lives less than a mile from here. When this anonymous caller phoned in, what did he say exactly?"

"He told us there was a dead cop that got run over on the PCH."

"What else?"

"He said, and I quote, 'Don't trust the LAPD.'"

Dean closed the file. "What's your bet," he said, "that Mohr's the one who made the call?"

"You really think Mohr made the tip?"

"I think it's no coincidence that Mohr lives a mile up the road from here." Dean paced the sidewalk, the gears in his brain turning. "I think the guys in SMASH *knew* they were being targeted, boss. These guys did something that was blowing back on them, and I think they were all trying to work together to get ahead of it. This whole story that Eldridge gave about Vendrell and Harlow working some kind of CI was cooked up. He thought he'd be able to pin it on Haywood, that I'd buy that story, haul Haywood in, and the rest would be history. These guys are *scared*, Willy. Eldridge knows I'm sniffing out his bullshit, so he's going to do whatever he can to keep me from digging up the truth."

"So, what now?" Wilson said. "What's your next move?"

"I need to talk to the rest of the SMASH guys," Dean replied. "Sean Mohr first. He knows something, something he's trying to keep a lid on." A thought struck him. "That woman," he said. "Kara Shardlow."

"The woman who was with Marcus?"

"Yeah."

"What about her?"

"We know someone paid her to hang out with Marcus," Dean said. "Some anonymous caller who left cash, booze, and instructions to get Marcus liquored up. I want to find out who. I want to talk to her and see if we can suss that out a little more. Now that Marcus is missing, I'm starting to wonder if there's more to that story."

Minutes later, Dean and Wilson were on the way to Los Feliz to talk to Kara Shardlow, but halfway there, Wilson, who was on the phone calling up his local contacts, learned that Kara's roommate, a woman by the name of Ellie, had reported Kara missing twelve hours ago.

26

I t appeared that Kara Shardlow had disappeared from Los Angeles entirely. Her bags had been packed. Her cell phone had been left behind in her apartment, and her vehicle, a Honda Accord, had been left in a parking lot at LAX.

"She just left," Kara's roommate Ellie explained to Dean when he stopped by the apartment. "No note, no anything."

An hour of questions on Dean's end left him with even more questions than answers. It appeared that Ellie knew nothing about Kara's side hustle as a call girl and that as far as Ellie knew, Kara was just a girl who made a living doing cam-girl work and OnlyFans.

"I think someone made her disappear, boss," Dean told Wilson. "Whoever paid her to be with Marcus the night of the murders probably went to the trouble of making sure no one could ever hear from her again."

Dean figured—and relayed to Wilson—that it was one of the SMASH guys. The way he saw it, they wanted to pin the Vendrell-Harlow murders on Haywood, maybe even hope that Dean would assist in that when Eldridge sent him out to question the parolee. So they hired Kara, paid her to plow Haywood with booze and weed, and hoped that Haywood would get busted and sent back to jail.

"This thing keeps getting messier the more I dig, boss," Dean said. "I could use a cup full of aspirin and a cold plunge right about now."

"Right there with you," Wilson replied. "After Kara Shardlow was reported missing, her roommate rang up Kara's family in Reseda. They started ringing up my office line nonstop. They want answers, and rightfully so. Hell," he huffed, "I could hear Shardlow's kid crying in the background. Talk about adding insult to injury."

Dean squinted. "What are you talking about?"

"Shardlow's family's been calling me nonstop."

"I caught that," Dean inched closer to his SAC, "but you said something about a kid—*Shardlow's* kid. You never mentioned that before."

"Shit." Wilson pinched the bridge of his nose. "I meant to tell you that we rolled by Kara Shardlow's's apartment and questioned the roommate. I got the rundown that Shardlow has a son. Shardlow's parents took the kid in after she got busted for crystal in Long Beach last year. She cut a deal to do rehab and a stint in a halfway house. Her folks took custody of the kid while Shardlow cleaned up. Obviously, that didn't happen."

Dean closed his eyes.

She has a kid.

A kid who might not have a mother now.

"How old is he?" Dean said. "The boy."

Wilson took a beat. "He's six."

"*Jesus.*" Dean racked his fingers through his hair. "Un-fucking-believable."

"Focus on the task at hand, Deano," the SAC said. "You

said you had a feeling someone in SMASH might have set Kara Shardlow up, so tell me who you think that might be and why."

Dean had a thought.

He ran it through a filter.

Then, with all the confidence he could muster, he said, "Maybe it was Eldridge."

Wilson's eyes widened. "What makes you say that?"

"I had a feeling before. Thought maybe I was being paranoid, but..."

"Well, speak your mind."

"Maybe he didn't think I'd cut Haywood loose when I found him," Dean said. "Maybe he thought they'd haul Haywood in for them, they'd force him to confess to Vendrell and Harlow's murders, and that would be the end of it."

"That's pretty thin," Wilson replied. "If it wasn't Haywood who killed these guys, then it was someone else, and if it was someone else, who was it and *why* did they do it?"

Dean wanted to ask the SMASH guys a few questions in an effort to find the answers.

Before he did that, he had to scope out the funeral for Detective Mike Vendrell.

27

The funeral, held at the cemetery, was packed with onlookers. Dean stood at the far back, scanning the faces in attendance through his Wayfarers. An uncomfortable silence was shared by about 200 people in attendance. The Honor Guard raised their M1 rifles for the three-rifle salute.

From a distance, it was hard for Dean to make out people's faces. But it was clear, based on the three guys in front that they were the surviving members of the SMASH unit, the ones he wanted to pull aside and talk to individually to find out what was going on and why.

The funeral lasted just under an hour. A slew of cops—including Eldridge—took turns speaking at a podium positioned beside a blown-up police academy graduation photo of Detective Mike Vendrell positioned next to a blue-and-white wreath.

"Mike was an honorable man," Eldridge said during his speech, "a loving husband and devoted civil servant."

Dean rolled his eyes.

And possibly crooked, but we'll hold off on saying that out loud.

By the time all was said and done, after the rifles had been fired and the uniformed officers in attendance had paid their respects, Dean headed out to a coffee shop. He grabbed two black coffee to go and waited outside by his Pontiac for about two minutes before Layla Adrian arrived.

"There was a lot of good acting at that funeral," Layla said as Dean handed her a to-go cup of coffee. "You'd think that Vendrell was Jesus Christ himself."

"I didn't see you there."

"I was in my car parked about a half mile away."

"Were you watching through binoculars or something?"

"I was." Layla wrinkled her brow playfully. "I'm a modern-day Veronica Mars."

"Well, be careful, Miss Mars," Dean said. "Eldridge and his guys are on high alert now. He put in a lot of calls to stop me from looking into his people any further. The deputy director gave me one more week to finish looking into this thing. The timeline on the investigation is speeding up."

Layla nodded. "I find myself in a similar position. Eldridge had a conniption after Wyler got killed and then started hounding my editor. I was told to wrap up things on my end. Actually, I was told to back off of the story *entirely*, but—"

"But you won't."

"Never."

She's dedicated, Dean thought. *I'll give her that.*

"Does the name Kara Shardlow ring any bells with you?" Dean said.

"No," Layla replied. "Should it?"

Dean told her about the nights Kara spent with Marcus,

how someone paid for it, and that Kara's roommate had recently reported her missing.

"We need to find her," Dean said. "I think whoever paid her to hang out with Marcus might be responsible for her disappearance. See what you can do on your end to track her down."

Layla jotted down Kara Shardlow's name on her notepad. "Will do."

"You heed my advice about carrying a gun, by the way?"

"I did." Layla patted her messenger bag. "I picked up a Walther PPK, the James Bond gun. Took it a few times to the range in the past week."

"How do you like it?"

"I hate it, but," Layla shrugged, "I get what everyone is saying about guns making you feel more powerful when you fire them. I'd prefer not to use it, but better safe than sorry, right?"

"We're all making compromises," Dean replied. "I'd prefer kicking it with my kid right now, but unfortunately the circumstances require me to see this one through if I plan on spending more time with him."

Layla's face lit up. "You have a kid?"

"Yeah, a son. His name's Jeremy."

"Wow." Her lips curled into a subtle grin. "I guess I overlooked that particular tidbit when I looked through your file."

"That's why I came back to LA," Dean said. "I'm hoping to transfer to a full-time position here to be closer to him. That's why I took this assignment. Wilson told me that solving this thing, or at least taking a look into it, would help grease the wheels. But it's taking a lot longer than I expected."

It had been four days since Dean arrived in LA, and during that time, he'd only seen Jeremy once, on his birthday. He was planning to take him and his old man to a Dodgers game soon, but Dean wanted more with his son. He knew the only way to make that happen was to get to the bottom of the whole SMASH ordeal.

"Speaking of the investigation," Dean said as he reached through the driver's side window of the Pontiac, grabbed a file Wilson had given him, and handed it over to Layla.

"What's this?" she asked.

"The rundown on the members of the SMASH unit. It's everything we've got on them so far. We've managed to piece together an extensive history for each and every one of them."

"Anything of interest?"

"The bank transactions for Vendrell, Harlow, and Mohr are pretty suspicious."

"How so?"

"We'll still need one of our forensic accountants to go through them with a fine-tooth comb," Dean explained, "but they were making some pretty hefty deposits into their accounts in the past three years. When Mohr and Vendrell died, they were both sitting on close to $500,000. According to the file, they won that money playing craps and poker in Vegas. Every six to eight weeks, they took a weekend trip to the casinos and came back with some pretty solid winnings."

"Casinos," Layla said, "are the easiest place to launder cash."

Dean nodded. "It's the go-to for people looking to clean their cash as quickly as possible. You take the dirty cash to the casino, trade it for chips, and then cash it out for clean money at the end of the day. If you look at the transactions, Vendrell, Harlow, and Mohr were making sure to keep their winnings just under the threshold each time so they didn't have to report it to the IRS."

"If it was dirty money, where was it coming from?"

"That's what we need to figure out. Whatever these guys were up to was something that got them killed. Whatever that is, Eldridge and some of his cronies in the LAPD went to great lengths to cover it up, so whatever paper trail there may be is one we can assume has been covered up, destroyed, or redacted."

"If that's the case," Layla said, "what do we do? How do we expose the truth here?"

"By putting the squeeze on the members of the unit that are still alive," Dean explained. "I want to talk with this guy Mohr first. We think it's possible he may have made an anonymous call to the Bureau's field office. I've tried to get in touch with him, but Eldridge won't let us near any of the SMASH guys with a 10-foot pole. They're not taking any of my calls."

Layla pointed to a photo of a younger man with blonde hair and a buzz cut. "You also might not get much from this guy either."

"Tyler Adams." Dean scrutinized the younger man in the photo with the strong jaw and a thoroughbred, all-American boy complexion. "Boy looks like Captain America."

"He's the newest recruit in the unit," Layla said. "He got assigned to SMASH just under a month ago. He's green, but he's good. He did a stint over at the Newton Division until he graduated up to the big leagues. I don't get the impression that he's like the other guys in the unit. The most thorough info I've gotten on any of the SMASH guys is Adams, but even then, I can't get within 5 feet of him."

"How'd you pull the info on Adams?"

"I have a friend in the LAPD who works the complaints desk," Layla said. "Long story short, my contact has her own grievances with the guys over in SMASH. Turns out Vendrell, well, *fondled* her back when they were rookies."

"Your contact must really trust you pretty well. She's taking a big risk spilling her guts to a reporter."

Layla smirked. "As are you."

"Does your source know Adams?"

"She does. And the word is that Adams is a good kid. I think it was a move on Eldridge's part to try to add some polish to SMASH, considering the fact that there's been some labels of corruption that never came to light."

"Eldridge knows something." Dean clenched his jaw muscles. "Bureaucratic *prick*. He says he despises corruption, but he'll dismiss it or cover it up if it affects his legacy. I'm pretty sure he was trying to pin this whole thing on Marcus Haywood who, by the way, is still missing."

"I heard." Layla's lips twitched down into a frown. "It's probably safe to assume he's 6 feet under by now."

"Probably," Dean said. "The way I see it, Eldridge agreed to let the FBI handle this initially because he thought we'd pin it on Haywood and that would be the end of it."

"You really think so?"

"Most definitely. Maybe when I question Sean Mohr he can shed some light on that," Dean said. "What do you know about him, by the way?"

"I know he got placed on a 5150 for twelve hours after his wife left him six months ago," Layla said. "The guy's been in kind of a tailspin since then."

"How would you know that he got held in a psych ward? Those files are sealed seventy-two hours after the fact."

"They are, but I have a friend who works at a psych clinic in Culver City."

Dean laughed. "You got a lot of connections, don't you?"

"That I do," Layla said. "And this friend I mentioned told me how they took a cop into their clinic one night. She made some subtle hints about who it was. Wasn't hard to piece it together."

"Why did Mohr get placed on a 5150?"

"Well, *allegedly*, Mohr got drunk, made a few calls, and then a black-and-white came to his place and found him with a gun in his hand. Mohr flashed his badge to try to get out of it. The arriving officers tried to talk him down, and then Mohr held the gun to his head and threatened to blow his brains out. I'm pretty sure Eldridge tossed him in a clinic for the night to calm him down."

"So Mohr's on the edge." Dean flexed his brow. "Makes him the perfect guy to talk to. He's ready to break. I'll move in on him soon."

"How are you going to get some face time with him?" Layla said. "Eldridge is keeping a close eye on these guys."

"Let me worry about that. Once I corner Mohr and have a chat with him, I'll give you the head's up, and we'll go from there. Until then, keep your head down."

Layla nodded. "I'll keep digging and compiling on my end until then. And if you plan on going to that Dodgers game in the meantime, let me know." She winked. "I'd be happy to tag along."

"That won't upset your..." Dean shrugged, "*boyfriend* or anything?"

"You're in the FBI."

"Last I checked."

"That means you probably pulled my file."

"Possibly."

"Then that means you probably know," Layla said as she turned and made her way down the sidewalk, "that I *don't* have a boyfriend."

"Yeah," Dean whispered. "I do."

28

T he second Dean opened the door, the light from the streetlamp outside flooded into the dive bar in Simi Valley. Five patrons huddled over the drinks as daylight washed over them.

Rats in a cage.

And I used to be one of them.

Dean did a scan of the room. Neon beer signs buzzed in the windows. "The Wreck of the Edmund Fitzgerald" played over the house speakers. At a table in the corner was Detective Sean Mohr, dressed down in boots, jeans, and a leather jacket, swirling the Jameson in his glass as he took a drag of his cigarette burnt down to the filter.

Dean approached the counter with his hands stuffed into his pockets, throwing a look toward Mohr as he flagged down the bartender. "Cranberry juice, please."

The bartender, a thickset woman in a leather vest, snarled. "Nothing else?"

"Just the juice."

"You on a cleanse or something?"

"Trying to shed my midsection." Dean pulled up his

shirt and showed off the FBI shield on his belt. "Is it working?"

With a huff, the bartender went off to fetch Dean's drink, brought it back, and slammed it down. "Fifteen bucks."

Dean took out his wallet. "No discount?"

"Now it's sixteen."

Dean laughed, slid the woman twenty bucks, made his way toward Mohr's table, and sat down across from him.

"Find another table," Mohr grumbled, his eyes fastened to his drink as he dabbed at the whiskey drops that clung to his handlebar mustache.

"Hey, man," Dean raised his cranberry juice, "it's a free country, isn't it?"

Mohr grunted, took his LAPD shield out of his pocket, and slapped it on the table. "Do me a solid, yeah?" he said. "Find another seat."

Dean reached into his jacket pocket, fished out his FBI badge, and placed it beside Mohr's. "It's a lot smaller than yours," he said, "but it carries a heck of a lot more weight."

"*Christ*," Mohr hissed, staring at the badge like it was a positive paternity test. "You gotta be shitting me."

"You look a little toasted, Sean. How many have you had tonight?"

"I'm not in the mood."

"Neither am I," Dean spread out his arms, "but here we are."

"Get bent," Mohr said. "I've got nothing to say to you, Blackwood."

"You know who I am, huh?"

"Of course I do. Eldridge told all of us to steer clear of you. All it's gonna take is one call to him," Mohr held up a finger, "just one, and you'll be sifting dead letters at the post office for the rest of your career."

"You stole that line from a Tom Cruise movie, dipshit."

"I mean it, Blackwood." Mohr stared deep into Dean's eyes. "*Get. Fucked.*"

"Pump the brakes, Sean," Dean said. "I saw you at Vendrell's funeral today. You seemed a little upset, so I'm just stopping by to offer my condolences."

"Three of our guys got killed," Mohr replied before he downed the last of his drink. "I'm fucking pissed."

"I'm sure you are." Dean pushed his glass aside. "It's like you said. Three of your brothers got put 6 feet under, and now you and this other guy Adams are probably thinking you're up next. Hell, maybe you know who's responsible for Vendrell and Harlow getting fitted for toe tags."

"I don't know who's doing this, Blackwood. If I did," Mohr's eyes narrowed into slits, "it would have been dealt with by now."

"Don't pull that 'vengeance for my fellow officer' crap with me. I know more than you think I do."

"Eat shit." Mohr snapped his fingers, held up his glass, and signaled the bartender for a refill. "I'm done talking to you."

"I bet I can get you to keep talking."

"Is that so?"

"Big time," Dean said. "You see, the FBI got an anonymous tip the night of Vendrell's murder. We traced the call to a spot in Silver Lake, and *you*," he pointed, "live about a mile away from that spot."

Mohr clenched his jaw.

"Not bad, right?" Dean winked. "Man, working for the FBI can be fun sometimes. To be fair, though, you had to have known that we'd be able to trace the call back to you. If you didn't want us to find out it was you, you would have taken more steps to prevent that."

Mohr didn't utter a word.

But Dean knew he had the guy right where he wanted him.

"Sean," Dean said, "tell me what's going on. This whole thing is going to spin out of control, and you don't need to be the next guy having a folded flag handed to his family. Whatever family you have left, that is."

"I don't need this shit." Mohr took a drag of his cigarette. "And you're just throwing shit up against the wall to see what'll stick."

"I know you made that anonymous call, brother." Dean narrowed his eyes. "You could have driven 50 miles up the road and made the call, but you didn't. You did it close to home because part of you, conscious or not, *knew* that someone would figure out it was you."

The detective averted his gaze and tapped the ash off the tip of his cigarette.

"I know you called us, Mohr," Dean said. "And you did it because you can't trust anyone in your department. You know that ratting on someone to Internal Affairs would blow back on you quicker than a backdraft."

Mohr shuddered, the cigarette between his fingers trembling. "You don't get it." He crushed out the butt on the ashtray next to him. "This whole thing is—"

"Bigger than I can imagine?"

"It is." Mohr's eyes widened. "You can't fuck around with this, Blackwood. I'm serious."

"So am I," Dean said. "Spend some more time with me, and you'll see that's the case."

Mohr buried his head in his hands. "This is so fucked." He traced his fingers through his hair, secured a grip, and squeezed. "This whole thing got way out of hand."

"Three cops are dead," Dean said. "Three members of

your unit who have been implicated on several occasions of doing things they're not supposed to. It's only a matter of time 'til it catches up with *you*, Mohr, and the more you wait this out, the more likely you are to get caught in the wheels, pun intended."

Mohr clenched his fingers into a fist.

"You *know* something, Sean," Dean said. "So, blow the lid off of it. No one else needs to get killed over whatever is happening here."

A few seconds ticked by.

Mohr smoked another cigarette.

Dean, seeing the glimmer in the cop's eye, knew he was about to break.

"I know," Mohr said.

"What do you know?"

"*Everything*," Mohr said. "And it's more complicated and dangerous than you can imagine. I don't know who to trust. Fed or no Fed, what guarantees can you give me?"

"All I know is that your life expectancy is dwindling by the second," Dean said. "The way I see it, Mohr, you can either work with me or you can roll the dice and hope you live to see the sun come up tomorrow."

"I need to know that you can protect me," Mohr said. "The people involved in this aren't screwing around. They'll take out a family of five if they have to. Look, I may have nothing to lose. I may not have anyone on my side, but the last thing I'm looking for is to get killed by these guys if they find out I ratted them out. You don't know what they're like. I'm serious."

"I can offer you protection," Dean shrugged, "but you'll have to tell me everything you know. All of it, no detail unspared."

The frazzled detective took his time to answer. "I'll do it," he finally said. "I'll come with you," he held up a finger, "but I'm not saying a word until I have guarantees with your SAC. If I feel like I'm going to get burned or brought up on charges, I walk. I want the deal of a lifetime for giving this info to you."

"You got it."

"*And* you're paying the bill."

Dean produced a twenty and slapped it on the counter. "Leave your car. I wouldn't be surprised if someone is tailing you."

"There's a ton of surprises in store for you, Blackwood," Mohr said. "*Boatloads.*"

Mohr crushed out his cigarette and followed Dean to the door. The moment they stepped outside, Dean's cell rang. "Talk to me," he answered.

"We just did a search of Haywood's residence," Wilson said. "We were hoping to find something that might give some hints about where he might have gone."

"And?"

"We found nothing. Looks like the guy just packed his bags and split."

"That doesn't mean anything," Dean said. "Someone could have thrown a bunch of Haywood's shit into a suitcase and made it look like he left town."

"Well, Eldridge put out an APB on him," Wilson replied. "As of two hours ago, they've pegged Haywood as their number one suspect."

"Of course they have."

"They're citing, and I quote, 'a slew of evidence' that has been uncovered linking Haywood to the murders of Mike Vendrell and Shane Harlow."

"What evidence?"

"They're holding their cards close to the chest, kid," Wilson said. "I'm not sure. At least not yet."

"*Sweet*," Dean grumbled as he padded down the sidewalk, Mohr beside him, the cop scanning the block feverishly for signs of a threat. "They're gonna pin this on Haywood, wrap it up with a bow, and call it a night in the next few days. You mark my words."

"Unless you can get Mohr talking," Wilson said. "You make any leeway with that?"

Dean flicked a glance at Mohr "He's with me right now."

"No shit?"

"I'll bring him to the office."

"The hell with that," Mohr protested. "Eldridge might have eyes on us. It needs to be somewhere private.

"I just heard him," Wilson said. "Look, there's a safehouse in Glassell Park. I'll text you the address. Bring Mohr there, and we'll get him on the record."

"Copy that."

"We'll talk it over with him. Nice work, D."

Dean pocketed his cell. Mohr walked alongside him on the sidewalk.

"All right, Blackwood." Mohr hunched his shoulders like a timid kid on the first day of school. "Where are we going?"

"Glassell Park," Dean said. "We need to—"

An engine throttled a few paces behind them.

Dean spun around.

Then the banshee-like shriek of tires burning rubber pierced the air as he saw a vehicle barrelling toward them. He grabbed Mohr by the collar.

"*Mohr!*" Dean shouted.

The car was going at least 40 miles per hour. The phrase "deer in the headlights" popped into Dean's mind even though it was daytime. He tackled Mohr.

The vehicle zipped past.

Dean pulled out his SIG.

Then the car made a hard right turn, booked it up the street, and disappeared from sight.

Remember the vehicle, Deano. It was a red car. Older model. Early 2000s.

No plates.

Just like the vehicle that took out Vendrell and Harlow.

Dean holstered his SIG, stood up, and offered his hand to Mohr.

"Nice job, Agent Man," Mohr said as he got to his feet. "You just became a target."

He's right, Blackwood.

Dean clenched a fist.

You're caught in the crosshairs now.

29

A half hour after nearly getting run over, Dean and Mohr were seated in the living room at the safehouse in Glassell Park, a one-story bungalow nestled against several others on a residential block a half-mile from the I-5. Dean had a coffee in his hand, and Mohr—per his insistence—nursed two fingers worth of scotch in a tumbler that Wilson had retrieved for him.

"It was a red vehicle," Dean said as he paced the living room floor. "Older model. No plates. Thing was waiting for us when we walked out of there."

"Were you followed?" Wilson said as he closed the curtains. "Did you pick up any tails?"

"No, we're clean. I made it a point to do parallels on the way over here." Dean scanned the room. "No one knows about this place, right?"

"Right."

"Good." Dean took a final swig of his coffee, placed it down, and looked at Mohr. "Then let's get to it."

"Detective Mohr," Wilson said as he offered his hand. "I'm Special Agent in Charge Kent Wilson."

The brittle cop gawked at the SAC's hand like it was covered in grime. "I want full immunity," Mohr said. "I also want to be put in witness protection. Don't put me anywhere too cold though. I hate the cold."

A chuckle slipped out of Wilson. "The man wastes no time."

"With what I know," Mohr said, "the both of you could get promoted to senior level positions inside the Bureau by the time you bring this story to light."

"Is that so?"

"You have no idea, man." Mohr threw back the last of his scotch and winced. "This shit makes that whole Bulger and Connolly business look like child's play."

"All right." Wilson loosened his tie and took a seat beside Mohr on the couch. "Lay it on me."

"I want my guarantees first."

"I want to know that you have something of *value* first."

"That's not how this is going to work." Mohr's eyelids tapered. "It's fuck or walk time, right now, and until I get something in the way of a notarized guarantee on your end, I'm staying more tight-lipped than a mute."

Wilson and the cop went back and forth for several moments, the tonality of the conversation remaining unchanged to the point that Dean checked his phone, saw that it was past 9:00 p.m. and decided—since it was going to take Wilson a moment to break Mohr—to put in a call to his son.

"I'm stepping outside for a second, Willy."

Wilson shrugged. "What for?"

"Gonna check in with my kid." Dean motioned to Wilson. "You got this?"

"Yeah." Wilson stood and moved toward the kitchen.

"I'm gonna get this guy a cup of joe. I need him to clear his head."

"I don't need to clear my head," Mohr said. "I need you guys to clue into the fact that the shit I know could get me killed."

"Easy, Mohr." Wilson held up his hand. "You need to—"

"*Fuck easy!*" Mohr shot up from the couch, his eyes manic as he backed up toward the door. "You guys don't get it, do you?"

"You're good, Sean," Dean said. "Everything's cool. No one knows about this place. You're safe."

"I'm not safe. With *these* guys..." Mohr hung his head. "Christ," he closed his eyes, "none of us are."

Dean narrowed his eyes.

These *guys*.

What the hell does he mean by that?

"I'll be back in a flash, Sean," Dean said. "Just have some coffee and try to relax, okay?"

A frazzled Mohr, mumbling under his breath, plopped down on the couch and held his head in his hands. Moments later, Dean was behind the wheel of the Pontiac parked in front of the safehouse, appraising the area to make sure no one was wandering about as he punched in Claire's number.

"Hey," his ex-wife greeted. "Everything okay?"

"I'm just checking on everything."

"Jeremy's asleep."

"Yeah, I figured," Dean breathed a sigh. "Just thought I'd take a stab at saying goodnight to him."

"Are you okay?" Claire said. "You sound tired."

"Things have been a bit crazy." Dean opted out of telling her about the car that almost ran him over. "I've just been running around a lot, that's all."

"You know," Claire took a brief pause, "I remember the last time you sounded like this."

"What do you mean?"

"You sound just like you did when you were running a million miles an hour when we were still together," Claire said, "back when you were..." Her voice trailed off.

But Dean knew what she was insinuating.

"Something's wrong," Claire said. "I can tell."

"No." Dean tried to maintain a composed tone. "Everything's fine."

"I don't believe you."

"Claire—"

"You sound *scared*, Dean. Whatever it is you're doing is obviously a bigger deal than you're letting on."

You can't tell her.

If she knows, you'll run the risk of losing your kid.

"Things are a little stressful with the case Wilson has me working on," Dean said. "That much I can say."

"Then walk away from it, Dean," Claire replied. "You told me yourself that you don't do this kind of work anymore."

"We're too far in it, now. I have to see this through. Believe me, once it's done, I'm *here*. I'll move back. I'll do whatever I need to do to make sure—"

"I've heard this before, Dean," Claire said. "If you slip right back into this routine, it's only a matter of rolling the dice before it catches up to you. And me." She paused. "*And* Jeremy."

"It's not like it was before," Dean said, his heart racing, his mind spinning. "Those days are over."

"Apparently not."

Dean didn't know whether to apologize or say nothing at all. Before he could figure out how to react, his cell phone buzzed with a text from Wilson telling him to get back inside.

"Everything's fine, Claire," Dean said. "I mean that."

"I hope so," Claire replied. "And I gotta go. I'll talk to you later." With that, she terminated the call. Dean closed his eyes as a wave of defeat washed over him.

You're going to lose your son.

You're going to lose him if you keep this up.

He pocketed his cell.

Slipped out of the car.

Then Dean heard something rustle near the front of the safehouse.

30

Instincts drilled into Dean by the Army Rangers took over. He pulled out his SIG and slipped out of the Pontiac, his senses on high alert as he moved in a crouch toward the safehouse.

Slow, Blackwood.

Slow, smooth, and easy.

He dashed onto the lawn of the home next to the safehouse, his eyes fastened to the rustling bush that stood a little over 3 feet tall. Dean tightened his grip on his weapon, moving swiftly in a straight line to flank whatever was in the shrubs as he lined up the SIG's sights.

"Put your hands up," Dean growled. "*Now.*"

The rustling stopped.

"You've got two seconds." Dean coiled his finger around the trigger. "*One.*"

Nothing.

"Two!"

Something ran toward him.

Dean prepared to fire.

Then a raccoon burst out of the foliage, chittered, and hissed in retreat toward the street.

"For fuck's sake." Dean exhaled deeply, relief triggering a cool sensation that swelled inside his chest. "I almost shot a trash panda."

The front door opened. Wilson poked his head out, a Glock in hand as he scanned the street. "Where are they?" he said. "Who is it?"

Dean holstered his SIG, laughing as he gestured to the critter fleeing down the road. "It's Rocket Racoon," he said. "Pretty sure he's packing too."

Wilson holstered his weapon and motioned for Dean to join him inside. Dean closed the door behind them as he saw Mohr pacing in the living room with a sidearm in his hands.

"Who's out there?" Mohr said, his eyes wide, his breaths heavy. "Is it one of Eldridge's people?"

Dean appraised the weapon in Mohr's hand—a Colt M1911, the kind of gun with rounds that could blow acorn-sized holes into a man's chest.

"Hey," Dean said. "Let me have that for a minute, yeah?"

Mohr huffed. "You kidding me?" He caressed the trigger on the Colt with his index finger. "No fucking way."

"We've got you covered, Mohr. We're not going to let anything happen to you."

"I'm not giving you my gun."

"I don't think you should have one right now, boss."

"And I didn't ask for your opinion." The detective gestured with the business end of the Colt at Dean. "The gun stays with me."

"Sean." Dean slowly inched his way toward the cop. "I can't stand in a room with you comfortably if you're waving around a piece."

Mohr's eyes shimmered. "You probably heard about my 5150," he said. "Didn't you?"

"This doesn't have anything to do with that."

"Bullshit." Mohr raised the gun, fire in his eyes. "Don't patronize me. Everyone walks around on eggshells with me like I'm some kind of schizoid."

"*Easy*, brother," Dean coaxed as he stepped closer to Mohr and stood 2 feet away from him. He was close enough that he could reach out toward the gun and touch it. "Just hit the pause button, all right?"

"Don't talk to me like I'm a perp!" Mohr's hand that was clutching the gun quivered. "You don't get it. I told you—"

Dean shot out his hand and swiped the gun from Mohr. Then he racked back the slide. The bullet in the chamber spit out from the breach, and he caught it with one hand before palming the weapon over to Wilson.

"Sit down," Dean said as he pointed toward the couch. "*Now.*"

A wide-eyed Mohr complied.

"Enough fucking around." Dean snagged a chair from the kitchen, placed it in front of Mohr, and sat. "Talk."

"I want a deal first."

"And you'll get it. You have my word. Just tell us what you know."

Mohr hung his head. "Look here, man," Mohr said. The department is hell bent on resolving this thing and being done with it as soon as they can. Internal Affairs, the murder team, and all the other departments are all over this thing like flies on a corpse. The LAPD wants this to end *their* way." Mohr's eyes widened. "Eldridge wants this to end *his* way. You've got no idea what kind of pull this guy has. He's the king of the city, and anything he says goes."

"Then we need to move fast," Wilson said. "And you need to tell us a story."

"I already told you." Mohr perched forward as fear coated his expression. "You have no idea who these guys are, the ones that are really running the show." His hands trembled. "The people behind this will do things to me that'll make the tactics those narcos down south use look like a deep-tissue massage."

"Who are they?" Dean said. "What are you talking about?"

The detective's complexion took on a ghostly shade. "These guys are real pieces of work, man. They have this one enforcer. He works for the guy pulling the strings on this whole thing."

"You mean Eldridge," Wilson clarified. "Correct?"

"No." Mohr shook his head. "Eldridge isn't the guy in charge. He's not the one at the top of the pecking order. And this enforcer I'm talking about..." he closed his eyes, "he's the most wicked, *evil* son of a bitch that ever walked the planet. One time he flayed a guy's genitals off with a potato peeler. Then he did the same to the guy's legs, his arms, his torso, his face. He skinned every *inch* of him. You know what the guy did after that?" Mohr's eyes widened. "He put it all on a pizza, cooked it, and made the guy *eat* it."

Tremors snaked up Dean's spine. "Who's the enforcer? Who does he work for?"

Mohr's lips tightened into a fine line.

"You have my word," Wilson said, "that we will do whatever we can to protect you. But you need to tell us who these people are, what's going on, and why it got three cops killed. You're the key here, Detective Mohr. What you tell us is going to help bring this whole thing to an end."

Dean saw the lines in Mohr's face slacken. The cop's

composure shifted into something akin to that of an innocent child.

He's sobering up.

He's coming to his senses.

"Haywood didn't do this," Dean said. "Did he?"

Nothing from Mohr.

Dean inched closer. "Nod your head yes or no, Sean.
The ball is in your court. I'll ask you again. Did Haywood
have anything to do with this?"

Mohr shook his head. "No."

"Vendrell, Harlow, and Wyler were dirty, correct?"

"We all are. Everyone except Adams. He's clean. He's just
a rookie. Eldridge put him on the squad just to put a good
face on the unit." Mohr turned up his gaze. "We're Eldridge's
foot soldiers, man. We're just the pawns in this crooked little
scheme of his."

"What scheme, Sean?" Wilson said. "What is SMASH
involved in?"

"It's complicated. Eldridge and his partners are involved
in a slew of side hustles, and he's paid off everyone from the
deputy chief to people in the DA's office to make sure he's
protected. He's been doing this for *years*, man. He even…"
Mohr turned down his gaze, "he even covered up that shit
with your brother way back in the day."

Dean looked at Wilson.

His eyes turned into silver dollars.

Then the memory of Tommy's death began to play back
at high speed.

31

The air felt like it had gotten snatched out of Dean's lungs, his legs feeling like they were composed of rubber as he inched his chair closer to the couch. "Say that again, Mohr," he grumbled. "Say what you just said so I know I'm hearing you correctly."

"Your brother, Tommy," Mohr replied. "That was his name, right? The official story was that he got killed by a drunk driver."

"It was," Dean said. "But I never believed it." He got down on one knee, his eyes widening. "Sean, what are you saying? How do you know about my brother Tommy?"

"I only heard about it one time from Eldridge," Mohr replied. "He said your brother was killed on purpose. He just never said why." Tears welled in his eyes. "I've been swallowing secrets like this for *years*, man. I've been a sin-eater for Eldridge for a quarter of my life, and everyone wonders why I got placed on a 5150."

"Sean..." Dean pulled air deep into his lungs, "tell me what happened with my brother."

"Only Eldridge knows the whole story."

"You must know *something*."

"I don't."

"God damn you!" Dean jerked Mohr up off the couch and pressed his nose against the detective's, his anger swelling to the point that the vein in his neck jutted out. "Tell me what you know!"

"*Dean!*" Wilson yelled. "Put him down."

Dean released his grip.

Mohr shook uncontrollably.

Then Dean angled his body away, his mind fixated on Tommy, his brain struggling to process the information that Eldridge—allegedly—had something to do with his brother's demise.

"This was a mistake," Mohr said as he backed away toward a corner of the room. "I shouldn't have come here. You guys have to cut me loose. You have to let me go. You have to act like I was never here."

"Sean," Wilson said, "you came to us. You were the one who gave us the anonymous tip."

"And I shouldn't have." Mohr made a move toward the door. "I have to go."

Dean pressed his hand into the detective's chest. "You can't leave."

"You have to let me go!" Mohr shrieked. "They probably know I talked to you." He grabbed a fistful of his own hair and pulled. "Oh *God*. They're going to kill me! You don't understand, man. Eldridge has connections with big people. He has *everyone* in his pockets." Mohr cast a suspicious glance at Dean and Wilson. "I mean, how do I know you guys aren't in on this? Huh? How do I know that?"

"We're not going to hurt you," Wilson said. "Look, I get that you're scared. Maybe it's best if you take a load off before we keep talking. There's a bedroom in the back you can crash in. Just take the night to recharge. You've been through a lot, and your nerves are exhausted."

Dean, his nerves spiking, felt his heart race to the point that he thought he might pass out.

Eldridge had something to do with Tommy's death?

Is it true?

If it is, then why did he do it?

Jesus Christ.

What the hell is happening?

Mohr, tears streaming down his cheeks, slowly made his way to the couch and sat. "I've done a lot of bad shit," he said. "I don't think there's ever any coming back from it. We all participated. They're trying to pin this on Haywood, but it's not him. *Christ.*" He hung his head. "How did this get so bad?"

"Listen to me, Sean," Wilson said. "Just relax. We'll pick this up in the morning, okay?"

Mohr said nothing as his crying slowly subsided. Dean gestured for Wilson to join him in the kitchen as Mohr mumbled to himself incoherently.

"What do you think?" Wilson said. "Is he paranoid, or is he telling the truth?"

"I don't know. He's only painting with broad strokes at the moment." Dean cut a glance toward Mohr. "First and foremost, I want to know more about what he said about Tommy."

"Hold off on that."

"He's talking about my *brother*, Willy."

"I know."

"It has to be true. I mean, how could he know about that unless Eldridge said something to him? Huh? *How*?!"

"We will in good time, kid," Wilson said. "But we need to get him to talk about what Eldridge is involved in, the grander scheme before anything else." He rested his hands on Dean's shoulders. "One step at a time, okay? We'll get the whole story from him, but I need you to focus."

Dean nodded, checked his pulse, and heeded his superior's words. "You're right," he said. "*You're right.*"

"Mohr needs to cool down," Wilson replied. "As do you. In the meantime, I'll get a few of our people to watch over Mohr for the night. You and I will need to get prepped while they do that. We need to get our ducks in a row, so get this guy to the field office in the morning, and put him on the record."

"I'm sure Eldridge is looking for him," Dean said. "If Mohr stays off the radar too long, it'll look suspicious."

Wilson pulled out his phone. "I'm going to make a few calls. We need to wait until—"

A gunshot rang out.

Dean and Wilson spun around.

When they rushed into the living room, they found Mohr slumped lifelessly on one side of the couch, the left side of his head blown off. In his hand was the .38 Special he had used to do the deed.

32

R ed and blue emergency lights lit up the street as Dean watched a pair of medical examiners load Mohr's bagged-up body into the back of a van.

"I screwed this up," Dean said to Wilson who was seated with him on the hood of the Pontiac. "I should have frisked him." Dean took out his toothpick and slipped it between his lips. "I should have my goddamn head examined for not frisking him when I first pulled him in."

"No point in dwelling on the past, Deano," Wilson said. "What happened, happened."

"This whole thing is fucked now. Mohr was our best lead. He was about two minutes shy of telling us the whole story, my brother's death included." Dean clamped down on his toothpick and broke it in half. "I've been out of the game for too long, Willy." He nodded toward the coroner's van as he pulled out the busted bits of his toothpick. "And we pretty much just handed Eldridge a layup here. Now that Mohr is dead, he's gonna use that against us."

"I hate to say it," Wilson turned up his gaze and fastened it on Dean, "but you're right."

"So it's over."

"Looks that way. The Deputy Director's gonna hang us out to dry on this." A depleted chuckle slipped out of the SAC. "I wouldn't be surprised if we got posted up in some backwoods field office before the week is out for this whole thing."

Dean angled his body away from the ME van, the anger welling up inside of him triggering his face to flush red.

He knew about Tommy.

He said that Eldridge had something to do with it.

Dean clenched a fist.

I'm not done with you, Eldridge.

Not by a long *shot, you motherfucker.*

"I'm gonna make a few calls, kid," Wilson said. "Pretty sure Eldridge is a few moments out from rolling up. I gotta try to implement something in the way of damage control here."

"Same here." Dean pulled out his cell. "Sorry I let you down, boss."

"This one's on me, too, Deano."

The pair exchanged silent apologies before Dean threaded his way through the uniformed cops on the street and plugged Layla's number into his cell, the line ringing twice before the reporter answered.

"Hey," Layla greeted, her voice weak. Dean figured she had just woken up. "What time is it?"

"It's late," Dean said. "Sorry to wake you."

"That's okay. What's going on?"

"Sean Mohr just killed himself. I thought you'd like to know."

"Oh *God.*" Layla held the line for a moment. "When did this happen?"

Dean told her the whole story—rousting Mohr from the

bar, the car that tried to run them over, bringing Mohr to the safe house, the line of questions he and Wilson threw at the detective, Mohr putting a gun to his own head.

"Mohr was our best lead," Dean said. "This guy knew everything, and now he's being carted over to a meat locker."

"Did he give you anything?" Layla replied. "Anything at all?"

"Nothing specific. We were still working on him when he put the gun to his head."

"I mean..." the reporter sighed, "Mohr was a bit scrambled. After that 5150, I guess it was only a matter of time before he did something like this."

"There's more to it than that. I know Mohr was a bit whacked out of his mind, but there was something else. He was *scared* of somebody."

"Who?"

"Whoever is puppeteering this whole thing. Someone I probably haven't crossed paths with yet." Dean gnashed his teeth. "I should have known he'd have a backup piece on him. I screwed this up, Layla."

Tires squealed from around the corner. Dean cut a look over his shoulder toward the inbound, unmarked sedan that pulled up to the curb. Seconds later, Eldridge got out of the car and started barking orders at the uniformed officers on the scene. All Dean could think about was Mohr's statement about the captain being involved in the death of his brother.

"Eldridge is here," Dean said. "I gotta go."

"Is there anything I can do?" Layla replied. "What do you need from me?"

"I'm not sure yet. It's kind of a fluid situation at the moment."

"What about you? Are you okay?"

"All things considered," Dean laughed. "Pretty sure my shield is going to get turned into scrap metal by the time this is finished."

"You don't know that." Layla's tone brimmed with defiance. "It's not over yet."

"Our best lead just blew his brains out."

"Then we'll find another lead. Mohr offing himself simply validates the fact that SMASH is up to something —that *Eldridge* is up to something. We're getting closer to the truth, Dean, and I still plan on finding out what that is."

"Your resolve is outmatched, Layla." Dean smirked. "I'll give you that."

"Call me when you can," Layla said. "We'll figure this thing out."

"Understood."

"Be safe."

"You too."

Dean terminated the call and walked over to Wilson. The SAC held up his cell as the pair watched Eldridge beeline toward them with a pair of clenched fists.

"I just got off the phone with the Deputy Director," Wilson said. "Apparently, Eldridge and some of his cronies made some calls to the DC office."

"So what's our status?"

"I've got a conference call here in about ten minutes. I can only assume my ass is going to get chewed out to the point that it'll look like bubblegum by the time it's finished."

"Don't be so hard on yourself, Willy." Dean clapped the SAC on his back. "All those squats and incline running you do, you've got the rear-end of a man half your age."

"That's not funny."

"Yeah, well," Dean fished a fresh toothpick out of his

pocket and put it between his teeth, "I still got a kick out of it."

The two men ceased speaking the moment Eldridge approached. The captain stared them down with a fiery gaze.

"So," Eldridge said as he held out his hands, "you gentlemen mind explaining to me why one of my men just put a gun to his own head?"

"Mohr came to us," Wilson replied. "He came forward to the FBI with some information he felt necessary to divulge."

"Bullshit."

"You know," Dean chuckled, "if I had a nickel for every time you said that, Captain, I could pay my phone bill for the month."

"*This*," the SMASH captain pointed to the van that housed Mohr's corpse, "is on you, and I'm going to see to it that you pay for it with your careers." His gaze ping-ponged between Dean and Wilson. "The both of you."

"Your detective had some interesting yarns he was spinning," Wilson chimed in. "He was about two seconds shy of telling us something he felt was substantial enough to warrant our protection."

"That man had a litany of mental health problems," Eldridge grumbled. "I pulled him off of active duty two weeks ago. The man was fried, and whatever you two said to him pushed him over the edge."

"That's not what happened," Dean said. "Mohr came to us willingly."

"All I know is another one of my guys is dead, and you two were in the room when he did it. Far as I'm concerned, you two coerced him into making some kind of horseshit confession without the presence of a lawyer or one of his reps from the department."

A curt, intemperate reply was on the cusp of slipping out of Dean, but before he could rattle it off, a carob-skinned gentleman sporting a gold USC football ring walked over and stood beside Eldridge. "I'm Deputy Chief Alan Howard," he said. "I've spoken with your Deputy Director, and he seems to be inclined to think that your involvement may have contributed to Sean Mohr's suicide."

"I just got off the phone with him," Wilson said. "And he didn't say it exactly in those terms."

"You understand how this looks, Special Agent Wilson?" Howard said. "One of our people shot himself in an FBI safehouse. Why was he not brought in for official questioning? Why did you do it at a safehouse instead of a field office? Nothing he told you will be on any kind of record."

Wilson looked at Dean.

Tell him.

"I approached Detective Mohr earlier this evening," Dean said. "I was asking him a few questions in regard to the murders of Mike Vendrell, Cole Harlow, and Ronald Wyler. He said he wanted to speak to us. Considering the high-profile nature of these murders, we felt that a secure, off-site location would put him at ease. He was looking to say whatever it was that was on his mind."

Howard shrugged. "Why wasn't he searched? Why didn't you confiscate his weapons? This doesn't bode well for either of you *or* the FBI for that matter." He looked straight at Dean. "And I've heard about you, Agent Blackwood."

"Is that so?"

"That I have. And your reputation as a rogue agent is one that adds all kinds of implications to this ordeal."

"You shouldn't be on the streets," Eldridge said, "let alone in a room with a seasoned LAPD detective. God only knows what you said or did to drive Mohr to put a gun to his own head."

Dean flexed his brow. "You're saying this is *my* fault?"

"Precisely," Howard replied. "And I'm pretty sure your superiors at the Bureau will back me up on that."

"This is unfathomable, Dean," Eldridge said, his tone like that of a parent scolding a child. "God only knows what your father is going to say about all of this."

"He might have some questions," Dean replied, his eyes narrowing and teeth gnashing, "about my brother Tommy, about his death that happened over twenty years ago."

"Come again?"

"You heard me, fuckwit." Dean stepped closer to the captain. "And don't act like you didn't."

Eldridge grinned.

Dean clenched a fist.

Then a uniformed officer walked over and inserted himself into the conversation. "Captain," the cop held out a cell phone to Eldridge, "Detective Benavidez for you."

Eldridge swiped the phone from the officer and moved away. Dean stared the captain down as he conjured up mental images of clocking the man upside his head.

"Look," Wilson said, "our people were tipped off about this case from the start, and every crime scene has raised nothing but suspicion."

"The Bureau's involvement in this matter has ended, Agent Wilson," Howard said. "The LAPD will handle this internally. These are *our* people, *our* officers, and after what has transpired here tonight, I'm going to be sure to pursue something in the way of formal charges for Agent Blackwood."

Dean's eyes widened. "All right, hold the fucking phone—"

Wilson flattened his palm against Dean's chest. "*Cool down*," he whispered as his gaze remained fixed to the deputy chief. "And I don't appreciate the posturing here, Howard. You know damn well my agent wasn't responsible for how this case turned out, so don't try to make it sound like the reason this whole thing has been so unprecedented and complicated is because of his doing."

"Regardless," Howard said, "I'll still be pressing something in the way of formal charges."

"Do what you need to do." Wilson's eyes narrowed. "But stay away from my agent in the meantime. Anything you have to say to him, you say to me."

Howard snickered.

Dean suppressed his urge to clock the deputy chief in his jaw as Eldridge rejoined the group.

"Well," the captain said, "looks like the search for who killed my guys is over."

Dean squinted. "What are you talking about?"

"Marcus Haywood was just shot to death outside of Tyler Adams' residence in Glendale. Apparently, Haywood showed up and tried to kill him."

33

D ean stared at the body of Marcus Haywood. The bullet-peppered corpse was positioned face-down in the middle of a residential street, a revolver clutched in his hand, his eyes wide and vacant of life, staring straight at Dean with a terror-stricken expression.

This is wrong.

Someone set him up.

Dean closed his eyes.

Eldridge is tying off loose ends before the truth has a chance to come out.

Dean made his way toward Wilson who was by three patrol cruisers parked at canted angles outside the apartment complex off Brand Boulevard. Near the entrance of the complex was Eldridge, speaking off to the side with Tyler Adams and Deputy Chief Howard.

"Neighbors called in a suspicious vehicle," Wilson said as he motioned to the cops on the scene. "When the patrol units arrived, they found Haywood inside his car in front of the complex."

"Let me guess," Dean replied. "The vehicle Haywood

was in matched the description of the one used at the Vendrell, Harlow, and Wyler crime scenes."

Wilson nodded. "When the officers approached the car, Haywood stepped out and started firing. He managed to get off three shots before the officers put him down."

"This is bullshit, boss," Dean said. "Eldridge is doctoring the scene. For all we know, the guys who took down Haywood are probably on his payroll."

Wilson held up his hand. "*Easy.*"

"They're trying to pin this whole thing on Haywood," Dean said. "Mohr said it himself that he wasn't responsible. And now they got Haywood's body *and* the car outside Adams' apartment? This has to be the most doctored crime scene I've ever seen in my life."

Eldridge approached.

Wilson looked at Dean and held up a single finger to his lips.

Save it for later.

"Gentlemen," Eldridge said. "It looks like Marcus Haywood is the guy who came after our people. We've got everything on hand to substantiate that." He gestured to the scene behind him. "Looks like he has a burner phone on him, and Vegas odds tell me that once we dump it, we're going to find out that he was the CI Harlow and Vendrell were talking to."

Wilson crossed his arms. "You think it's a good idea to be making such definitive statements before the scene gets worked?"

"It's pretty straightforward, don't you think? I had a feeling that Haywood was the one pulling the strings on this from the start. I gave that information to you days ago, and you proceeded to berate my men and their families instead of working with them. You had Haywood." Eldridge pointed at Dean. "And you let him go."

Dean furrowed his brow. "*Berate your people?* Is that what you really think happened?"

Eldridge reached into his pocket, produced a pack of gum, and then popped a piece into his mouth. "All I know is that Adams was spared the same fate. Haywood did this, gentlemen. Make no mistake about that."

Dean's nostrils flared as he bored his gaze into the SMASH captain.

You told Sharon to tell me about Haywood, didn't you?

You coached her in advance.

You knew I'd come to both of you, so you tried to set it up so I'd go after Haywood.

You thought I'd play ball, that I'd bring the guy in. But I didn't.

Dean gestured around the crime scene. "What part of this jives with you? If Haywood did this—a repeat offender with the IQ of a grapefruit, by the way—then why is he rolling up to Adams' place with a gun to put him down when he allegedly went through the trouble of running down the others with a car?"

"It's pretty simple, Agent Blackwood," Eldridge said. "Haywood probably got desperate after he missed hitting you and Mohr outside the bar. He figured maybe he was getting close to being caught. So out of desperation, he takes a gun and marches up to Adams to try to put him down."

"That doesn't explain the vendettas against Vendrell and Harlow. If they were Haywood's target, why would he go after the rest of the SMASH guys?"

"Because Haywood was a criminal," Eldridge said. "*Period.* He simply wanted anyone close to Vendrell and Harlow dead.

Haywood blamed them and the system for what happened to his life, so he decided to take it out on that system. It's the same MO that happened with Christopher Dorner."

"Horseshit," Dean replied. "It's not the same thing at all. And besides, Haywood coming after Adams like he did was tantamount to a suicide run."

"It's probably what Haywood wanted."

"You know what I think?" Dean nodded at the uniformed cops who took down Haywood. "I think you got your boys over there to cap Haywood and stage the scene to make it look the way you *wanted* it to look, Captain. I think you set this up. I think you planted that burner phone on Haywood that you claimed to have found. I bet if we dusted the thing for prints, we'd find a partial of your fingerprints on the goddamn thing."

Wilson grabbed Dean's arm. "That's enough."

Dean shrugged off his boss's grip. "No, this is bullshit. If Haywood was pulling a 'Chris Dorner,' why not go after Harlow and Vendrell's families? Why take out other cops? Why the elaborate ruse and this nonsense of running those guys over? And how in the hell could he have managed to track down, stalk, and kill *three members* of one of the most elite units in the LAPD?"

"Listen here, kid," Eldridge said, "we've got Haywood, the car used in the murders, and circumstances lining up with the narrative that *Haywood* is the man responsible for the deaths of Detectives Harlow, Wyler, and Vendrell. The report writes itself. And I'm fairly certain once all the dust is settled that the story I told you is the final one that will be given to the press."

Dean's fury swelled inside his chest. His skin prickled as he tried to collect his thoughts before he said anything he would regret later on.

Crooked bastard.

Classic LAPD coverup.

He can't get away with this.

He killed Haywood.

He probably killed Kara Shardlow too.

And if what Mohr says holds any weight, he killed my brother too.

"Mohr said that Haywood isn't responsible for this," Dean said. "And he seemed pretty convinced of it too."

"I told you," Eldridge replied, "Mohr was a mentally afflicted man. I'm sure once the ME gives us back the test results, we're going to find that he wasn't all there. Plus, you've got nothing official on the record but your word that Mohr said what he did."

Dean turned away.

A crock of shit.

An absolute fabrication.

Moments later, Howard approached and extended the cell phone in his hand like a ref holding out a yellow card. "Your Deputy Director," he said as he tossed the phone to Wilson. "And I suggest you take it."

Wilson caught the phone, glanced at Dean, and then moved away. Dean used the time that Wilson was on the phone to stare down Eldridge.

"If you think you're getting away with this," Dean said, "you're dreaming."

"You know," Eldridge wagged a finger and stepped closer, "I should have known you'd turn out the way you did. This whole cowboy persona of yours is as cliché as it gets. Hell," he flatted his palm across his chest, "if I watched my own brother get wiped out the way you did," he laughed, "I suppose I'd have a few screws loose myself."

The fingers on Dean's hand closed into a fist. "Choose

your next words very carefully, Captain. Because they may be your last."

"It's a shame really," Eldridge continued. "Maybe if your brother Tommy hadn't gotten killed, things would have been different."

Dean planted his feet.

He prepared to charge.

Then he felt Wilson secure a grip on his arm.

"That's it," the SAC said. "We're finished."

Dean narrowed his eyes. "What?"

"We're off the case. You and I need to report back to the field office first thing in the morning with OPR."

The anger welling up inside Dean was so palpable he could taste it. "Boss—"

"That's *it*, kid," Wilson pulled Dean away from the scene. "We're clearing out of here."

"We'll be in touch, Agent Wilson," Howard said. "This isn't over."

A litany of colorful curses and insults were on the tip of Dean's tongue as Wilson escorted him to the Pontiac. Dean threw a glance over his shoulder. Eldridge was smirking and waving as Dean and Wilson departed the scene.

"This is finished," Wilson said. "Everyone, the governor's office included, is spinning the story that the reason this all turned out the way it did is because of FBI obfuscation."

Dean felt like he'd been hit upside the head with a paperweight. "*Obfuscation?*" He threw up his hands. "This is so whacked, boss—completely fucktangular on all sides."

"It is what it is," Wilson said. "It's the LAPD's game, Dean. They have the ball now. We're *done*."

Dean moved away from his boss, feeling Eldridge's gaze burning the back of his neck like a schoolyard bully.

I can't believe this.

This sadistic shit is going to get away with it.
He looked at Haywood's body.
Adams' apartment.
Then he put his sights back on Eldridge.
Well done, asshole.
You got away with murder.

34

T he television in Dean's room was tuned to the local
news. Coverage of the shooting of Marcus Haywood
was being broadcast on several channels. Dean sat on the
edge of his bed, the remote clutched in his hand, his grip tight
to the point that the device was on the cusp of fracturing.

"In other breaking news," the reporter on the scene said,
"the pursuit of a suspect linked to a series of LAPD officer-
related homicides *ended* tonight in Glendale."

The mugshot of Marcus Haywood popped onto the
screen. Dean shook his head as the reporter continued on
with her coverage.

"The suspect, Marcus Haywood," the reporter went on,
"was killed earlier this evening after exchanging shots with
members of the Glendale PD outside an apartment complex
near Brand Boulevard. Captain Larry Eldridge," the screen
cut to a shot of the SMASH captain on the scene with
Howard, "believes that Glendale PD intervened while
Haywood was supposedly in the midst of targeting yet
another member of the same unit. An official statement will

be made during a press conference tomorrow. In related news—"

Dean pushed the mute button on the remote. His skin felt like it was on fire as he shot up from the bed and paced the room back and forth as he cursed repeatedly under his breath.

You're a lying sack of shit, Eldridge.

A crooked son of a bitch.

You covered this up just like you wanted to.

He threw the remote against the wall and busted it to pieces.

You killed my brother, and you got away with it.

For a few minutes, Dean stewed on the conversation he had with Mohr before the cop put a gun to his head. He weighed the truth of Mohr's statements about Eldridge being involved with Tommy's death, his mind racing and rage building as he paced some more.

Only Eldridge knows the truth.

One way or another, someone has to get it out of him.

Dean's cell rang. "Willy," he answered after the first ring, knowing who it was without bothering to look at the caller ID. "Where are you?"

"I'm calling from a burner," Wilson said.

"You taking hints from the SMASH crew now?"

"I need to make sure the call is untraceable. I can't have anyone knowing I called you. Are you at the hotel?"

"I am."

"Good. Then listen up. I've only got a few minutes."

Dean plopped down on the edge of the bed and waited for his boss to continue.

"We both know the LAPD is trying to cover this up," Wilson said. "They pinned this on Haywood, and now they're going to wrap it up with a bow and move on with their lives."

"And we can't do anything about it." Dean pinched the bridge of his nose. "Or the fact that Eldridge may have killed my brother."

"No, at least not *officially*, that is."

Dean had a sense of what was coming next. "You want me to keep digging," he said. "You want me to go after these guys."

"I want you to do what you *do*, kid," Wilson replied. "But the decision is up to you. If you decide to walk, it all ends right here. If you can figure this out, kid, if you can find out what's going on and nail these guys, that'll be enough to get us back into the Bureau's good graces."

"And if I go through with this, I run the risk of getting caught in their crosshairs, Willy. If I fail," Dean huffed, "I'm fucked."

And what about Jeremy?

What about Claire?

You told yourself you wouldn't live this life anymore, Deano.

You promised everyone *that you had turned your back on the old ways.*

Tommy or no Tommy, you're running the risk of losing the family you have left.

Dean shook his head. "I can't do this, boss. I came out here to be with my kid, to start over. Going through with this would blow my chances of seeing that through, even if that gives me a chance to find out what happened to my brother."

"Then we call it off," Wilson said. "It ends, right here and now."

On the television, the mugshot of Marcus Haywood popped up again. Dean stared deep into the man's eyes, his thoughts fixated on the fact that Haywood, Kara Shardlow, and God only knows who else had been turned into collateral damage as a result of Eldridge's crusade to cover up the truth.

Then the newscast cut to a mugshot of Kara Shardlow.

Dean squinted.

He walked over to the TV and turned up the volume. He sat down and told Wilson to wait a beat as he listened.

"The LAPD," the newscaster narrated, "also discovered the body of *this* woman, Kara Shardlow, an individual they believe was last seen with Marcus Haywood in the days leading up to the murders of the SMASH officers."

Son of a bitch.

No.

No, it can't be!

"Kara Shardlow's body," the newscaster went on, "was discovered earlier this evening in a drainage runoff in Los Feliz."

They'll find Marcus's DNA on her.

A slew of evidence to connect him to it.

All of it manufactured by whoever set this up.

"KCAL 9 news," the newscaster went on, "spoke with the family of Ms. Shardlow earlier this evening."

Dean was perched on the edge of the bed, watching with a slack-jawed expression as Kara's mother, Rachel, addressed the cameras on the porch of her home as she gripped the hand of the six-year-old standing beside her.

Kara's son.

"We are just *shocked*," Rachel said, holding back tears, her voice racked with strain. "We want to know who did this." She looked deep into the camera and locked eyes with Dean. "Whoever knows who is responsible for this, we beg you to come forward." She held up the young boy's hand. "We need to know." The grieving mother dabbed at her eyes. "We don't want the death of Thomas's mother to go unanswered."

Dean's heart shot into his throat.

He slid off the bed.

He tried to tally the odds that Kara's son—*Thomas*—had managed to have the same name as his late brother.

One in a million.

My God.

Dean's nostrils flared as he watched young Tommy Shardlow being paraded in front of the news cameras.

It all comes full circle.

"Kid," Wilson said through the phone. "You still there?"

Dean placed his cell on speaker. "You never told me," he said. "You never told me Kara's kid was named Tommy."

The SAC said nothing.

"You knew if I knew," Dean went on, "that I'd flip. That's why you didn't want to tell me about the kid."

"I know you," Wilson said, "and I didn't want to use that to motivate you. I didn't want to make this personal."

The face of Thomas Shardlow became Dean's sole focus.

I'm sorry, kid.

God, I am so sorry.

"Eldridge can't get away with this," Dean said. "He can't. Same goes for whoever else was involved, the people Mohr was talking about."

"So..." Wilson held the line for a moment, "what are you going to do?"

"If I go after Eldridge and the rest of these guys," Dean said, "I'd have to do things like I did in the old days. The only way this thing gets solved is if I go rogue. I can't have any contact with you. I have to do this under the radar. I have to be completely off the books."

"So you'll do it?" Wilson replied. "Be clear with what you want to do here, kid. State your intentions, and state them clearly."

Dean held the line, his fury brimming to the point that he thought he might shoot steam out his ears like a character in a *Looney Tunes* cartoon.

Eldridge can't get away with this.

He can't.

You have to take him down.

You have to do this for Marcus.

For Tommy.

For Kara.

For the kid and everyone else who got caught up in the wake of this.

"I want this prick, Willy," Dean told his boss. "I want him so bad I can taste it."

"This can't be a revenge mission, Deano," Wilson replied. "If you operate from that mindset—"

"I know." Dean angled his body toward the balcony, wondering where Eldridge was as he conjured up images of putting a gun to the SMASH captain's head. "But I want him, and I'm going to get him."

"Well..." Wilson took a beat, "I suppose that's the end of it."

"Stay by the phone, boss." Dean pulled air deep into his lungs. "I'll call you when it's finished." He hung up the cell, placed it on the nightstand, and unclipped his FBI shield from his belt.

He looked it over.

Tossed it in the nightstand drawer.

He closed the drawer, turned his back on it, and went to retrieve his SIG.

"We're back, Deano," Woody said. "You and me, the dynamic duo. Back in the saddle again!"

Dean said nothing.

Maybe Woody was right, maybe he wasn't, but he didn't have time to unpack it.

You got work to do, Blackwood.

He took out his SIG, chambered a round, and stuffed it in his holster.

Eldridge is yours.

Dean scooped up his car keys and moved to the door.

Now go out there and get him.

35

Two days passed. Eldridge's press conference was over, and Marcus Haywood was named the culprit in the murders of Detectives Vendrell, Harlow, and Wyler. And traces of Haywood's DNA were found on Kara Shardlow's body. The burner phone on Haywood's body had been dumped. To everyone's shock—save for Dean—it turned out that Haywood *was* the CI named Tookie who had taken extreme, elaborate measures to set up Harlow and Vendrell in, according to Eldridge, "an act of revenge."

According to the LAPD, the matter had ended. The case was closed.

But as far as Dean was concerned, things were far from over.

Standing on the second-story patio area at Universal CityWalk, Dean put his sights on Tyler Adams, the 200-pound SMASH squad rookie with looks on par with Chris Evans. He was strolling hand in hand with his girlfriend down the main drag of the tourist hotspot on the level beneath him.

Adams is the last of the SMASH officers.

He's on the inside.

And he's my best shot at getting closer to the truth.

Dean watched Tyler and his girlfriend climb the staircase to the second level, concealing himself behind a potted plant as they approached the hostess of the restaurant. Tyler gestured to the patio area, the waitress nodding enthusiastically as she guided the pair to a table.

They sat.

Ordered some drinks.

A few minutes later, Tyler's girlfriend stood up. Dean read her lips to find that she was going to use the restroom.

Now, Dean.

Go.

Dean moved inside and approached the table, Tyler's back to him, the rookie fiddling on his phone. Dean walked up and slapped Tyler on the back. "What's good, Tyler?"

Tyler spun around, his eyes narrowed and chest puffing in reply. "Do I know you?"

"Dean Blackwood."

The rookie's eyes widened.

"Yeah." Dean pulled out a seat and slipped down onto it. "Figured that name would ring a bell."

"Look, man." Tyler held up his hands. "I'm not supposed to—"

"—talk to me. I get it. I'm sure Eldridge warned you about me in advance." Dean forked a thumb toward the inside of the restaurant. "Look, your girlfriend Kelly is about two minutes shy of coming out of the bathroom, so I'll keep this simple. You can tell her to wait here because you're pretty sure you dropped your keys downstairs, or we can make her part of this conversation, but I don't think we need to ruin her afternoon."

"You..." Tyler squinted. "You know her name?"

"I know all about her." Dean pointed a finger. "*And* you. You're twenty-six. Bright beyond your years. You went to UCLA, your GPA was 3.8, and Kelly works at the Solheim Senior Care facility five days of the week. I also know that Gladys, the woman Kelly tends to the most at the nursing home, knits her mittens every year for Christmas."

A slack-jawed Tyler said nothing.

"I'll be downstairs," Dean said as he stood up from the table. "Think it over. All I want is a few moments of your time. I'll be waiting down there by Jamba Juice."

Minutes later, Dean, sipping a protein smoothie outside Jamba Juice, caught Tyler Adams walking toward him with his hands in his pockets. The timid looking SMASH squad rookie threw the occasional glance over his shoulder, his expression sheet-white as he nodded in greeting at Dean.

"So," Tyler said, "what do you want?"

"Walk with me," Dean replied as he took one more sip of his drink and tossed it into a waste bin. "This won't take long."

The two walked down the strip, Dean feeling the tension radiating off of Tyler like the kid was radioactive.

"Look," Tyler said. "I'm new to the unit. I don't know anything. I shouldn't even be talking to you."

"Four dead cops, Tyler." Dean held up the corresponding fingers. "*Four.* That doesn't sit well with you, and if you got half a brain, which I know you do, you know that Haywood wasn't the guy who did this."

Tyler said nothing.

"You know something was off about this whole thing," Dean said. "And you're too smart and too scared to screw with someone like Eldridge, considering all the connections he's got. I'm sure he sat you down. He probably told you not to talk to anyone." He gestured around. "Hell, he probably bankrolled this little excursion today, didn't he?"

Tyler's gaze shifted down toward the VIP pass around his neck.

"You didn't sign up to be like the rest of those cops," Dean said. "I'm sure of it. I pulled your jacket, Adams. You served in the Rangers."

"Yeah," Tyler said. "I did."

Dean slipped off his leather jacket and then rolled up the sleeve of his flannel to his bicep and showed Tyler the 75th Ranger tattoo inked into his flesh. "Busted my knee and got discharged not long after it," he said. "Some of the best *and* the worst years of my life." He covered up the tat. "I need your help, kid. The SMASH unit is bent. People are dying because of it. I know this doesn't sit well with a guy like you. Something's off, and I learned a lot about it from Mohr."

Tyler winced. "Mohr?"

"He shot himself in front of me because he was too scared to confess to what was going on. He admitted that SMASH has some kind of side operation, but he swallowed a bullet before he could tell us more."

"Well, Mohr was right." Tyler did a scan of his surroundings. "They are up to *something*, but the specifics were something I was never let in on. I'm not part of the inner circle. Look, I want to help you. I do. I just don't know a hell of a lot. Plus," he averted his gaze, "the word now is that Eldridge is going to shut down the unit."

Dean's eyes widened. "He said that?"

"Not long after the press conference. Eldridge said they're going to rally and rebrand, essentially. I'm on leave until then. Eldridge says he's got a slot for me in the new unit as soon as he gets the ball rolling." Tyler huffed. "He's been making it a point to make it as cozy as possible for me until then."

Eldridge is sweeping it all under the rug

He's trying to burn this thing to the ground before the truth comes to light.

"Was there anything you knew about?" Dean said. "Anything suspicious? Anything that seemed off to you?"

Tyler thought about it. "I was always a little spooked by Vendrell and Harlow."

"How so?"

"I rode with them a few times. They were a different breed of cop. Dyed in the wool cowboys. I was pretty taken aback by some of the unit's strong-arm tactics, but the guys insisted that was how the game was played, that SMASH had to be as edgy as the guys we were taking down." Tyler stepped in closer. "But it was pretty clear to me after a while that Eldridge and some of the higher-ups might have been using the unit to pad their pockets. I got the sense that they were, well, doing stuff during their off-hours that I didn't know about."

Dean took mental notes. "Keep going."

"I never saw the other guys in the unit participating in anything illegal," Tyler said, "if that's what you're getting at. Frankly, I don't think they wanted me to know either."

"Because you're a boy scout," Dean replied. "I know a little bit about you, Tyler. You're a good guy. That's a big reason Eldridge put you in the unit. He wanted someone clean to make it look good."

"Maybe." The rookie's gaze drifted. "I still think they were trying me out though."

"What do you mean?"

"I think that Vendrell and Harlow were sizing me up when I first started out. They were testing me, seeing if I was on their side. After a while, I think they realized I wasn't like them. I stopped participating in a lot of the raids and got stuck being their paper bitch. Hell, I'm surprised I didn't get canned from the unit altogether."

"What's your relationship with Eldridge like?" Dean said. "How close are you guys?"

"Not that close," Tyler replied. "Wyler was the one who ran the unit. I worked with him the most. The guy was intense too. He never said much. He was always working alongside Eldridge though. He was his right-hand man. Anytime there was a problem, beef, whatever, Wyler was the one who made it go away."

A thought popped into Dean's brain—an angle. "How loyal are these guys to you?"

Tyler winced. "What do you mean?"

"As in, if you came to them asking for a favor, saying you were in some kind of trouble," Dean shrugged, "do you think they'd help you?"

"Yeah," Tyler nodded. "Most definitely. These guys love having favors owed to them."

"When's the next time you're talking to them?"

"I'm seeing Eldridge and a few others at his house tomorrow. He's having a barbecue. Some kind of, I don't know, wrap party for the unit. His words."

A wrap *party.*

Dean rolled his eyes.

Oh, for fuck's sake.

Eldridge, you are a gem.

Dean reached into his jacket and pulled out a scrap of paper. "Call this number," he said. "It goes to me and me only. Call me when you get back tonight after your girl falls asleep. Got it?"

Tyler took the paper and glanced at it. "I don't want to

cause any problems, Mr. Blackwood. I've got a career to think about." He nodded toward his girlfriend waiting for him on the upper level. "I've got, you know, a *life* I need to consider."

"And I need your help, Tyler," Dean said. "Eldridge is dirty. He's a piece of shit. And if this asshole continues to go unchecked, a lot more people are going to get hurt because of it."

A forlorn expression washed across the rookie's face. Dean sensed that the kid was mulling over everything he had said to him with serious consideration.

"We'll work this out, kid," Dean said. "You have my word. Until then, just enjoy your day. That girl of yours is having a blast, I can tell."

"Yeah." Tyler smirked. "Yeah, she's pretty great."

"She loves you." Dean clapped the rookie on the shoulder. "The Bureau footed the bill for a bunch of nifty little profiling classes—reading body language, stuff like that. Long story short," he threw a glance in Kelly's direction, "I'd put my money on that girl of yours being in it for the long haul—kids, family, the whole thing."

Dean walked away, leaving a beaming Tyler Adams to go on about his day. As Dean made his way to the parking structure, he thought about the last comment he made to Adams. It occurred to him that it had been several days since he saw his own son, so once he was behind the wheel of the Plymouth, Dean fished out his cell phone and plugged in his ex-wife's number.

"Hey, Dean," Claire greeted. "Everything okay?"

"I'm good. Is Jeremy there?"

"He just got back from playing with a few friends a few minutes ago."

"Can I talk to him?"

Moments later, Jeremy's voice came on the line. The kid was panting and heaving from whatever copious amount of physical exertion he had on display moments before. "Hey, Dad!" he said. "Where are you?"

"I'm working, Pally."

"Are you coming by soon?"

"Pretty soon. What are you up to?"

"I was playing a basketball game on the Xbox with Josh and Bryan."

"Which team were you?"

"The Lakers."

"Good man." Dean cleared his throat. . "Listen, Pally. I just, uh...I wanted to say that I'm sorry I haven't been by yet."

"It's okay," Jeremy said, a touch of disappointment in his voice. "I talked to Grandpa, by the way."

"Was he grumpy?"

"Big time."

Dean laughed. "I'm not surprised." He took a beat. "Listen, buddy. I need you to know that I'm really trying to make it a point to be around more."

"I know."

"I love you, kiddo."

"I love you, too, Dad," Jeremy said. "But I gotta go. I'm supposed to play another four quarters with Bryan online."

"Hop to it, Pally," Dean replied. "Make the Lakers proud."

"Bye, Dad!"

"Bye, kiddo."

Dean listened as Jeremy ran away, the sounds of the phone changing hands as he tamped down his feelings of regret and shame and remorse for not being with his son.

"Dean?" Claire said. "Are you still there?"

"I'm here."

"Everything okay?"

"Yeah, everything's good."

"Listen," Claire said, "I was thinking maybe we could have you over for dinner in a couple days—if you're up for it, that is."

"Absolutely," Dean said, forgetting for a brief moment that he was working a case off the books for the Bureau. "I'm there."

"I'll get the details to you in a little bit, then. Talk soon?"

"Talk soon."

Dean hung up the phone, turned over the engine, and drove his Pontiac through the parking structure. As he turned onto the freeway, he ruminated on what Tyler Adams told him about the barbecue taking place the following day.

That's it, Deano.

He throttled the engine.

That's *how you get to Eldridge.*

36

"Here's the deal," Dean said into his phone, lingering on the balcony of his room. "When you arrive at the barbecue tomorrow, you're going to tell Eldridge I confronted you."

The pitch was met with severe resistance on Tyler's end. The rookie offered his protests—at one point even saying he wasn't up for it—but Dean managed to calm the kid down and continued on with the outline of his plan.

"You're going to tell Eldridge that I approached you yesterday," Dean said, "that I grilled you pretty hard and tried to get you to break. After that, you're going to tell him that your girlfriend is pregnant, and another man is responsible."

A noise that sounded like a cross between a gasp and a laugh slipped out of Tyler. "Why the hell would I do that?"

"Because you need to sound desperate. You need to make Eldridge feel like you need his help, that you essentially want the guy who supposedly got your girlfriend pregnant dead."

"*Jesus,*" Tyler groaned. "This is nuts."

"You'll go to Eldridge," Dean continued. "You'll turn on the recording device you have on your phone. Just keep it in your pocket or somewhere where it's not visible but can still pick up sound. Tell Eldridge everything I just told you. Improvise if you have to. Just feel out the situation and respond to Eldridge accordingly. What's important is that you tell him everything I've just told you."

"What does telling Eldridge all of this accomplish?"

"We know Eldridge is covering up for something," Dean said. "I need to provoke him. He might contact this enforcer we spoke about, try to help you take care of this guy who knocked up your girlfriend. Hell," Dean laughed, "he might send the guy after me."

Tyler held the line. "This sounds thin, man," he finally said. "How do we know it's going to work?"

"We don't," Dean said, "but desperate times call for desperate measures."

The pair went over the plan a few more times to make sure Tyler had it ingrained in his mind. Once Dean was satisfied the kid was on board, Tyler requested one last thing from Dean.

"If anything happens," the rookie said, "look after Kelly for me."

"*Nothing* is going to happen, Tyler," Dean replied. "We're just trying to rile up Eldridge a little bit, get him to make a mistake."

"What if he makes me? If he knows I'm working with you..." The rookie's voice trailed off.

"I've got your back, Tyler. Nothing is going to happen to you. Or Kelly. Or anyone else." Dean narrowed his eyes. "You have my word."

At 1:00 the following afternoon, Dean was seated behind the wheel of the Pontiac four doors down from Eldridge's residence, with a Dodgers cap hung low over his head. Ten minutes into waiting, his cell phone buzzed, and when Dean answered, a timid-sounding Tyler greeted him.

"I'm here," the kid said. "I'm ready to go. I just pulled up."

"I see you." Dean craned his neck and saw Tyler approaching the front of Eldridge's residence. "And there's a slight change of plan."

"What do you mean?"

"I need you to keep this call going. I need to hear it live. I'll be recording it on my end. Just stick the phone somewhere on you where it can pick up sound." Dean fiddled with his phone, pulled up a voice memo app, and pushed the little red button that recorded everything on the call. "Can you do that?"

"Yeah…" Tyler breathed a sigh. "Yeah, I'm wearing board shorts. The fabric is pretty thin, so it should pick up voices easily."

"Good." Dean tracked the rookie as he rapped his knuckles on the front door of Eldridge's home. Tyler shifted his weight and looked like he wanted to crawl out of his own skin. "Just act normal. Have a couple of beers or something in the meantime. Try to look a little distraught, but don't make too big a show of it. Just wait it out until Eldridge has thrown back a couple. Once he has, pull him aside for a little chit-chat."

"Understood," Tyler said. "What happens when it's finished?"

"You go home," Dean said, "and you wait for me to call."

"Okay."

"You got this, Tyler. Easy in, easy out."

Dean saw Tyler place the call on speaker and slip the phone into his board shorts. Moments later, a petite, blonde woman answered the door, embraced the rookie, and motioned him to come inside.

All right.

Dean watched the front door close.

Here we go...

The sound on Dean's phone—to his satisfaction—was picking up everything. He could hear Tyler greet Eldridge's wife. Kids playing. The rookie cracking open a beer. Bullshitting with other police officers in the backyard, even the soft reverb of "Reach Out I'll Be There" by the Four Tops playing from a pair of speakers in the backyard.

Dean closed his eyes, recalling all the details of Eldridge's domicile, seeing things from Tyler's POV as the kid glad-handed his way through the party.

"Yo, Adams!" Dean heard a male voice greet Tyler. "What's going on, brother?"

That's not Eldridge.

That's someone else.

"What up, Sly?" Tyler replied. "How's it going?"

"It's going. The captain's in back. We've got burgers and dogs on the grill." The guy named Sly took a pause. "Where's your lady friend?"

"She's not feeling great," Tyler said. "She's going to sit this one out. Think she's got a stomach flu or something."

Good, kid.

Keep it up.

"*Damn,*" Sly remarked. "Sorry to hear that. Well, grab a brew. The party's just getting started."

Fifteen minutes passed. Most of the conversations sounded innocuous to Dean. After a few minutes *more* ticked by, Dean heard the voice of Captain Larry Eldridge.

"Ty!" Eldridge said. "Good to see, buddy. How are you holding up?"

Tyler huffed. "Hanging in there. Been a long couple of days."

"How was Universal?"

"It was great. Thanks again for hooking that up."

"Well," Eldridge said as Dean heard ice cubes rattle against a glass, "maybe this will get you to the finish line."

Dean furrowed his brow.

What're you up to, shitbird?

"Oh, *man*," Tyler groaned. "Jameson is a slippery slope, Cap."

"Come on," Eldridge replied. "You need a bit of wheel greasing after that fiasco with Haywood. Come on, kid. Have a sip."

"I don't—"

"It's a party, kid." Eldridge's tone ticked down an octave. "Have a drink."

The music playing in the background changed over to "Get Down on It" by Kool and the Gang. The song pulsated through the phone as Dean listened to the rookie throwing back the whiskey Eldridge had palmed him.

"Hot damn," Tyler said. "That hits quick."

Eldridge laughed. "Atta boy."

"I think I needed this."

"Are you sure you're okay?" Eldridge said. "You look like you've got something on your mind."

Dean shifted his weight.

Here we go.

The rookie is up to bat.

"Yeah," Tyler said. "Yeah, I uh…I don't know, sir. I'm having a bit of a problem."

"Wait here one second," Eldridge replied. "We'll talk it out. I just need to address the troops really quickly."

"Sounds good."

Doing good, kid.

Keep it up.

You're almost there.

"Everyone!" Eldridge announced. "Can I have your attention for a moment, please?"

The guests stopped speaking.

The music died down.

Dean perked up in his seat and waited for the rest.

"I, uh…" Eldridge cleared his throat. "I want to thank you all for coming today. It's been a rough go of it for all of us. We've lost several members of our family, and I know it seems a bit selfish of us to be having this little get-together of ours, but I know that Mike, Cole, Ron, and Sean would have wanted it this way. They were our brothers. We knew them well. And we are fully aware that they would have wanted us to have a good time here today."

Dean rolled his eyes.

I'm sure they would.

Even though they're all rotting in a box somewhere.

"Even though these men aren't with us today," Eldridge continued, "they are in our thoughts and prayers. We will continue on with the legacy our fallen teammates forged and make today a celebration of their lives, their commitment to the greater good, and the steadfast dedication and loyalty we all have to one another. So please, raise your glasses to the fallen members of the SMASH unit, whose lives were cut short by a vindictive criminal who took the coward's way out. But even though they are gone, they will forever live in our hearts and minds. *Cheers.*"

Glasses clinked.

Applause followed.

Dean clenched his fist as he listened to what he felt was one of the biggest snake oil salesman pitches he had ever heard in his life.

"Okay," Tyler whispered into the phone. "He's coming back."

Dean shook his head.

Don't talk to me, kid!

You'll flag yourself down.

"Tyler," Dean heard Eldridge said. "Let's talk in my office."

The sounds of the party faded as Dean heard Tyler pad his way inside the house with Elridge. He heard a door swing open. Footsteps clacked along hardwood floors, and then a few moments laters, Dean made out what sounded like Eldridge slipping into a leather chair.

"Talk to me, Tyler," Eldridge said. "What's going on?"

"Well..." Tyler's voice was racked with nerves. "I'm not sure where to start."

"Start wherever."

"I...think I'm in trouble."

"What kind of trouble?"

"It's my girlfriend," Tyler said. "She's pregnant."

"Why is that troubling you?" Eldridge replied. "Are you not ready for that kind of thing?"

"I would be..." Tyler said, "if it were mine."

Dean held his breath.

Here we go.

He slowly released it.

The moment of truth.

"I see," Eldridge said. "And you're certain it's not yours?"

"I'm pretty sure," Tyler replied. "I had suspicions for a

while that she might have been unfaithful to me. I just never had the balls to ask her."

"Who is the other guy?"

"I don't know. That's what's driving me nuts. This whole thing is...it's fucked."

"You sound paranoid," Eldridge said. "I mean, is it possible that you're—"

"It's not mine," Tyler cut in. "Believe me, I know."

"Okay, kid. I believe you." Eldridge adjusted his weight in his leather chair. "So what were you hoping to do about it, son?"

Tyler took a moment to answer. "I want to know who it is, sir," he said. "And once I do know who it is...well, I want him out of the picture."

Keep going, kid.

Keep. It. Up.

"I see," Eldridge said. "To be frank with you, I'm surprised you came to me with this. You know where I stand with this kind of talk."

"I know, sir," Tyler groaned. "I'm just...well, I'm frustrated. I'm not saying I'm going to follow through with it. I only wanted to tell you because I feel like I'm going crazy. I gave everything to this woman—*everything*—and now she's stabbing me right through the heart. It kills me, sir. And I don't know what to do about it."

The sounds of a drawer being pulled open on Eldridge's desk came over the line.

A moment later, Dean heard the clinking of a glass followed by the dribble of liquid being poured into it.

"Glenlivet," Eldridge said. "After everything that's gone down with the boy recently, well," he chuckled, "I've had more than a few fingers' worth."

Tyler said nothing.

"I'll help you out with this little problem of yours," Eldridge continued. "But to be frank with you, son..." his voice took on a grave timbre, "I feel like there's something else you're not telling me."

"There is," Tyler said. "I just wasn't quite sure how I was going to present it to you."

"Just talk it through. I'm sure we can hash it all out."

Tell him

Dean clenched a fist.

Do it.

"That FBI agent," Tyler said. "Blackwood. He confronted me at the theme park the other day. I think he's been following me."

Eldridge took a pause. "Really?"

"Yeah."

"Interesting." Eldridge took another pause. "Well, what did he have to say?"

"He's trying to get me to snitch on you guys," Tyler said. "I'm not sure why, but I told him to piss off. But he told me he'd be back. The sick bastard thinks I'm gonna betray my people. It took every bit of restraint I had to not haul off and hit him."

"I'm glad you didn't give in to that impulse," Eldridge replied. "And I can't imagine what he thinks I'd be up to. That Blackwood character is, well, tenacious to say the least. He's got a hard-on for me."

Dean smirked

You have no idea.

"I don't get it, sir," Tyler said. "What's this guy's deal?"

"He's touched in the head, son," Eldridge replied. "Blackwood used to be an undercover agent. I think he dabbled in the trade a bit too long. I think all his experiences messed with his head a bit. Ever since his brother passed—"

Keep it up, you piece of shit.

"—well, he's never been the same." Eldridge gave Tyler a brief rundown of what happened with Dean's brother, and the more Dean listened in, the more he felt himself tamping down the urge to bolt out of the car, run upstairs, and use a blunt object to beat Eldridge within an inch of his life.

Cool down, Dean.

Easy.

Focus on what's in front of you.

"You want a drink, Adams?" Eldridge said. "How's about a bit of Glen? It might calm you down a bit."

"That's okay, sir," Tyler replied. "I think I'm—"

"Sit down, kid."

The beating of Dean's heart rate intensified as he heard the SMASH captain pour another drink.

Something's not right.

Something feels off.

"We're going to get this sorted out," Eldridge said. "I'm sorry you're going through this. I don't like knowing that you're in pain, son. And I'm going to dismiss this comment of you wanting someone dead as nothing more than venting. Also, rest assured, Blackwood will be dealt with. He's overstepping his boundaries jamming my people up. I'm sure it's going to come back to bite him in the ass. Come on. Let's go back to the party."

Dean clenched his jaw.

Damn it.

He knows.

Somehow, he knows.

"Sure thing, Captain," Tyler said. "Sure thing."

"You're doing good, trooper," Eldridge replied. "I'm

proud of you." A wood-on-wood screech came over the line —the sound of the door to the office being opened. "Careful on those steps. You're looking a little wobbly there, son."

Tyler shrieked at the top of his lungs.

A loud thud followed swiftly after.

Dean's eyes widened when he picked up on what sounded like the rookie toppling head over heels down a staircase.

Dean reached for the door handle to his car.

Slipped out.

Then Dean froze when he felt the barrel of a gun being pressed into the back of his neck.

He held up his hands.

Turned up his gaze.

Then he saw a mustached man with a crew cut, an LAPD shield attached to his hip, and a SIG P226 in his hands pressed against Dean's neck.

37

Dean was seated outside of Tyler's hospital room, listening to the machines the rookie was tethered to beep and whirr.

This is your fault.

You fucked this up.

Dean cut a glance toward Tyler. The rookie was lying on his bed in a coma that, according to the doctors, he might not ever wake up from.

And even if he does, it won't matter. Even if he tells the truth, Eldridge will spin the story however he wants to.

Dean hung his head. He was at a loss, unsure of what to do and feeling like he had thrown an innocent kid under the bus in the process.

"This is a mess, laddie," Woody said. "All of it. Every *inch* of it."

Dean clenched his jaw.

"How does it feel, chum?" Woody cackled at the top of his lungs. "How's it feel to be the magnet for chaos you know you've always been?"

Dean brushed Woody off once he saw Eldridge

approaching from down the hallway, the fingers on the captain's hand curled into a fist as he padded his way briskly toward Dean.

"You son of a bitch," Eldridge grumbled. "What are you doing here? What the fuck were you doing snooping outside my *house*?"

Dean rose from his chair—no fear, no intention of backing down. "I'm surprised that some trigger-happy flunky of yours didn't put a bullet in my head."

The captain came nose to nose with Dean. "What the hell are you still doing around here? You were given direct orders from your Deputy Director to back off this."

"Drop the act, you crooked piece of shit. We both know that you're about as clean as a viewing booth in a peep show."

Eldridge's nostrils flared, the vein in his neck protruding. "You're in deep shit, son," he said. "Mark my words. You're going to be sitting in San Quentin for the next ten to fifteen by the time I'm done with you."

Dean pointed to Tyler's room. "You're responsible for this. I may not be able to prove it right now, but I won't stop until I do."

Eldridge pressed a finger into Dean's chest. "Keep talking, shithead. You're giving me nothing but ammo." He gestured toward Adams' room. "And that officer, that *kid* in there, is most likely going to have brain damage and paralysis for the rest of his life, and it's all because of you," Eldridge sneered and backed away. "Now get out of here, and if I see you again, I'm going to assume you're rolling in hot, and I'll give my guys shoot-on-sight authorization."

It took every ounce of restraint for Dean not to lunge after Eldridge and pummel him into oblivion, but he couldn't. The moment the weeping Kelly Mayer, Tyler's girlfriend, came running around the corner and jumped into Eldridge's arms made the remorse Dean felt over Adams' condition intensify.

Dean padded his way down the hallway, fuming as he got in the elevator. He arrived in the lobby and headed toward the Pontiac parked in the lot.

Wilson would call him once he caught word.

Probably a few others.

There would be repercussions of some magnitude.

And then Layla popped into his mind—the only person he knew he'd be able to talk to without feeling grilled over the whole ordeal.

38

"Good man," Woody whispered. "Just look at it. Take it all in. You don't have to drink it—not yet, that is."

The whiskey in Dean's glass caught the light above the hotel bar. He traced the rim of the glass with his finger, the scent of the high-shelf booze lapping at his nostrils as Woody beckoned him to take a sip.

"Just one. One and done. You can handle that. That's all you need. You've earned it.

Just take one sip, laddie, and the pain will go away."

Everything played back in Dean's mind at high speed—Marcus Haywood, Kara Shardlow, Jeremy, Claire, Layla, Tyler Adams. A heavy weight was on his shoulders, bearing down on him with overpowering strength.

As Dean slipped a toothpick into his mouth, he looked down at his glass, the whiskey tempting him to dive in head-first in a bid to numb his pain.

That was the draw of the sauce.

The appeal of the drink.

It was the medication Dean knew would make all his pain go away.

"Dean," Layla called out.

Dean angled his body around. "Yellow Ledbetter" by Pearl Jam pumped softly through the bar's speakers. "Hey," he said, puttering out a deep breath as he nudged his glass to the side.

Layla placed her bag down and slipped down onto the stool beside him. "How long have you been here?"

"Long enough."

"How..." Layla hesitated as she gestured to his drink, "how many have you had?"

"Zero," Dean said as he gestured at the glass. "I've just been staring at it. This is the first glass of booze I've asked for in years."

"Are you...?" Layla furrowed her brow. "In recovery or something?"

"I am. I guess Adams getting put into a coma kind of did it for me." Dean sighed. "I'm having a rough night. I guess that's pretty obvious though."

"We all have them."

"Not like this," Dean said. "That kid is in a coma because of me. He may not even wake up. And if he does, he's got a long road of recovery ahead of him." Dean hung his head. "Wilson asked me to solve this thing, but I'm starting to feel like all I'm doing is making the situation more untenable, and more people are getting hurt because of it."

"You can't blame yourself." Layla pressed her finger into the counter. "*Eldridge* did this. He's the architect behind this whole thing. And he can't get away with it."

Dean pulled the glass closer, on the cusp of taking his first pull, ready to fire the starter pistol to kick off the race. "Have you ever heard of eidetic memory?"

"I have. It's essentially the ability to recall things in vivid detail."

"I was diagnosed with it when I was a kid—well, a version of it anyway. It happened right after my brother died."

"Yeah," Layla nodded. "I uh...I heard about that when I pulled your jacket."

"Well, ever since that day, my life has gone a million miles an hour. I can recall every *second* like it just happened—every memory, good and bad—and I just added Marcus Haywood, Kara Shardlow, and *now* Tyler Adams to my little home movie collection. That's what I call it, by the way, my little," Dean tapped the side of his head, "*penchant* for recall."

Layla listened in as Pearl Jam continued to play in the background.

"When my brother Tommy died," Dean said, "I started running—literally, I mean. I ran track all throughout high school. Set a record from clocking in a four-minute fifty-second mile."

"Not bad."

"Not bad at all. A lot of people, coaches included, wanted me to keep at it in college, but I opted for the military. Set a few records there, too, until I folded my knee 90 degrees in the wrong direction. They said I wouldn't walk right again, but I proved them wrong. I got back up, did all the rehab, and," Dean shrugged, "now I'm still running, and for the life of me, I don't know how to slow myself down."

Dean prepared himself to take a pull of the whiskey, the rim of the glass near his lips—but then he stopped, shook his head, and put the glass down. "I'm no different."

Layla cocked her head to the side. "I don't understand."

"I'm no different," Dean said, "than all the rest of the sob cop stories everyone's heard before. I'm the guy who caused a rift in his family. The one who nearly drank himself into oblivion. The lawman with the oh so clever mind that stands out from the rest." Dean rolled his eyes. "I'm a cliché, Layla. A run of the mill story people have heard a thousand times before."

Layla inched closer. "We're *all* a bunch of clichés. We've all made mistakes. We all have something that drives us and some kind of pain that motivates it. I mean," she threw up her hands, "I was a chain-smoking, Adderall fiend for years when I first started this crusade of mine to right the wrongs of the world. I ended up crashing pretty bad one night and ended up in the ER. After that, I split from my husband, cleaned up." She waved her hand through the air. "It was a whole thing."

"Woe is us," Dean said as he flexed his brow. "Right?"

"No." Layla shook her head. "No, not at all. Maybe you're seeing things through that kind of lens right now, but it's a warped way of looking at things. I know. Believe me. I was a pent-up, pissed-off cynical person for *years* before I changed my outlook on things."

"What changed?"

"Nothing," Layla said. "That's what I had to realize. I finally recognized that the world *can* be shit, things *can* suck, but the way I saw it, I didn't have to bring myself down to that level. I had to do what I could to impact things in a positive way."

Dean shook his head. "I've tried to do that, Layla. I have. The only problem is, the more I try to fix things, the worse they get," he huffed, "at least that's how Woody views it."

"Who?"

"*Right*." Dean shook his head. "You don't know." He sat up straight. "In rehab, we learned that there's a voice in our head, the one that implores us to make bad decisions. Have you ever heard the Robin Williams routine where he talks about it?"

Layla shook her head. "Enlighten me."

"That voice," Dean went on, "is the same one you hear when you stand on the edge of a building, that irrational part of your subconscious that tells you to jump. You know you *won't*, but when you're an addict, that voice is louder. When you're in the throes of addiction, that voice kind of takes control of the wheel." Dean tapped his skull. "My voice is called Woody. I named him that after that night I had in El Paso. I was shitrocked on Woodford Reserve, and he was telling me to pick a fight. I did and then nearly got myself killed, and after that I got on the straight and narrow." He rolled his eyes. "That son of a bitch still shows up every once in a while. He tries to lure me back in, but I learned to dismiss him. Took some practice, but I got him right where I want him."

"Sounds rough," Layla said, "having to put a thing like that in check, I mean."

Dean nodded. "It has its moments. Like I said, I've got it under control for the most part. It's only when things go really south that Woody decides to rear his head and flap his gums more than he usually does." He closed his eyes. "I'm good at what I do, Layla. Maybe it's luck, maybe it's because of what happened to Tommy that turned me into who I am, I don't know. The one thing I *do* know is that I've left a lot of destruction in my wake, and...well, Woody's got me rethinking a lot of things."

"Well," Layla leaned in close, "you know what I think your pal Woody is failing to see?"

Dean furrowed his brow.

Tell me.

"Your pain," Layla said. "History. Conflict. Mistakes. He

also doesn't talk about your loyalty, your strong work ethic, and the moral compass you have. He also doesn't acknowledge a man who loves his son, a guy who loves a lot of things and is committed to defending them."

Dean smirked. For the first time in his life, he felt like he had an angel on his other shoulder to counterbalance Woody.

"You're a good man, Dean Blackwood," Layla said. "That's what I see. And as far as the clever cop clichés go, I'd embrace it. The world *needs* people like you, Dean. They need to put their faith in people who will do whatever they can to stop people like Eldridge. They need men and women who take a stand and say, 'Fuck you—you're not getting away with this.' And if the world can't put stock in people like that, then," Layla threw up her hands, "what's the point?"

Dean looked Layla deep in her eyes. It had been years since he was able to confide in someone, to know a person who could put him at ease as effortlessly as she did. "Not bad," he said. "You have a knack for pep talks."

"Practice makes perfect," she replied. "I do the whole *Truman Show* thing in front of the mirror once or twice a week to pump me up. It keeps me going."

Dean laughed.

Layla did the same.

"So," she said as she motioned to his whiskey, "are you going to drink that and turn into another sad cop cliché, or are you ready to dump it, pivot away from the sad boy routine and help me nail Eldridge? I have some info I think you might want to know."

Dean pinned his gaze to the whiskey.

"Don't be an arse," Woody hissed. "Just have it, for cryin' out loud!"

The hell with you, dipshit.

Dean placed a $20 bill on the counter, pushed the glass aside, and told the bartender to dump it.

Now leave, and don't come back.

"All right," Dean said to Layla. "Lay it on me."

"After what you told me about what happened with Sean Mohr," Layla replied, "we know that the SMASH guys were working with someone. The question we have to ask is *who*."

"Did you make any leeway on that on your end?"

"There was a name that came up twice when I was interviewing a couple former LAPD officers in the past couple of days, cops who were willing to tell me a few things about the SMASH guys."

"How did you manage to pull that off?" Dean asked. "The LAPD is a brotherhood. There aren't a lot of guys who would want to give out that kind of information."

"Remember my contact in the complaints department?"

Dean nodded.

"Well," Layla said, "she gave me a short list of a few people who had run-ins with Vendrell, Harlow, and a couple other guys in the unit. I went to their houses and interviewed a few of them. I mean, I had a few doors slammed in my face, but a couple of them were willing to talk."

"What did they tell you?"

"Two of the people I interviewed," Layla said, "mentioned that Vendrell and Harlow had helped clear an 'associate' of theirs, a civilian. This guy had all sorts of charges against him, ranging from weapons charges, domestic assault, and drug possession, all that got dropped in the blink of an eye thanks to Vendrell and Harlow."

Dean squinted. "Who is he?"

"All I got was a first name: Hayk. These two people I

interviewed also alluded to this guy Hayk having connections to the Armenian Mob. Whoever Hayk is, Vendrell and Harlow weren't going to let him get in trouble. Needless to say, the fact that this guy Hayk might have mob connections has the wheels turning in my brain."

Dean ran his palm across the stubble on his chin. "It would make a lot of sense. Maybe Vendrell and Harlow were dealing with him, offering protection, something like that. Maybe this guy Hayk was working with SMASH somehow."

"Possibly," Layla said. "I'm not sure what kind of lead it is, but at this point, it's the only thing I have to go on. Maybe you can run that name by some of your people. Maybe that will take you somewhere."

"Me," Dean flexed his brow, "or *us*?"

The reporter winked. "Don't worry, Blackwood." She grabbed her bag. "I'm not through with you yet."

39

Dean surveyed the FBI field office through the Pontiac's windshield. He had been ducking every call from his superiors for the past several hours. Wilson even went so far as to feign that he was attempting to bring Dean in on behalf of the Bureau in regard to Tyler Adams' "accident."

Eldridge had made more calls.

The heat had been turned up.

The way Dean figured it, he had forty-eight hours to make some headway before, as his old man would say, "Shit would start to get thick."

"How are you going to find out about Hayk?" Layla said. "Now that the Bureau wants you in for questioning, your resources are kind of limited, and there's nothing else I can really uncover about the guy on my end."

"There's a slew of databases the FBI and other agencies have access to," Dean explained. "They've got all kinds of snazzy stuff stored in the computers at the field office."

"You can't go there."

"Yes, I can."

"Aren't they looking for you?" Layla's eyes widened to express her incredulity. "Won't they grab you the second they spot you?"

"They might," Dean said. "But I don't have much in the way of choices here. I'm going to stroll right in there, access the databases, and see what I can pull on Hayk."

"And if it's a bust? If Hayk doesn't pan out, what then?"

"Then we're back to square one. Like you said, we need to see this through. After all…" Dean took a beat, "rumor is that Eldridge had something to do with my brother's death."

He told her the story that Mohr told him.

By the time he was finished, Layla was at a loss for words.

"We start with Hayk and go from there," Dean said. "If we turn up nothing, we pivot. We're flying blind now, Layla. It's dead reckoning every step of the way."

Dressed in a muted-tone suit to blend in with the rest of the agents, Dean marched into the lobby of the Los Angeles FBI field office. He flashed his credentials. Walked through the metal detectors. Hotfooted his way toward the elevators while angling his face away from the cameras positioned throughout, and then spotted a directory that indicated the database/tech level was on the fifth floor. Moments later, he arrived on the fifth floor, stepped out, and kept his head low in the off chance that someone would recognize him as he threaded his way through the hallway.

The floor was packed cheek-to-jowl with cubicles, a cacophony of agents clacking on keyboards inside of them. Dean glanced to his left toward the west at a long row of plexiglass windows. Dozens of technicians were inside, huddled around large monitors tethered to big black servers glowing like lights on a Christmas tree.

Bingo.

It had been some time since Dean had been on this floor, and he only recalled one technician who would assist him in his plight.

Richie Baumgardner.

He checked his watch.

Move fast, Deano.

Easy in, easy out.

Dean entered the database room. A few heads turned in his direction as he made sure to look away while he looked for signs of Baumgardner. He was a hard man to miss, a portly individual who bore the appearance of a turtle, his mouth always slightly ajar like someone squatting in front of a television too long. It took all of five seconds of looking before Dean spotted Baumgardner nestled in his little corner on the left side of the room. The tech was hunched over his keyboard and typing with a speed that probably would break the *Guinness Book of World Records.*

Dean approached.

Stood behind Baumgardner.

Then he cleared his throat, which triggered the tech to yelp.

Baumgardner angled his body around, adjusting the Coke-bottle spectacles on his face as he rolled up the sleeves on his dress shirt. "Blackwood?"

"*Shhh.*" Dean held a finger to his lips. "Don't tell anyone."

"What are you doing here?"

Dean pulled up a chair. "I need you to do me a favor."

Baumgardner glanced around the room. "Why do I have a feeling this isn't approved?"

"Because it's not," Dean said. "And last I checked, you owe me more than a few favors."

The portly tech puttered out a groan. "This is just like El Paso.."

"This is *nothing* like El Paso," Dean said. "Look, I need you to run a name for me."

Baumgardner gestured to his screen. "All my searches are logged and filed. If I run something that wasn't approved, they're going to know."

Dean's eyes narrowed. "Like that's ever stopped you before."

Baumgardner said nothing.

"Come on, buddy," Dean said. "I just need you to run a name for me."

The tech crossed his meaty arms. "What's in it for me?"

"The fact that you'd be contributing to the Bureau's mission of justice for all."

"Oh, *please*," Baumgardner huffed. "I'll get eighty-sixed from this place if they find out I was doing something unsanctioned."

Dean fished around in his pockets, pulled out a $5 bill, and held it up. "Then maybe, *just maybe*, someone was using your computer while you were out snagging something from the vending machines. You can have total deniability."

"No way." The tech shook his head. "They'll rake me over the coals if they find out my station was unattended."

"Horseshit," Dean said. "You've been here for years. You're too valuable of an asset for them to fire you. The worst they'll do is say, 'Don't let it happen again.'" Dean held the cash in front of Baumgardner's face. "Two minutes. Grab yourself a pair of Snickers on me."

"I'm supposed to cut down on the sweets."

"Well, I won't tell if you don't."

Baumgardner stared at the cash.

Dean waved it around.

After a few seconds ticked by, the portly tech took the money, stood up, said nothing, and left the room.

"Beautiful," Dean said as he positioned himself in front of the keyboard, pulled up the NCIC search engine, and typed in the name Hayk. Dean cross-referenced the name with Armenian Mob connections—LA based. Then he followed up by searching the same thing on the Interpol site. It took six minutes of searching before he pulled up three names that held criminal records sultry enough that the interdepartmental databases felt the need to log them away for the record.

Hayk Garagosian

Hayk Hakobyan

Hayk Adiamy

Dean noted the names and the last known addresses where the men resided in LA and logged them away in his memory.

He stood.

Pushed away from the desk.

Made his way back to the elevators.

Then someone shouted out, "Hey, buddy!" the moment he stepped into the elevator.

Dean sighed.

Turned around.

He greeted a lanky agent with thinning hair who ogled him from head to toe.

"I know you," the agent said.

"No." Dean shook his head. "I don't think so."

"Yeah, I do." The agent squinted. "And you're in big trouble, boss."

Dean held his ground.

The agent stepped closer. "You're that guy from Dallas. The one who dinged the SAC's car in the parking lot, right?"

"You got me." Dean laughed. "Can't navigate tight turns to save my life."

"Well, good luck." The agent chuckled. "Pretty sure the insurance people are going to have a field day with you."

"That they will."

"Take it easy."

"You too."

Dean entered the elevator. The doors closed. As his heart rate lowered, he laughed. Once he was out of the building and back behind the wheel of the Pontiac, he put his focus back on the three names that now served as his new leads.

Easy in.

Dean took one last look at the field office, removed his tie, and tossed it in the back seat.

Easy out.

40

There were twelve missed calls on Dean's phone from the FBI brass and the same number of voicemails. On top of that, Wilson—still pretending he had not allowed Dean to work the case off the book—had left a series of texts and voice messages insisting that Dean bring himself into the field office of his own accord.

"They're not tracking your phone," Wilson said on a voicemail that he left on a secured line. "At least not yet."

Behind the wheel of the Pontiac, Dean focused on the three names he pulled from the database, three possible leads that could point him in the right direction.

"I've got three possibilities," Dean said to Layla over the phone, the device on speaker as he weaved his way through the traffic on Highway 101. "Hayk Garagosian, Hayk Hakobyan, and Hayk Adiamy. I could go the old-fashioned route of looking them up in the phone book, but I figured maybe you could lend me a hand on this one. I need you to cross-reference those names with the weapons, assault, and drug charges you were mentioning."

"I'll need about an hour," Layla said. "I have someone here who can look those names up."

Dean drove.

Debated moving his stuff out of his hotel.

An hour and a half and a drive-thru gas refill later, Layla rang him back.

"Okay," she said. "Looks like Hayk Garagosian is out. He's serving time in Lompoc for a Ponzi scheme he was running in the '90s. He has no drugs, weapons, or assault charges. Plus, the timelines don't add up. Vendrell and Harlow were kids when he went away."

"So it's not Gargosian," Dean said. "Next."

"Adiamy is also out. He's been dead since 1996. If I'm reading this right, Hakobyan might be your guy. The only thing I could find on him was a snippet from an article back in 2002 concerning a shooting at a nightclub. Hakobyan was detained by the cops after the incident but got off."

Dean smirked.

It's him.

"You got anything in the way of information on him?" he said. "Picture? Description? Addresses? Anything like that?"

"No, unfortunately," Layla replied. "But it sounds like Hakobyan has a stake in this nightclub in Glendale. It's called Private Selection. Maybe you can start there. According to what I'm seeing, the place has been raided a couple of times by the PD for drug charges."

"I'll check it out. You got an address?"

Layla dished Dean the info, and minutes later, he was on his way to the nightclub as the sun was setting, a warm tangerine glow coating the lanes of the 134 freeway. After twenty minutes of driving, Dean found himself in the city of Glendale, a suburb of LA with a dense Armenian population.

Dean brought the Pontiac to a stop outside a squat, one-story nightclub off Santa Monica Boulevard, tucked between a liquor store and across the street from a Honda dealership. No windows. Innocuous. Dean did a scan of the joint, logging away the entrances and exits in his home movie collection.

One on the northeast corner.

One in the south.

A service entrance on the west.

They probably have people posted up there at any given moment.

Dean parked the Pontiac down the block 30 yards from Private Selection, far enough away that he couldn't be seen but close enough that he could get a good visual on the club. He checked his watch: 2:00 p.m. The place wouldn't be open until 10:00 p.m., according to his Google search.

Dean cranked the window, propped his elbow, stared at the front of the building, and waited for fifteen minutes. After those fifteen minutes passed, two men exited the building wearing dress shirts, slacks, gold chains, and rings. Their complexions were darker, their hair slicked back, a menacing appearance projected by the both of them. They lit up a pair of cigarettes, standing close to one another as they threw occasional and suspicious glances over their shoulders.

Howdy, boys.

What are you up to?

Dean watched as the men finished their cigarettes, flicked them into the streets, and headed back inside the building. The next move for Dean was simple—get a visual on Hayk. The only way he knew he could go about doing that was slipping into a nice suit and rubbing elbows with a few criminals on the dance floor.

He opened his phone.

Did a Google search. He found a menswear store six blocks away and decided to get himself fitted for a three-piece, and while he was getting fitted, he booked a rental for a Mercedes from Enterprise Rent-A-Car.

41

Night had fallen, and the denizens of the city who lived under the radar were out and about, scurrying around like rodents in dark corners away from the watchful eye of the law. In his hotel room, Dean Blackwood was set on blending in among them, dressed in a silver-toned suit with a white shirt, the collar crisply pressed and starched with angles as sharp as a knife.

Dean stood in front of the full-length mirror in his room to double-check that his appearance was immaculate and on par with a wealthy guy headed out for a night on the town. He checked the five grand in cash—bribe money—that he procured from the ATM, held together with a gold clip he purchased with his suit in Glendale.

Make sure you get the Bureau to reimburse you, Deano.

If *this all works out, that is.*

Dean took the SIG P226 from the bed. Checked the rounds. Stuffed it in the back of his pants before he shot his cuffs, puffed his chest, and headed toward the elevators.

The entire ride down, Dean thought back to the incident

in El Paso. The situation he was in felt similar to that night, but there were some differences. Instead of biker threads, he was in a three-piece suit. In lieu of riding in a shoddy elevator in a shoddy hotel in a shoddy part of town, he was in a 300-bucks-a-night, semi-upscale hotel in a suburban area of Los Angeles. While the factors going into the situation may have differed, the end result was the same.

He was undercover, pretending he was someone else, and the high of it all prickled his skin and triggered a jolt of adrenaline that left him craving a smoke.

"Maybe start with that," Woody coyly suggested. "Just one smoke to tamp down your nerves."

No.

"Okay, well, you're going to a *club*, laddie. They'll have drinks there. Maybe a gin and—"

Get fucked, pal.

Last time I'll tell you.

Once the elevator doors opened, Dean walked through the lobby, made his way to the parking lot, and slipped inside the pearl-white Mercedes he rented for the night..

He flexed his hands.

Tuned the radio to a classic rock station.

Huffed amusedly because he heard the *exact same song* his Ranger unit would put on when they were gearing up to go into battle.

"Man in the Box," Alice in Chains, a quintessential hard rock classic (Dean's opinion) that got his pulse pounding and took his mind off the adrenaline coursing through his body.

It was a little past 7:30 p.m. when Dean rolled up to the club. He decided that making note of his presence would assist with his bad boy cover, so he pulled up to the valet in front of the northeast entrance, hopped out, and palmed the guy the keys wrapped in a $50 bill. The valet drove off as Dean appraised the line of people in front of the club, all of them dressed up and revved up, though a handful of them appeared perturbed at having to wait in line.

Get the layout, Deano.

Make a map of everything.

He clocked a bouncer up at the northeast entrance.

A pair of valets on a smoke break by the northwest service entrance.

Two points of ingress.

Neither has a good view of the other.

Dean fixed his sights to the south entrance where a pair of guys—the same men he spotted earlier that day—cackled, fist-bumped, and hacked on their Euro-brand cigarettes.

Try the front first.

Easiest way.

Bribe your way in.

Dean cut through the line, nudging a couple of patrons aside to show he gave all of two shits. He was living a role, playing the part of an ecstasy dealer looking for a new supplier—that was his cover, and from what little he had gathered on the Armenian Mob element, he knew the sects working on this side of town made most of their profits in drugs and insurance scams.

Dean knew it was a long shot that he'd actually strike up a deal with anyone. The caliber of guys he was dealing with didn't operate with outsiders, but his mission statement wasn't geared toward earning their trust.

He just needed to put a face to the name.

He had to draw Hayk—and whoever he was in league with—out in the open.

Dean approached the bouncer—Armenian, 6'7", 210

pounds. Dark blazer. Dark pants. Dark shirt. Typical bouncer attire. The kind of guy Dean knew he'd have to shoot in the knee or kick in the nuts instead of going fist-against-fist with.

"What's good, brother?" Dean greeted before he switched to Armenian, one of three languages he knew how to speak—decently. "*Inch'pes e dzer gishery?*"

"Get fucked." The bouncer forked a thumb to the line and didn't make eye contact with Dean. "Back of the line."

"*T'et'ev tar.*" Dean fished out two $100 bills and held them up. "I'm here to see Hayk."

The bouncer said nothing.

Dean peeled off another hundred. "I'm supposed to have a talk with him."

The bouncer bored his hollow unblinking gaze into Dean. "Last time." He took a step forward and pressed a meaty finger into Dean's chest. "*Korel.*"

Get lost.

Dean smirked, stepped away, and resolved himself that going through the front was a bust, that his only option at getting inside was the south entrance—the rear—where the two guys he'd spotted smoking cigarettes were holding court.

Bribing them would be his first move.

His second would require more of a physical angle.

Don't forget the cameras, Deano.

You're not getting far if they spot you.

He surveyed his surroundings. He saw a camera by the front entrance and another near the service entrance. And based on the way the two guys up there were sucking down their cigarettes, bullshitting, and paying no attention to what was going on around them, he slapped together a plan.

Dean padded his way toward the club's service entrance.

The men spotted him.

Then the one in the red shirt stood forward, flicked away his cigarette, and took on a defensive stance. "Hold up, bro," he said. "You gotta go through the front."

"I'm here to see Hayk," Dean replied as he eyeballed the camera above the rear door. "I'm a friend of his."

The two men exchanged knowing glances.

Then the one in the blue shirt shrugged. "Don't know no Hayk." He nodded over Dean's shoulder. "Now leave."

Dean pulled out his wad of cash. "I'm not in the mood, fellas. I've got a meeting with my homeboy Hayk, and I don't take him for the kind of guy who likes to wait." He peeled off a pair of Benjamins. "Hundred bucks if you guys let me in the back there."

Red and Blue laughed, ballooning their postures to appear bigger as they stalked their way toward Dean.

"You stupid or something, man?" Blue said. "*Bounce*."

"Listen," Dean pocketed the cash, checking over his shoulder to make sure he was clear out of view of the patrons in front, which he was. "You can either let me inside, act like you never saw me, and then go back to chipping away at whatever lung capacity you've got left..."

Red approached Dean on his right.

Blue came in on his left.

Then Red cracked his knuckles and held his fists at his sides. "Or what?"

Dean shot his palm out and struck Red in the nose. He dropped to the pavement.

A wide-eyed Blue reached toward the Glock nestled in the back of his pants.

Dean whipped out his SIG, cocked back the hammer, and lined up the guy's head flush between the sights before he had a chance to draw.

"Or *that*."

Blue cut a glance toward his unconscious buddy and swallowed the lump in his throat.

He held his hands high and requested that Dean give him a pass.

"I'll think about it," Dean said as he motioned to Blue's Glock with his SIG. "Two fingers. You know the deal."

Blue—slowly—reached around, pinched his Glock with a pair of fingers, and held it up for Dean to see.

"Over there," Dean said as he nodded toward the dumpster on his left. "Toss it."

Blue gnashed his teeth and grumbled something in Armenian. Then Dean instructed him to haul Red's body into the dumpster and hop in with him. Once Blue complied, he informed Dean about the fleet of security personnel inside who were seconds away from flooding the scene.

"Thanks for the heads up," Dean said as he jutted his chin toward the dumpster. "Now tell me your name."

"Why?"

"Because I said so."

Blue took a beat. "Artin."

"Artin *what*?"

"Sarkissian."

"Got it." Dean winked. "Enjoy your siesta, brother." He pistol-whipped Artin in the face and watched him crumble into unconsciousness beside his buddy. Then he closed the dumpster's lid, secured it with the lock bar, and took a look around to make sure he was still in the clear.

Dean holstered his SIG and padded his way to the service entrance, the dull throb of music pulsating from inside the club.

He drew a breath.

Just like the old days, Blackwood.

He released it.

Time to go to work.

Then he flayed open the door and slowly made his way inside.

42

Dean emerged in a cramped, dark hallway, the only source of illumination coming from a few slivers of light trickling in from an antechamber on his right. The volume of the music intensified the closer he came to the antechamber. It was a shitty, bass-heavy melody that triggered a throb deep inside his skull.

Slow and easy, ace.

Slow. And. Easy.

Dean cracked his neck and stepped into the antechamber.

He saw a brute of a man rushing into the vestibule ahead of him, a radio in his hand and a wide-eyed look on his face, indicative of a guy who just saw two of his pals getting their asses beat on a security monitor.

The guy's mouth dropped open.

Dean waved.

Then he kneed the guy in the nuts, watched him keel over, got behind him, and locked the guy's neck between his arms before he choked him into a slumber.

The brute sputtered his lips.

Passed out.

Then Dean kicked open the door on his left—the security room—and dragged the guy inside.

"Looks like you got a little distracted with the PornHub there, slick," Dean mumbled to the comatose brute once he saw that one of the monitors was tuned to an adult-oriented short film.

The brute remained still.

Dean slipped back into the antechamber.

Then he strolled up to the curtains, parted them, and stepped into the club.

Sixty to seventy people were packed on a dance floor coated in a sea of multi-colored lights from projectors in the ceiling. In the corner of the room, Dean picked out the DJ, a college dropout pumping his fist in the air as he changed the track to something even more bass-saturated that shook the walls of the club.

The patrons cheered.

Dean rolled his eyes.

Then he resumed his appraisal of the club, noted the bar on his right, and then a throng of clubgoers dressed head to toe in high-ticket attire congregating in the VIP lounge on his left.

Dean approached the bartender working the counter, a younger kid with a defeated countenance in the process of mixing a martini.

"What's good, man?" Dean shouted over the music. "How's your night going?"

"What can I get you?"

"I need to speak to Hayk."

The kid pulled his focus off the mixer, his eyes widening upon hearing the name. "I don't know no—"

"Cut the shit," Dean said as he placed a twenty on the

counter. "Talk to whoever you need to. Just take the cash, and go get your boss."

The kid took a pause. Said nothing. Then he picked up the cash, told the barback beside him to cover for him, and slipped into the sea of patrons on the dance floor.

Dean sat up at the counter.

He kept a close eye on the antechamber in case the brute woke up.

Two minutes later, he felt a presence brush up beside him.

Dean angled his body around, his posture relaxed as he laid eyes on a 6-foot man with a dark complexion, goatee, a bald head, and a pair of brown eyes that looked more dead than alive. Circles were under his eyes. A gold chain hung from his neck. A thick scar traveled from east to west above the collarbone.

Jesus.

What lab did they brew you *in?*

"There a problem?" the guy said.

"You Hayk?" Dean replied.

The guy tapered his eyes curiously. "Who are you?"

An alias Dean used from his undercover days came to mind: "Kelso."

"I don't know anyone named Kelso."

"*I'm* Kelso." Dean flexed his brow. "I got referred to you from a buddy of mine."

"Who?"

"Artin Sarkissian," Dean said as he flashed a cocky, self-assured grin. "I'm looking for a supplier, and he referred me to you."

"Is that so?"

"So, you *are* Hayk? I got the right guy, yeah?"

"I am," the guy said. "But you're speaking Chinese, bro."

Good job, Deano.

A face to the name.

Now, make your exit and get the hell out of here.

"I work with a group in New Mexico," Dean said. "Word has it that you—"

Hayk snapped his fingers. Three men came up behind him, the trio dressed in suits with bulges sticking out through the fronts of their jackets.

"Go," Hayk said. "Now."

Dean held up his hands. "Point taken." He buttoned the top of his blazer. "I'll be in touch." He turned his back on Hayk, feeling the man's gaze boring into the back of his neck as he made his way to the entrance, the three men Hayk called to his side following him every step of the way.

You got 'em, man.

You've seen him.

Now pray that they don't shoot you in the back on your way out the door.

Dean left the club via the front entrance. The bouncer gawked at him inquisitively as he walked through the door. After Dean handed the valet his ticket, his car arrived a minute later. Two minutes after that, he was on the road and calling Layla.

"How's it going?" Layla said.

"I paid a visit to Hayk's nightclub," Dean replied. "I just met him about two minutes ago."

"You're kidding."

"I'm not."

"Well, how'd it go?"

"Time will tell," Dean said. "I'm on his radar now. The whole point is to try to stir things up a bit. Based on what I know about this kind of crew, they'll poke their heads up soon. His guys followed me out, so they probably clocked my ride." He cut a glance toward the side mirror. "Wouldn't be surprised if they were tailing me either. They'll want to have a little chat with me sooner rather than later."

"Wouldn't they want to lie low after this?"

"I knocked out two of Hayk's guys and put them in a dumpster," Dean said. "He'll come around."

"*Jesus*, Dean," Layla groaned. "Be careful."

"I will."

"What's your next play?"

"I'm going back to the hotel. I need to catch some sleep for a quick minute."

"Call me in the morning?"

"You got it."

Dean hung up the phone, unbuttoned one of the buttons on his dress shirt, and looked at his mug in the rearview mirror.

"Felt good, didn't it?" he heard Woody say. "Just like the old days."

"Get lost."

"You're acting the maggot, laddie—you *enjoyed* it. You *know* you did."

You did, Deano.

Part of you dug that whole entire thing.

Just admit it, and quit lying to yourself.

Dean slipped in a toothpick.

For the first time in a while, it did little to curb his craving.

43

The adrenaline had subsided by the time Dean made it back to his hotel. Once he was in his room, he slipped off his club attire, donned his T-shirt and jeans, and placed his SIG on the nightstand.

Dean sat on the bed and implemented a box-breathing technique to slow his heart rate. The thrill of the hunt dissipated slowly with each breath he pulled into his lungs, his senses dulling, less sharp, his mind returning to a state of neutrality.

"Hell of a feeling, no?" Woody said. "Better than a shot in the arm."

"I never went that far," Dean replied. "*Never.*"

"You came close."

"Hell if I did."

"*Suur* you did, laddie. I was there. Remember that time in Caldwell? You were shoving marching dust up your nose like it was your job. That little mafioso goon you were building a case against offered you some H, but you turned him down."

"Get lost, Woody." Dean closed his eyes. "I mean it."

"You know you wanted it," the Irish bastard teased. "Just like you knew you wanted to go into the club tonight. You *wanted* to kick those guys' arses and—"

Dean chucked the television remote at the wall. It came apart but still worked. He cursed under his breath for losing his cool.

"I'm doing this for Marcus," Dean whispered. "For Kara. For her kid. For all of 'em."

"That's your *excuse*," Woody clarified. "You do this because you like it."

"No, I don't."

"Quit the lying."

"You're just a goddamn voice in my head," Dean said definitely. "You're *me*. You're just the unreasonable part of my mind. That's all you are."

"That's a *lie*, laddie," Woody replied. "That's what the folks in rehab told you to make you feel better about yourself. You're a *junkie*. You're a no-good, adrenaline-seeking conman who gets his jollies off doing stuff like you did tonight. No matter what you tell yourself. No matter what that reporter—"

Enough.

Go away.

Woody's voice receded into the catacombs of Dean's mind.

I'm done talking with you for the night.

Dean rubbed the back of his neck, his stomach rumbling from the lack of consistent meals he had in the past two days.

Eat something, dummy.

You're running on fumes.

Twenty minutes ticked by after Dean called room service. Then knuckles rapped on his door. He switched off the television that was tuned to the news, relishing that a hot meal was waiting for him as he twisted open the locks and palmed the handle.

"You guys are quick," Dean said. "I just called—"

The door flew open, struck Dean in the face, and knocked him flat on his back.

He sat up.

Gnashed his teeth.

Then a guy with a silenced pistol in his hand rushed into the room.

44

The intruder wore a black wool mask. A black sweater. Black leather gloves. The gun in hand was a Beretta 92F outfitted with a suppressor, and the barrel was aimed point blank at Dean's face.

The prowler mumbled something in Armenian.

Dean wasted no time trying to figure out what it meant. He shot out his foot, caught the intruder in the shin, and then rolled to his left.

The intruder squeezed off a shot as Dean moved out of the way. The round punched into the carpet and missed Dean's head by a quarter of an inch.

Dean pushed off the ground, dashed toward the intruder, and seized the man's wrists. The two men then wrestled for possession of the weapon, the intruder squeezing off another shot in the process that drilled its way into the television.

Dean shot his forehead into his opponent's nose and broke it. The intruder howled as he brought a hand to his face and lost his grip on the Beretta.

Dean, left hand gripped onto his opponent's throat, shot

out right in a bid to grab the weapon, his fingertips steel, but the intruder kicked him in the ribs. Dean spewed out a grunt as his opponent pushed him to the floor.

The intruder made a move for the Beretta.

Dean kicked it with his heel and caused it to fly into the bathroom, the weapon skidding across the tile before it came to a stop against the base of the toilet.

Dean shot to his feet.

He charged at the man.

Then he threw a jab and followed it with an uppercut. But when he attempted to plant a haymaker into his opponent's chin, the intruder blocked the blow, pulled Dean inward, and coiled his right arm around his throat and his left arm around the back of his neck.

Dean's vision slowly faded to black, air evacuating in a hiss through his lips as his complexion tinted to a deep shade of crimson.

Hell no.

This is not how it ends.

Dean planted his feet.

Pushed back.

Drove his opponent into the wall and heard the guy's head strike the doorframe of the bathroom.

The indruder's grip slackened.

Dean buried his elbow in the man's gut.

Then he turned out of the hold, heel-kicked his opponent in the rear to the floor, and booked it toward the bathroom.

Dean dived toward the floor and slid against the tiles, his hand outstretched toward the Beretta lying at the base of the toilet. He slapped his palm on the weapon's grip—but then Dean felt his body being pulled back swiftly. Losing his hold on the Beretta, he glanced over his shoulder and saw his opponent dragging him out of the bathroom by his ankle.

Dean spun onto his back. Drew back his heel. Shot it out into his opponent's face and felt a tinge of satisfaction when he heard some bones break.

The intruder recoiled, releasing his grip on Dean's ankle as Dean sat up, pushed off the ground, and rushed his opponent with an NFL-worthy tackle. Dean drove his attacker into the wall, threw two gut punches into the man's stomach, and then his attacker responded with an uppercut that struck Dean in the chin and forced him to tumble over the bed.

Dean sat up, shot a look toward the nightstand, spotted his SIG resting on top of it, and secured a grip on the weapon as his opponent ducked into the bathroom.

Dean toggled the safety.

His opponent reappeared, the Beretta in his grip and the business end trained in Dean's direction.

Dean fired off one shot.

The shooter did the same.

Both rounds missed by a wide several inches.

Dean ducked below the bed, the SIG gripped tightly in his hands as he prepared to reengage.

He drew a breath.

Counted to two.

Went into a crouch, and then took aim over the bed. But the door leading into the room was ajar, and his attacker was nowhere to be seen.

"Shit," Dean hissed, standing up as he scanned the room with his weapon. He dashed toward the door to his room, terminating his run before he pressed his back against the wall and poked his head out.

Two rounds registered from Dean's left, the bullets

striking the door just above his head and forcing him to retreat back into the room.

He cursed under his breath.

Waited.

Then Dean counted to three before he stuck his head back out, his gun raised in the direction the shots had been fired from, only to discover that no one was there.

He's running, Deano.

Go after him.

Dean dashed down the hallway, came to the stairwell at the end of the hall, and kicked open the door. No one was there, but the clanging of footsteps against the stairwell, clambering down toward the lower levels, indicated that the intruder was on the run.

Dean hotfooted down the stairwell, skipping every third step until he came to the ground level, arrived at the door for the service entrance, and booted it open.

Dean ducked into the alleyway behind the hotel.

Scanned the terrain with his weapon.

A moment later, he picked up on the squealing of tires 10 yards away on his right.

Dean ran as fast as his feet could carry him toward the street, his lungs on fire as he dashed out of the alleyway, cut a glance to his right, and saw a black Audi making a hard right at the end of the street.

"Well," Dean said as he toggled the safety on his SIG, "looks like you got their attention, bud."

45

At 10:23 p.m., four Pasadena PD officers were in Dean's room taking pictures, noting the damage that had been done as a result of the scuffle. Dean was seated on the edge of the bed with an ice pack pressed against his lip. Wilson was standing a few feet away with his arms crossed and a scowl on his face as an EMT did an appraisal of Dean's wounds.

"A few bruises," the EMT said. "Maybe a cracked rib." He shot his chin at Dean. "Do you need anything for the pain?"

"Negative," Dean replied. "I'll suck it up."

The EMT smirked.

Dean thanked the man for looking him over.

Then Wilson requested "a moment alone" with his agent, waited for the cops to leave, and got down on one knee. "Is this your idea of wrapping the case up in an expedited manner?"

"I've got a killer headache at the moment, Willy," Dean said. "Mind if we pick this up in the morning?"

"I've been trying to get you on the phone for a couple of days now."

"You told me to go off the reservation."

"I told you to go off the *book*," Wilson clarified, "not off the *rails*." He stood and shrugged his defeat. "What happened? Who was that guy?"

"Well," Dean tossed the ice pack down on the bed, "he sure as hell wasn't the concierge."

"Your second-rate jokes aren't amusing."

"I'm just as disappointed in them as you are, boss. Usually I'm spinning gold."

"All right, enough. What's going on, kid?" Wilson softened his tone. "Talk to me."

The two moved onto the balcony, Dean closing the door behind them and feeling the chill of the night air pleasantly cooling his skin. "I went to a club tonight," he said. "I got a line on someone with possible connections to the SMASH crew."

"Who?"

"A guy named Hayk Hakobyan. He has alleged Armenian Mob connections *and* connections with Vendrell and Harlow apparently. I went there tonight, asked a few questions, and then I almost got my head ripped off by what I can only assume was one of his guys."

Wilson crossed his arms. "And who tipped you off to this?"

Don't tell him.

Don't throw Layla under the bus.

"Some old confidential informants," Dean said. "I was pursuing a lead based on a tip I got, that's all."

"Well, we've got everyone from the DD on down wanting

to burn you for this. I've been running as much interference as I can, but I can't keep doing it."

"I'm getting close, Willy." Dean held up his thumb and index finger, an inch of space between them. "*This* close. I just need a little more time. That's all. I'm about to blow the lid off of this whole thing. You knew what asking me to do this would entail. So you either let me do what I need to do, or you send me home."

A moment passed before Wilson answered. "You have two days," he said. "You come up with nothing, you're done."

"Copy that."

"As far as Hayk Hakobyan is concerned, I'll do what I can on my end." Wilson tapered his eyes inquisitively. "And this guy who came after you—you said you busted him in the jaw, yeah?"

"*And* his nose," Dean clarified. "You might want to do a sweep of the local hospitals in case he stopped in for some stitches and a stint."

"He's not that stupid."

"I'm sure he's not. Odds are you won't come across him, but if you do, give him a wide berth. Try to put a tail on him."

"While I'm doing that," Wilson glanced toward the tattered hotel room, "check yourself out of here and find somewhere to lay low while I clean this mess up. Go somewhere you know you can ride this out. In the meantime, I'll do what I can to look up this Hayk Hakobyan character. No more of this sneaking around shit, or did you think I didn't know about your visit to the field office the other day?"

"Baumgardner," Dean hissed. "Thought that portly little putz had my back."

"Just stay by the phone." Wilson motioned toward the hallway. "I'll clear things up with the Pasadena PD and the hotel in the meantime." He held up a finger. "Get this done, and get it done fast. And I was never here. The brass finds out I'm helping you, I'll be manning a toll both before the week is out. You read me?"

"Yeah," Dean said. "I read you."

Wilson said nothing and headed toward the door, Dean bracing himself against the balcony railing as he surveyed the twinkling lights of the city.

Somewhere out there the bad guys were waiting. Somewhere out there, his name was floating around all the wrong inner circles—and he knew that meant he was getting closer to the truth.

46

"Blackwood," George said as he angled the computer monitor around. "Dean Henry. Born August 29th, 1985. Father's a former LAPD captain—robbery homicide. Mother is deceased. He's also got two siblings. One of them—"

"Skip that for now." Hayk held up his hand. "Just tell me who he works for."

George, huddled over the computer in the office above the club, nodded and scrolled through a few pages of the background for Dean Blackwood, the database provided to the "organization" by a few bribes to some "friends" in the federal government.

"He's a former Army Ranger," George said. "Looks like he was in the midst of being recruited for Delta Force before he fucked up his knee and got discharged. After that, he went into a kind of tailspin—booze, pills, shit like that." George peeked over the monitor. "Then he joined the FBI."

Nothing about the background was amusing to Hayk—or alarming. "What kind of agent is he?" he asked, his tone

—as always—calm and cool and without any shred of emotion. "What does he do?"

"The files are not accessible," George informed him. "I can't pull up anything."

"So he's a *secret* agent man." Hayk stroked his goatee knowingly. "Probably works undercover is my guess."

"You think?"

"Absolutely. The FBI's known for recruiting guys like Blackwood for their little black bag operations, guys with skill sets they assign to take on the cases that are much more dicey, the stuff those suit-wearing paper pushers can't handle. I'm talking about wet-work kind of operations, brother. Shoot-to-kill kind of jobs."

"I thought that kind of stuff was the CIA's business."

"You'd be surprised." Hayk snickered. "The Feds have all sorts of little side hustles they don't want the public to know about. I heard all about it from one of our sources inside the DOD. The FBI has a small score of operations they don't disclose to the general public, and my guess is *this* man," he motioned to Dean's photo on the screen, "is or was a part of them."

"So he's a ringer," George said. "He's a potential rule-breaker that'll overstep his boundaries if need be."

"We'll hope for the best and plan for the worst in terms of that." Hayk sat on the edge of George's desk, produced a Dunhill cigarette, and lit it. "Our people in the LAPD have gotten sloppy. This whole Haywood mess of theirs led this Blackwood character—*and* the FBI for that matter—right to our doorstep."

A cold shiver traced up George's spine. "Does Aram know about this?"

"I'm not sure. My guess is that our friends in the LAPD tried to handle this without him knowing. Either way, I'll inform him shortly." Hayk blew a smoke ring out of his mouth. "I think it's safe to say this long-standing arrangement Aram and our people have had with the LAPD is, at least it seems at the moment, on the verge of collapsing. They should have told us." He tapped his ash into the crystal tray beside him. "They should have warned us about this," he eyeballed the picture of Dean on the computer monitor, "*Blackwood* long in advance."

"Should I call Aram?" George said as he fished out his cell. "Should I tell him about Blackwood?"

"No, leave that to me." Hayk stubbed his cigarette out. "I'll let him know what's going on. Until then, I want to know if Blackwood has any family in town—parents, a wife, siblings, a child."

"He does." George pointed to the monitor. "An ex-wife and his child. They live in Santa Monica. I've got the address right here from the DMV."

A half-second later, someone knocked on the door. George opened it to reveal Artin, his face broken and swollen from where Dean Blackwood had punched and pistol-whipped him. His focus was on the carpet beneath him, his demeanor similar to a dog caught red-handed for piddling on a rug.

"Come in," Hayk said as he motioned for the cowering subordinate to join him. "*Voch'inch'*."

Artin walked in. Took a seat. Didn't look Hayk in the eye as he twiddled his thumbs and asked George for a smoke.

"Relax, brother," Hayk said. "What are you so stressed about?"

"Because I fucked up." Artin's trembling hand took the cigarette from George. "I let that guy—"

"*Hangstats'ek'*." Hayk brushed Artin's comments aside

with a swipe of his hand. "What happened, happened. It's over." He patted him on the back. "How's Alex?"

"He's got a concussion." Artin leaned in toward the open flame of George's Zippo lighter. "When he woke up in the dumpster, I had to tell him what happened. Fucker didn't know what hit him." He turned his gaze up to Hayk. "I'm sorry. Truly. I should have—"

"Should. Would. Could." Hayk shrugged it off. "Again, Monday morning quarterbacking won't help us here. I'm actually glad this happened in a way. It exposed some of our weaknesses with the club's security. We can," he cut a glance at George, "how would a white boy phrase it? 'Beef things up.'" He chuckled. "We'll sort it out, Artin. *Ink'nerd mi anhangstats'ek'.*"

Artin took a long drag of his cigarette and blew out the smoke with an even-tempered exhale. "What can I do?" he asked. "How can I make this right?"

"You want to square this up?"

"Yes."

"You want to save face?"

"Of course."

"Is it possible," Hayk came up behind Artin, leaned in close, slipped one hand into his pocket, and the other on top of Artin's shoulder, "for you to go back in time and stop that guy from getting into the club?"

"N-no," Artin stammered before he swallowed the lump in his throat. "No, it's not."

"Well," Hayk produced a switchblade from his pocket, clicked it open, and jammed the blade into the back of Artin's neck, "then there's nothing more to talk about."

Artin's body slumped to the floor.

Hayk casually wiped the blood off the blade. "Get rid of

that," he said as he gestured to the corpse, "and do the same with Alex once they discharge him from the hospital."

"What about Emin?" George asked, completely unfazed by what had just happened.

"Who?"

"He ran into Blackwood in the hallway. The idiot was surfing through PornHub when his ass got knocked out."

"*Himarner.*" Hayk checked the time on his gold Bulgari wristwatch. "Dispose of him too. And start putting better people on the doors of the club from now on." He nodded toward the computer monitor. "You said you have the address for Blackwood's family, yes?"

"*Ayo'.*"

"Forward it to me." Hayk's lips twisted into a sneer. "I think a simple solution to dealing with this white boy just presented itself."

47

O nly one person came to Dean's mind when Wilson told him to find somewhere to lie low—his father's place. If there was anyone he knew he could stay with who would take up arms if the situation arose, it was—former—Captain Donald Blackwood. After checking out of the hotel in Pasadena, Dean arrived at his father's place and found the old man dead asleep on the couch. *Magnum Force* was playing on the television at a dull roar.

Dean slowly closed the door, Clint Eastwood in the midst of mumbling, "Go ahead—make my day," as he fastened the deadbolt, chain, and handle locks.

Dean fixed his gaze on his father, the glow of the TV on the old man's face as he sat half slumped over with his arms crossed over his chest. Not wanting the risk of Donald thinking someone else was in the house and drawing down on him with a .357, Dean placed his duffel bag beside his father as a sign, told him to "sleep well," and proceeded to grab a Coke from the fridge. It was almost 2:00 a.m., but Dean knew he wasn't getting any sleep that night.

Dean took a few sips and then leaned against the island

in the kitchen, thinking about his next play and how he'd go about wrapping things up in two days.

Where do I go now?

I've got the bad guys on my trail, but where do I go from here?

Wait until they find me?

Have a huge shootout in the middle of the street?

He shook his head.

I need evidence.

I need a lead.

If Eldridge or any of his cronies are in league with this guy, I need to find out how and why.

The fatigue of the night's events started to set in. The muscles on the back of Dean's neck constricted.

Just chill for now.

Pick this back up in the morning.

Dean dumped his half-depleted Coke down the sink. Flicked the lights off. Then he padded down the hallway, approached the guest bedroom, and stopped to take a glance up at the attic space above his head. Dean eyeballed the padlock securing the attic, recalling the one back at the old family home in Pasadena that Donald used to keep under lock and key.

"Don't go up there, boys," he could hear his father say in his mind. "It's off-limits."

Screw it.

I'll be up for hours anyway.

Dean peeked over his shoulder toward his comatose father.

What's he going to do, ground me?

The smell of mildew tickled Dean's nostrils as he poked his head up into the attic and looked around. A single light bulb hung from a chain overhead. Dean switched it on, the glow of the bulb coating a series of legal boxes stacked waist-high with a dull luminescence.

The labels on the boxes dated from 1985 all the way up to the early 2000s. Dean pinpointed a series from the '90s. Rifled through them. Arrived at the box labeled "1993"—the year his twin brother died—and found an *LA Times* snippet that mentioned Tommy's death.

His eyes misted.

He put the article back.

Then he sifted through another box.

And then another.

And another.

And another.

Most of the contents pertained to highlights of Donald's career, the rest of them mementos from family vacations, graduations, and even a few co-pay invoices for his late mother's cancer treatments.

The box marked "LAPD" caught Dean's eye. Inside, he discovered Donald's old innocuous police reports, nothing that caught his interest until he found an article from the *LA Times* that made him pause in his tracks.

There was a black-and-white photo in the article, the headline "LAPD RAMPS UP ITS CRIME SWEEP" in big bold letters.

Several officers were in the picture.

All of them were smiling from one ear to the other.

Dean's heart sank when he realized he recognized each one of their faces.

"*Son of a bitch*," he muttered softly, his hands shaking as he appraised the mugs of Larry Eldridge, Mike Vendrell,

Cole Harlow, Ron Wyler, Sean Mohr...and then Donald Blackwood, Ron Wyler's arm around his shoulder like he had known him for years. According to the article, Dean deduced that Vendrell, Harlow, and Wyler used to serve under his command.

48

Dean nudged his father in the foot, the article he had found in the attic clutched in his hand. "*Dad*," he grumbled. "Get up."

Don Blackwood's eyes fluttered open as he sat up. "What is it?"

Dean tossed the paper on his father's lap.

Donald's color paled when he gazed at the photo on the page.

"What about it?" Donald said. "Is this supposed to mean something to me?"

"*Don't*," Dean growled. "Just..." He drew a breath. "Just make it make sense."

"Make *what* make sense?"

"The men in the paper." Dean gestured to the article. "You knew each and every one of them, didn't you? According to the article, Wyler, Harlow, and Vendrell were *your* officers."

Donald took a beat.

Cleared his throat.

Then he tossed the paper to the floor.

"What do you want me to say, son?"

"The *truth*, Dad," Dean said. "You told me you never crossed paths with the SMASH unit before."

"That's not what I said."

"Don't try to pull one over on me. We're in the same line of work. I know when someone is deceptive," Dean crooked a finger, "and that's *precisely* what you're doing right now. People are dying, Dad. An innocent man was convicted of a crime he didn't commit. I know you know something. I knew you knew those guys in SMASH, and I need you to tell me why you lied about it."

A sheepish Donald, eyes glued to the floor, said nothing.

"You need to tell me what you know," Dean insisted. "This is only going to get worse if you don't tell me the truth."

Donald's hand trembled.

His posture slackened.

Then he got up off the couch, walked over to his recliner, and slid down onto it defeatedly.

"I never wanted this," Donald said. "I never wanted *any* of this."

Dean got down on one knee, looking at his old man like he would an innocent child who was being bullied on a playground. "Dad," he said, taking a beat between his words. "What did you do?"

A single tear slid down Don's cheek. He wiped it away, holding a finger to his lips like he was trying to dam up the truth. "They made me do it," he replied. "I had to do it to protect you and your siblings. I had no choice."

"Who?" Dean said. "Who made you do what?"

"It was Eldridge," Donald replied. "He's responsible for all of this. *Everything*. He's the one who's been pulling the strings since day one."

Dean stood up, his back to his father as he clenched a fist. "Start from the beginning. Tell me everything. All of it."

A few moments ticked by as Dean's father summoned the courage to speak. "It all started back in '92," he finally explained. "Eldridge was, and is, the most corrupt son of a bitch in the LAPD. He knows how to pull strings. He knows how to con and manipulate the system to his advantage. He asked me years ago to use my position in the department to help him clear a guy who killed three people."

"Who?"

"A guy named Hakobyan—Hayk Hakobyan."

Dean closed his eyes.

Unbelievable...

"Eldridge has been in league with Hakobyan and his crew for years," Donald went on. "Eldridge has been offering protection, murder-for-hire, you name it. I told him I didn't want anything to do with it. I knew that Eldridge had the pull, so I didn't cross him or rat him out. I thought I could turn my back on him, and it would go away." He shook, tears streaming freely down his face. "My *God*, what have I done?"

"Tell me your part in it, Pop." Dean turned around, approached his father, and looked him square in the eyes. "And don't leave anything out."

"I...I helped launder his cash. I did it for years. One day, I said I wanted out. Eldridge told me I had no choice. When I refused to give in, he..." his father slowly turned up his gaze, "he sent me a message. He gave me a warning, something he knew would scare me off if I ever tried to turn my back on him."

"What warning?"

Don gripped his son's hand tightly. "Eldridge..." he hung his head, "had your brother killed. He...he had one of

Hayk's men run over Tommy. After it happened, I got a call. I was told all my family would suffer the same fate if I didn't comply. Eldridge had Tommy *killed*, Dean. It was always him, and I had to keep my mouth shut so the rest of you could stay safe. I could never tell you the truth. I couldn't tell anyone, and I've been holding onto that for years."

Dean's ears buzzed.

His stomach twisted into a knot.

A pounding headache thumped inside his skull.

"I'm so sorry, Dean." Donald reached out his hand. "I never—"

"*Don't*," Dean grumbled. "Just..." he held up his hands, "just don't."

He wanted to curse his father out. Yell. Scream. Break everything in the living room. Everything he had known his whole life had been nothing more than a giant lie covered up by LAPD's best and brightest.

His brother had been killed.

And his father had played a hand in keeping the truth from getting out.

"God damn you," Dean hissed. "God *damn* you." He turned into the hallway and rushed into the bathroom before he slammed the door shut behind him.

The home video of Tommy's death played in vivid detail in Dean's mind. He felt on the verge of passing out, not knowing what to think or say as he slipped down onto the bathroom floor, fighting the whirlwind of rage that stirred inside his chest.

They'll pay.

All of them.

Every single last one of them are dead.

49

I t took Dean thirty minutes to calm himself. Once he did, he walked into the kitchen to find his father seated at the table, hands folded, staring straight ahead. Dean didn't utter a word as he took the seat across from Donald, staring at him with a heated expression as he stroked his upper lip with his index finger.

"You know what happens now," Dean said. "Right?"

His father said nothing.

"I'm going to burn the whole thing down," Dean explained. "The whole thing."

Donald met his son's gaze. "You can't, son. These people aren't the type of guys you mess with."

Dean leaned in close. "*Watch me.*"

"You don't know these guys."

"Acquaint me with them."

Don lowered his head. "The man who's in charge of the family is named Aram Sarkissian. He's a drug dealer, among his other trades, and Hayk Hakobyan, his cousin, has been his number one muscle for years."

Dean nodded. "Yeah, I met him not that long ago. Steely-eyed prick. He smells like Aqua Velva."

"That's the one."

"How have you been helping them?" Dean asked. "You said you assisted them in laundering their cash."

"I did, and I do."

"Whose money?" Dean said. "Eldridge's? Sarkissian?""

"Both," Donald said. "Every penny of it. I launder the cash, store it in the Airbnb, and someone from the Sarkissian clan stops by every once in a while to make a withdrawal. I've been doing it for years. My methods have changed, but I've always been in charge of the spreadsheets."

"What about your end?" Dean said. "What's in it for you?"

"Nothing," his father said. "I just keep my mouth shut. My family being spared from what happened to Tommy is the trade-off. I never get a dime of what they make."

"Where's the money? Where are you stashing it?"

"You know my little trips to Tahoe I take twice a year? The cabin out there?" Don huffed. "I stop by Reno on my way. I take the cash the SMASH unit has and launder it through the casino and a few other shell corporations I set up. Once I've cleaned the hard cash, I store it away in that Airbnb unit I have out in Silver Lake, and the Sarkissian guys stop by every few months to take a slice. Occasionally, I'll get the call from the Sarkissians to skim off the top to the SMASH guys. That's how the Sarkissians pay Eldridge and his people."

Dean took in the information. "One big pot. It keeps things simple." He looked at his father. "And having an ex-cop run the operation for them is an ideal proposition."

Donald said nothing.

"So," Dean said, "Eldridge formed an alliance with the Armenian Mob years ago. Then he creates SMASH to operate as the mob's enforcers, the guys who will provide the muscle and cover for them when they have to. In turn, Eldridge gets a payday, and he and the Sarkissians use *you* as the bank. How am I tracking?"

"You're right on the mark, kiddo," Donald said. "That's the long and short of it."

"What about Eldridge? Has he contacted you since I got tangled up in this case? He must've sent word to you, pressuring you to back me off of this."

"No, not yet. It's only a matter of time though."

"It is," Dean said. "Eldridge knows I'm onto him. Same with the Sarkissians. He'll try to contact you sooner or later to turn up the heat, if he hasn't already."

"Not yet," Donald said. "No one wants to see their money compromised. I know Eldridge. He'll put off putting the squeeze on me until he's desperate. He probably figured he could deal with you, be done with it, and go back to life as usual. It's foolish on their part, really, and at this point, I'm ready to shoot it out with the bastard after what he did to our family. And, if he takes me down, so be it."

"Knock it off, Pop," Dean replied. "That's not going to get us anywhere. I'll keep you safe. Eldridge and his cronies won't get within 10 feet of you. I guarantee it."

Donald sank into his chair, the weight of his mistakes making him feel like he was on the verge of collapse.

"What I can't understand," Dean said, "is why the SMASH guys are getting knocked off. Who's doing this? And what do they have to gain from it?"

"I don't know, son," his father said. "Truly, I don't."

I have the truth about Eldridge.

About the Sarkissians.

About why Tommy was killed.

I know the whole smash—no pun intended—but who the hell is knocking off these cops?

And why?

"Tell me one thing," Dean said.

Don furrowed his brow. "What?"

"Who killed Tommy, Pop? You said it was deliberate, that Eldridge was sending you a message. What I want to know is who was behind the wheel of the car that ran over Tommy."

Defeat washed across Donald's face. "I never found out. I was too scared to try to pinpoint the man who did it. I was trying to protect you and your sister—my *family*. The only thing I do know is that it was one of the guys in the Sarkissian family."

"How can you be sure?"

"Something that Eldridge said." Don closed his eyes. "He said, 'Now you know not to mess with these guys.'"

Dean's anger had never been so potent. Part of him felt like he was actually *thirsting* for blood.

"Eldridge is shutting down the unit," Dean said. "I got word from the kid he put in the hospital that it is happening."

"It makes sense," his father replied. "He's trying to burn the thing down before anything can bite him in the ass. He'll put some space between him and everything, and rebuild it once the dust has settled."

"Well, if he's tearing the operation down," Dean paused as he slapped together a plan, "he'll want to take out all the cash you've been holding for him and move it somewhere else. It makes sense. It's what I would do if I were trying to clean this whole thing up."

That's it, bucko.

The money is the key.

That's your bait right there, slim!

Dean shot up from his seat, snagged the keys to the Pontiac, and tossed his father his windbreaker.

"Where are we going?" Donald rose and slipped on his jacket. "What do you plan to do?"

"We're going to the AirBnb." Dean twirled the keys on his finger. "We're going to seriously fuck with Eldridge's cash flow."

50

Dean broke every speed and traffic law getting to the Airbnb unit in Silver Lake. Donald gripped onto grab handle the entire ride over, completely silent as Dean drove like a bat out of hell. The entire ride was silent, Dean's heated gaze fixed to the road as he steered with a white-knuckled grip.

Dean pulled into the driveway of the one-story ranch unit nestled between two other homes on a residential street, a sky-blue paint job with white trim that reminded him of the Brady Bunch estate.

Dean looked around. The coast was clear, and after taking one more look over his shoulder, he slipped out of the car and moved to the front door with his father in tow.

"Open it up," Dean said.

Don unlocked the door and pushed it open. Dean moved in first through the pitch-black foyer, his SIG drawn as he cleared the room just like the Rangers had taught him. He spotted the living room on his right. The dining room on his left. Ahead of him was a hallway that led to two bedrooms, a study, and a kitchen. After Dean cleared all the rooms, he rejoined his father in the foyer.

"Where is it?" Dean said. "Where's the money?"

Don gestured around the residence. "Everywhere," he replied. "Walls, floors, you name it."

Dean padded his way toward the yard at the rear of the house where there was a small space with a patch of grass and a portable aluminum shed. He threw open the doors to the shed and saw a pair of hedge clippers, a rake, a crowbar, and a sledgehammer hanging neatly from hooks.

Dean grabbed the crowbar and the sledgehammer.

Strolled back into the house.

Stripped off his jacket, turned in a circle, and eyeballed the wall beside the couch.

He flattened his hand against the wall.

Patted it.

Then Dean stood back, raised the crowbar, and began striking away piece after piece.

Ten minutes later, sweat clinging to every inch of his body, Dean swung the sledgehammer and surveyed the contents inside the wall—copious amounts of cash stuffed in plastic bags. Hundreds of thousands of dollars.

Millions.

Eldridge's Fort Knox.

"How much?" Dean asked as he tossed down the crowbar. "How much is there?"

"In that one wall?" Donald shrugged. "10.1 million."

"Good *lord*." Dean laughed. "You're lucky none of your guests got wise to this, Pop. You'd have been paying for some dipshit's VIP passes to Coachella."

"To what?"

"Never mind." Dean started ripping out one bag after

another. "Just help me take this out. I'll move to the floors after we stack it up."

"What are you going to do with it?"

"It's what *you're* going to do, Pop."

"What's that?"

"You're going to call Eldridge tonight. You're going to tell him that someone broke in here and stole the cash."

Don's eyes widened. "That's insane."

"Yes, it is."

"They're going to try to hunt down whoever did it."

"That's my hope," Dean said.

His father grabbed him by the arm. "*Dean,*" he pleaded. "Son, please, don't do this. I've let this go on long enough already. I can't put you in harm's way. If anything happened—"

"You're going to stay in a motel," Dean said. "The Days Inn in Encino. Check in under the name Gibbons so I know how to get in touch with you. I'll call you later tonight to make sure you're safe, and once I know you are, you're going to make the call to Eldridge. After that, you lay low until I tell you it's safe to come out. This is how it's going to be. We're not negotiating—*this* is the plan."

Dean pulled his cell phone from his pocket, dialed Layla's number, and waited three rings before she answered.

"Hey," Layla greeted him. "What time is it?"

"I need your help."

"What's going on?"

"I need you to meet me at an Airbnb unit in Silver Lake. I'll text you the address. Pick up two prepaid cells." Dean eyed the bills scattered at his feet. "And bring a hell of a lot of bags and suitcases while you're at it."

51

Two knocks sounded on the front door of the Airbnb. Dean shot up from the couch, SIG in hand as he approached the door, stood in the foyer, and told Donald to stay in the kitchen.

"Who is it?"

"DoorDash," Layla replied. "Open up, please."

Dean safetied his weapon, opened the door, and greeted a bleary-eyed Layla with a weak grin.

"The bags are in my car," she said as she stepped in the foyer. "Three suitcases, six duffel bags, and a few other odds and ends pieces of luggage."

"That'll work."

Layla held up a 7-11 bag, opened it to show the two prepaid cell phones inside, and handed them over. "Good enough?"

Dean nodded. "Good enough."

"All right," Layla said. "Now do you mind telling me why I rolled over here at midnight?"

"Over here." Dean motioned to the living room. "Take a look."

Layla strolled into the living room as Dean locked the door, her wide-eyed gaze glued to the cash strewn on the floors. "What..." she gasped. "What is all of this?"

He laid out the entire story. The Armenian Mob angle. Eldridge's alliance with them. His father's involvement. The culprit who killed his brother. Layla barely blinked as Dean explained things. Once he finished, she moved toward the kitchen sink and braced against it like she had just gotten off a tilt-a-whirl.

"This is big," Layla said. "And you solved it quicker than I ever could have. I've been working on this for years." She cut a glance at Dean. "And you managed to do it in *days*."

"I'm tenacious," he said. "For better or worse."

"I can't believe your father is involved. His name never came up in my research. You said that newspaper article you found tipped you off?"

"You would have found it sooner or later. I just happened to get there first. But there's no time to dwell on all that. I'll have plenty of time to digest my father's misdeeds once we wrap this thing up."

"Where is he?"

"He's safe." Dean checked his watch and figured his father was halfway to the motel in Encino. "I'm stashing him away somewhere until this is finished."

"Okay." Layla drew a breath and composed herself. "What happens now?"

"I'll set out the bait for Eldridge and his cronies. Once they know their cash is missing, I'll tip them off that I have it. After that, I'll reel them out into the open."

"And then what?"

Dean took a beat. "And then I kill them."

Layla brought a hand to her mouth, her skin turning to an ashen shade. "Dean, you can't."

"There's no other way this ends."

"That can't be how this plays out."

"It will."

"I'm a reporter, Dean. We can use what you've discovered and bring that to my editor—"

Dean held up his hand. "I can't take a chance on that. We don't know who Eldridge knows, who he's got connections with. And these people *killed* my brother, Layla. I can't let that pass. Far as I'm concerned, they deserve everything that's coming to them."

"You need to call your boss." Layla grabbed his wrist and squeezed. "You need to let me write this up, let your people take over, and do this the right way."

"Eldridge will do whatever he can to make sure none of his people get burned. Same for the Sarkissians. Doing things through the normal channels won't guarantee a slam dunk. No, I need to do this *my* way. I need to get Eldridge to confess, and I need to find out why the other guys in the unit were being killed off. That's the only way we can bring him down, to take him in and make him answer for what he's done."

"I thought you said you were going to kill him."

"No, not Eldridge." Dean shook his head. "He doesn't deserve that luxury." His eyes shimmered with lethal intent. "But I am going to kill the man who murdered my brother, and Eldridge is the only one who knows who it is." Dean fished into his pockets, pulled out a few bills, and placed them in Layla's hand. "Go to Encino. There's a Days Inn out there. I'll forward you the address. My father is there now, and I want you to stay with him. Leave your cell behind on the way out so no one can track you. I'll call you guys tonight when I'm ready to set this thing into motion. Also,

I," he sighed, "I need you to take an Uber or a Lyft. My old man took the Pontiac, so I'll need your car."

"Dean—"

Dean took Layla's hand into his. "Please, Layla. There's no other way. If we want to end this thing, *this* is how we do it. I have to do things my way here." He squeezed her hand. "I need you to trust me."

Layla waited, silent, and then palmed over her car keys and cell phone.

"I don't like this," she said. "I don't like this at all."

"But you trust me," Dean replied. "You *do* trust me, don't you?"

"I do."

"Then go write this up. Tell everyone what happened. Once I draw these guys to me and figure out the rest of the story, I'll make sure you know about it, even if something happens to me."

Layla shook her head. "Don't say that."

"Don't worry," Dean said. "I can take care of myself. Everything's going to be all right. Can you bring in the bags and suitcases before you leave?"

"I can," Layla said. Layla offered no more protest. She simply stood with Dean and looked him in the eyes with an affectionate acknowledgment that required no words to express.

"Go," Dean said. "Get as far away from here as possible. This is going to get ugly before it comes to an end, and you don't need a front row ticket for that."

Layla opened her mouth.

Tried to speak but found it a useless effort.

Once she brought in the bags, she made her way out of the house and closed the door behind her as Dean moved the duffle bags to the living room. "Okay, assholes." He grabbed a fistful of cash and stuffed it into one of the bags. "Let's dance."

Dean loaded the last bag of cash into the back of Layla's Honda Civic and covered it with a blanket he'd snagged from inside the rental unit. Once that was finished, he took out the pair of burner phones Layla purchased, set up both, and left one of them behind in the Airbnb unit's kitchen, jacked into a charger.

"This isn't gonna go well, laddie," Woody taunted. "You know that, right?"

"Maybe." Dean took out a toothpick. "But I bet you like that, don't you?"

"Going rogue? Full Rambo?" The leprechaun chuckled delightedly. "I *love* it."

Dean shook his head.

Slipped in the toothpick.

Then he pulled out his personal cell, plugged in Wilson's number, and waited for two rings.

"Dean," Wilson said. "Where are you?"

"I'm getting close, Willy," Dean replied. "This thing is almost wrapped up."

"We've got a problem, Dean." The strain in the SAC's voice was palpable. "A big one."

"What is it?"

"A warrant has been issued for your arrest. I can't cover for you anymore. If you don't come in within the next three hours, they're sending out a team to bring you in."

Dean's grip on the phone was so tight that he was on the cusp of breaking it.

I can't go in.

I can't turn back.

"Dean," Wilson said. "Talk to me."

"I have to finish this."

"Kid—"

"I gotta go, boss." Dean held his head high. "I'll catch you on the flip side." He terminated the call, was tempted to chuck the cell onto the lawn, but then spotted a pickup truck cruising toward him down the street.

The pickup cruised past and then stopped on the side of the street.

Dean padded his way toward it.

Then he tossed his cell in the truck's bed on top of several bags of fertilizer.

That'll buy me a little time.

Christ, how much of it do I even have left?

You gotta call him, Deano.

You gotta ring up the kid.

Dean locked up the Airbnb.

Slipped into Layla's Civic.

Then he pulled out the burner phone, checked the battery, and dialed Claire's number from memory.

"Hello?" Claire answered.

"It's me."

"Where are you calling from? What number is this?"

"I had to borrow a phone." Dean closed his eyes. "Can I talk to Jeremy really quickly?"

"It's 1:00 in the morning. He's asleep." Claire paused. "You sound off. Is everything okay?"

"I just wanted to check in with him."

Maybe for the last time ever.

"Dean..." Claire said. "Something's wrong."

"*Please*, Claire. I need to talk to him. It's important."

Half a minute ticked by before Jeremy hopped on the line, Dean doing his best to compartmentalize his feelings as he heard his son's voice.

"Dad?" Jeremy greeted weakly.

"Hey, Pally." Dean smirked. "How are you?"

"I was sleeping. Where are you?"

"I'm just working, kiddo. I'm about to wrap up soon."

"Will I see you this weekend?"

Dean's lip quivered.

Tears welled in his eyes.

Probably not, Pally.

Probably not.

"Of course," Dean lied to his son. "I'll figure out a time with your mom in a little bit."

"Are you okay, Dad?"

"I am."

"You don't *sound* okay."

Kids, man.

A million times more intuitive than adults double their age.

"I'm just a little tired, bud," Dean said. "But I'll be finished soon."

At the cost of this.

At the cost of your son.

The toll of this crusade is your family, Blackwood, and don't you ever forget that.

"You have a good day, Pally," Dean said. "I love you."

"I love you too."

"Be good."

"I will."

Dean terminated the call.

Breathed deeply.

Then he turned the key, revved the engine, and prepared to back out.

"Look what you're doing, laddie," Woody said. "Turning your back on your kid like that. If this doesn't *prove* you're a fiend for the action, I don't know what will."

"You don't know shit," Dean replied. "This has to happen. If I don't do this, my entire family is in danger."

"Because you got involved in this to begin with. You should have said no. None of this would have ever happened."

Maybe.

Possibly.

But it's too late to unpack all that right now.

"I'm interested to see how this pans out, my friend," Woody said. "Best of luck to you."

"Get bent, buddy," Dean replied. "And when I get back, I don't ever want to hear from you again."

"Yeah..." The leprechaun huffed incredulously. "We'll see about that."

Dean revved the engine.

Zipped down the street.

Then he made a beeline for his father's home and the cache of guns he knew the old man had stored away inside of it.

53

D ean recalled the combination to his father's standing safe from his mental movie collection. When he was twelve, he poked his head into Donald's study and saw the old man fiddling with the dial. Dean memorized the combo and logged it away for future reference, though he couldn't imagine when and why he'd ever need to get inside of it.

Until now.

Dean flayed open the door to the safe and appraised the contents: a Remington 700 Sendero SF II. Long range. Bolt action. A Vortex Razor HD GEN II 4.5-27X56 scope mounted on top of it, and a KABAR knife his father kept as a memento from his time in the Corp.

Forty-five for the SIG.

Dean palmed a box of .223 rounds and counted.

Twenty rounds for the Remington.

Sixty-five rounds total.

Dean wrapped the rifle in a blanket, press-checked the rounds in the SIG, and holstered it. Then he scooped up the KABAR, headed into Don's bedroom, and found a black shirt, black slacks, and the vintage black leather jacket the old man had worn back when he was a detective working the streets.

Dean slipped on the clothing.

He double-checked his appearance in the mirror. He felt a cold shiver trace up his spine when he saw that he was a spitting image of his old man.

Sins of the father.

Sins of the son.

Dean shot his cuffs and shook off the thought.

No time for that bullshit now.

Sort through it all once you get out of this.

Alive.

He exited the house and stepped onto the porch, checking around to make sure there were still no tails.

All Quiet on the Western Front.

He took out the burner phone from his pocket and dialed the number for the Days Inn that Layla and his father were hiding in and told the operator to connect him to the Gibbons room. Two rings later, his father greeted him over the line.

"Dean," Don said.

"Where are you?"

"We're here. Layla and I. We're safe."

"Good," Dean said. "It's time to make the call. Tell Eldridge that someone broke into the unit and stole all the money. I'll take it from there."

"Son," Donald said. "Please, I can't watch you—"

"Everything is going to be okay. You have my word."

Tremors crept into his father's tone. "I love you, my boy," he said. "I love you more than you'll ever know."

"Me too." Dean closed his eyes. "I'll see you soon." He hung up the phone, stuffing it in his jacket pocket as he climbed down the porch steps and got behind the wheel of Layla's Honda Civic again.

Finish this, Blackwood.

He revved the engine.

End it.

54

D ean parked the Civic across the street and six doors down from the Airbnb unit, his gaze fastened to the front door. He checked the time on his G-Shock—just past 2:00 a.m.

Only a matter of time.

Dean tapped his finger on the steering wheel.

Rested back in his seat.

Debated making the call to his father to see what the status was—but then a pair of headlights appeared up the street two doors from the Airbnb, and there was no question in Dean's mind who it was.

He slumped down in his seat as a black Escalade pulled in front of the Airbnb.

The SUV parked.

The front doors opened.

Two men in black attire slipped out and approached the front of the house.

That's Hayk.

Dunno who the other guy is though.

Hayk and his partner entered the house slowly, the pair

checking over their shoulders before Hayk closed the front door behind him.

Dean waited two minutes.

Pulled out his burner.

Then he placed a call to the one he had left behind in the kitchen.

It rang once.

Twice.

Shortly after the third ring, someone picked up the line.

"Howdy, shithead," Dean greeted. "Remember me?"

"I do," Hayk replied. "How's it going, Blackwood?"

"Hanging in there. Yourself?"

"Doing all right. Got a little bit of indigestion from the Zankou I ate earlier."

"Soda water," Dean suggested. "It'll settle your stomach."

"Thanks for the tip." Hayk's tone ticked down an octave. "Now, where's our money?"

"I have it—*all* of it. Every last penny and dime."

"You made a bad play, my friend." Hayk switched to his native tongue. "*Shat himar.*"

"Blow it out your ass," Dean said. "Like I said, I've got your cash, and unless you want me to start burning every last bill, you're gonna call your boss Aram and arrange a meeting."

"Do you know who I am? Do you know what I am capable of doing to your life?"

"Lemme guess." Dean recalled his conversation with Sean Mohr right before the man blew his brains out. "You're the kind of guy who'll flay my skin off with a potato peeler."

"So you've heard the stories."

"I have. And they mean fuck-all to me, dipshit. Now quit acting like a revved-up little spitfuck, and call your boss."

Hayk said nothing, his heavy breathing audible on the other end of the line.

"I want a face to face with Aram," Dean said. "If you screw with me, if you deviate from the plan, I'll start using your money for firewood."

"You really have no clue what you've gotten yourself into, Blackwood," Hayk replied with a biting tone. "I'll burn your world to the—"

"You've got two minutes. One second later, *I* start burning your green."

Dean terminated the call and tossed the burner on the seat beside him.

Just wait.

You've got the upper hand.

You've got them right where you want them.

One minute ticked by.

The burner rang.

Dean waited for three rings before he answered.

"Go."

Not a word was said. The only thing that was audible over the line was breathing—slow, guttural, a primal kind of respiration more akin to that of an animal than a man. "Blackwood," the voice finally said. "This is Aram."

"What's good, Aram?"

"You have my money."

"That I do."

"I'd suggest you give me my money back."

"We can do that—but in person."

"Why?"

"I want to meet you."

"And why is that?"

"Because I don't like you," Dean said. "And I want a chance to pummel your face in before I put a bullet in it."

"I see," Aram replied. "Well, perhaps *this* might force you to reconsider your proposal."

The burner buzzed—a text.

Dean opened it.

And his jaw dropped when he saw the photo of Jeremy sleeping soundly in his bed.

55

"Now," Aram said as Dean touched the photo of his son on the burner's display, "do I have your full attention?"

Dean's heart sank.

His temperature rose.

For a fleeting moment, he was tempted to dash outside, run into the Airbnb, and put a bullet in Hayk's brain.

Focus.

Easy.

You cannot *fuck this up!*

"You listen to me," Dean said coolly. "You hurt my son, and I swear to God I will rip you apart limb by—"

"Are you finished? Time is running out, so I'd suggest you listen carefully."

Breathe, Deano.

He tightened his grip on the phone.

Focus on the task.

Don't let your emotions get the better of you.

"Long Beach docks," Aram said. "One hour. Bring the

money. You won't walk away from the situation alive, but if you comply with what I ask, your son lives."

"You're lying." Dean shook his head. "You're going to kill us both, either way."

"Probably, but you still have a razor-thin chance of saving him. If I were in your position, I'd think I'd try to take that chance, no matter how slim the margins were. Correct?"

Dean closed his eyes. "Correct."

"Good," Aram said. "There's a ship; the *Nuevo Amanecer*. My men will be waiting for you near it. You know I don't need to say the obvious part about no cops or others being with you, yes?"

"I want you there too."

"Fat chance."

Dean clenched his jaw. "Then to hell with your money. I want you there." He ran his next proposal through a filter, accepted it, and stated it to Aram. "And I want the man who killed my brother. Whoever he is, you get him down there too."

"Blackwood—"

"*Try me*, asshole," Dean said. "I'll burn your cash. And by the time the reporter I've been working with breaks the story, you'll be out of business and stuck in Chino with your 300-pound gorilla of a bunkmate."

A few moments ticked by.

Dean waited for the reply.

Then Aram said, "I'll be there, but I'll have a gun to your kid's head the entire time. If you do anything stupid, you know what happens."

The line went dead.

Dean took a moment to process the situation as he stuffed the burner in his pocket.

You can't call Claire.

There's no time.

You have to move, and you have to move now!

"Look what happens, laddie," Woody said. "Look at the sum of your choices."

Dean said nothing.

He stared at the SUV as Hayk and his partner got inside, peeled away, and headed out.

Work the problem, Blackwood.

Dean turned over the ignition.

Go and get your son back.

56

Dean stepped out of the store at the gas station with four red plastic gas cans tucked under his arms. He placed the cans down by the pump. Filled them up. Tried not to think about Claire losing her mind, the cops being called, or the myriad of other problems that were hours away from catching up to him.

Find Jeremy.

Get him back.

Nothing else matters until that's done.

He knew it was a suicide mission. The chances of him walking out of the situation alive were slim, but a father's rage was on his side, and some of the most impossible feats on the planet had been accomplished when a parent found their child in harm's way. Jeremy would *live*, no matter what, even if Dean knew that meant his own life would come to an end.

Call her, Blackwood.

Put the word out.

Talk to her one last time.

Dean pulled out his burner.

Plugged in Layla's number and leaned against the Civic.

"Dean?" Layla answered. "Is that you?"

"They have my kid." Dean closed his eyes. "These bastards took Jeremy."

"Oh, my God!" Layla held the line. "Dean, I—"

"I need you to call my ex-wife. My father has her number. Tell her I know where Jeremy is, and I'm going to bring him back. I'm sure she knows. I'm sure the police are already involved."

"Where is he? Where are you going?"

"I'm going to the Long Beach docks. There's a ship there, the *Nuevo Amanecer*. I'll be meeting the Sarkissians there. I want you to wait for one hour before you tell the cops that. I need a little time."

"Dean—"

"*Promise me.*"

Layla took a beat. "I will," she finally said. "I promise."

Dean snapped his eyelids open. "I'm sorry, Layla. To you. To Jeremy. To everyone. I'm..." He briefly choked on his words. "I should have never touched this thing. I should have stayed far away from it. But none of that matters now. I just need to finish this."

"Dean..." Layla hesitated. "Am I going to see you again?"

"I hope so." *Time to go, slim.* "Take care, Layla. I'll call you when I can."

"Be careful," she replied. "Get back to us alive."

Dean terminated the call.

Pushed his emotions to the side.

Then he filled up the last of the gas cans and loaded them up.

57

Seated behind the wheel of the Civic that was parked under an overpass, Dean gazed through the windshield and did a scan of the Port of Long Beach 100 yards ahead of him. The dock roughly measured about three football fields and was filled to the brim with crates, loading cranes, and a container ship—the *Nuevo Amanecer*—docked beside a large body of water that melted into the horizon. The dull glow of the lamp lights peppered on the dock danced along the tides, the moon shining brightly in the night sky overhead.

Dean slipped out of the Civic. Popped the trunk. Took out a bag of supplies he had grabbed from his father's house, and jerry-rigged a homemade explosive device he learned how to make from a Delta Force guy back when he was in the Rangers.

He attached the device to the gas cans in the trunk.

He loaded up the bags of cash beside it.

Then he rigged the device to blow if someone popped the trunk. He figured he had a 50/50 shot of blowing the Civic sky high before the sun fully rose.

Sorry, Layla.

I'll try to explain it to the insurance company as best I can.

Dean scooped up the rifle wrapped up in the blanket on the front seat, squinting as he did another evaluation of the docks.

They've got snipers covering the area.

Find 'em, and mark 'em.

Dean took out the Remington.

Loaded it with rounds.

Then he fixed the scope on top of it. He took out the steel pipe he'd stuffed with insulation, wrapped it with strips of cloth, and secured it with duct tape. The Remington was now outfitted with his makeshift suppressor.

Dean got down on his belly.

He peered through the scope.

Then he drew a breath and whispered, "Okay, dickheads —where are you?"

Dean surveyed the dock for close to a minute until he located a pair of snipers that had been placed there before his arrival. The first one was lying belly-down on a crane off to the right of the *Nuevo Amanecer*—110 yards away. The second was posted up on a crane on the far opposite side— 90 yards away, both shooters looking about as big as pinky nails through the scope's lens.

Bingo.

Dean made sure when he crafted the suppressor that it would not only cut down on the noise but also conceal enough of the muzzle flare that it wouldn't flag his position. He was also covered enough by the overpass that the only way Hayk and whoever else was on the dock would know their men were down was when they failed to check in over the radio.

Dean lined up the sniper between the sights on the crane on his left.

Held his breath.

Slowly applied pressure to the trigger.

And then the horn of a ferry rang out from somewhere in the distance.

Now.

Dean squeezed off the shot, the sound muffled enough that only someone within 20 yards of him would have heard it go off. A half-second after he fired, he saw the round strike the sniper's skull and split his head in two.

One down.

Dean ejected the depleted round, chambered another, and quickly panned the rifle toward the second sniper posted up in his nest.

He lined up the target's head between the sights.

Breathed.

Squeezed.

Watched the sniper's head whip back as the round struck him in the skull.

Toast.

Dean took one last scan of the area for anything he might have missed.

Spotted nothing.

Then he slung the rifle, slipped into the Civic, and turned over the engine.

58

D ean pulled the Civic toward the gate that opened onto the docks, scanning through the windshield as he kept one hand on the steering wheel and the other on the SIG rested in his lap.

He stopped the car.

Pulled out his burner.

Dialed Hayk's number and waited for just one ring.

"Blackwood," Hayk said. "Where are you?"

"I'm here."

"Pull up to the ship. Do it slowly. You fuck around, your boy dies."

Dean ended the call.

Pocketed the cell.

He drove onto the dock, weaved his way through the obstructions, and parked the Civic next to the gangway that led up to the *Nuevo Amanecer*, the right side of the vehicle facing the containers in a bid to offer him cover.

Dean slipped out of the car, slivers of sunlight cutting through the clouds from the east. He cut a glance toward containers spaced out in 20- to 30-yard increments all throughout the docks, the pre-dawn chill licking at the back of his neck as he positioned himself behind the car's open front door.

Where are you, son?

Where the hell are these bastards keeping you?

Five seconds ticked by.

Ten.

Then two men appeared from around a Japanese shipping container. Dean clocked the Heckler & Koch UMP submachine guns tucked subtly into their leather jackets.

One of them was Hayk.

"Step away from the vehicle," the goon beside Hayk said. "Out in the open."

Dean flashed his middle finger.

"I'm not playing with you." The goon motioned at Dean with his UMP. "Move away from the car."

Dean shook his head. "No chance, idiot boy."

"*Idiot boy?*"

"Yeah, idiot boy. Don't know your name so I gotta call you something."

"Hands up," Hayk said as he and idiot boy spaced apart and drew down on Dean. "Do it now."

Dean squinted to get a better view of idiot boy. He made out bandages on the guy's face and fresh welts on the jaw wounds he had recently acquired.

"You were the one in my hotel room a few hours back," Dean said. "Weren't you?"

"I was." The man gestured to the bandage across his nose. "You broke my nose, asshole."

"Sorry about that." Dean flashed an approving smirk. "You know, you kind of look like that pig-faced fucker from *Star Wars* now."

The goon responded by squeezing off a round that bore

into the pavement by Dean's feet—2 inches shy of striking Dean in his boot.

"Ditch the hardware," he instructed Dean. "Now."

"No dice."

"Quit screwing around, white boy." The goon took aim at Dean's head. "Last time I'm gonna tell you."

"Get fucked, mouth-breather. I've got your money, and it's ready to get blown to hell. Test me. See if I'm bluffing."

A groan puttered out of Hayk. "Cut the shit." He nudged his partner. "The both of you." He fastened his eyes on Dean. "We've got your boy, Blackwood. Just throw down your gear, walk toward us, and he goes free."

Dean pointed to his jacket pocket.

Hayk and his goon raised their weapons.

Then Dean took out the portable radio from his pocket and held it up for them to see. "I click the button," he said, "and the money in the trunk turns to ash."

"Then we shoot you and take it." Hayk shrugged. "Easy fix."

"The device is tamper-proof, genius. You screw with it," Dean flexed his brow, "*Boom!*"

"Bullshit."

It is bullshit.

It's just a radio.

But you two dickheads don't know that.

"Test that theory out then, asshole." Dean tapered his eyes. "See how it works out for you."

One second ticked by.

Two.

Then Hayk raised two fingers, motioned to the cranes beside him, and shouted, "Take him!"

Nothing happened.

Only the sounds of the ocean breeze blew through.

Then idiot boy got on his radio and put out a command to the snipers who were no longer there.

"*Whoops,*" Dean said. "Looks like your boys might've taken five there, brother."

"Not bad." Hayk laughed and flexed his brow. "Doesn't change a goddamn thing though. You're outgunned and outnumbered, Blackwood."

"You think this is going to be that easy, huh?"

"I do."

Dean locked eyes with Hayk.

Hayk eased his finger around the trigger.

Idiot boy took a step forward and flexed his grip on his weapon.

Three.

Dean flexed his hand.

Two.

Hayk gnashed his teeth.

Go.

59

I diot boy focused his weapon, eyes narrowed.

Dean drew out his SIG.

Squeezed off a single round and struck the guy square in the center of his forehead.

One-point-five seconds flat.

Then Dean swept his weapon to the left, rattled off a pair of rounds, and shot Hayk in the sternum—but the bullets caught Hayk in the Kevlar strapped to his chest. The thug fired his HK blindly in response, the bullets chewing up the right side of the Civic as Dean dropped into a crouch behind the driver's door.

Shit.

Should've aimed higher, Deano.

Hayk side-stepped his way into concealment behind the container behind him, emptying his magazine into the hood of the Civic and perforating it with a series of rounds to the point that the car looked like Swiss cheese.

Dean peeked over the hood.

Fired off two shots.

As soon as Hayk ducked into cover behind the container,

he cut a glance to his right, saw a container 20 yards away, and ran toward it.

Dean arrived at the edge of the container.

Gripped his SIG in both hands.

Then he slowly peeked around the corner, saw Hayk stepping out from his position, and ducked back into cover as Hayk rattled off another series of rounds.

Dean hissed through his teeth.

He heard Hayk's gun go dry with a *click*.

Then he stepped out, squeezed off four more rounds toward Hayk, and saw the mobster sprint toward another series of shipping containers 30 yards behind his original position.

Go.

Move.

Now!

Dean sprinted toward Hayk's position, his legs and lungs on fire. Some CO back in his Ranger unit would've chewed his ass out, rung him upside the head for storming in head-first like he was—but he was pissed.

He wanted Hayk dead.

"*Kill* him, laddie!" Woody insisted. "Get him! Put your hands around his throat! Look him right in the eyes and *squeeze* the life out of him!"

Dean approached a container on his left.

Turned the corner.

And then Hayk came out of cover with his submachine gun raised and ready to fire.

Hayk swiped his UMP at Dean's SIG.

Knocked it out of his grip.

The weapon skidded out of Dean's hand and coasted along the pavement.

Dean seized Hayk's weapon with both hands, raising it

toward the sky as Hayk emptied the magazine before the gun racked back empty.

Dean ripped the UMP from Hayk's grip.

Struck him against the skull with it.

Hayk fell to the ground.

Dean tossed the weapon.

Hayk shot to his feet.

Then two men then squared off like boxers revving up in the ring, teeth clenched and eyes wide as they slowly closed the gap.

60

H ayk spit on the ground. "Okay, Blackwood." He held his head high. "*Hima du merrnir*."

Now you die.

Dean rolled his eyes.

How original.

The two men inched closer.

Hayk flexed his fingers.

Dean slipped off his leather jacket.

Then Hayk rushed toward Dean, cocked back a fist, and howled as he prepared to strike a blow against Dean's jaw.

Dean planted his feet.

Reached behind his back.

Then he whipped out his father's KABAR from the back of his pants, thrust it forward, and buried the blade in Hayk's windpipe.

"You're right," Dean hissed through his teeth. "That *was* easy." With one hand on Hayk's shirt, Dean lowered the thug to the ground as Hayk's skin paled and blood seeped slowly out of the wound.

The thug's eyes widened.

His mouth slackened.

Then his eyes rolled back into his skull as he sputtered out his final breath.

Dean released his grip.

Pulled out the blade and wiped the blood off it.

Then he sheathed it, scooped up his SIG, and did a press-check of the rounds.

He spun in a circle, a palpable silence settling over the docks, only the caw of a seagull and the distant blare of a foghorn cutting through the void.

Where are you, son?

Dean's nostrils flared.

Where are they holding you?

"I'm here!" he shouted. "Show yourself or I swear to God I'll blow the money."

No reply.

Silence.

"*Answer me!*" Dean grumbled. "You've got five seconds!"

One second ticked by.

Two.

Then a familiar, gravelly voice called out, "In here," from an office unit 20 yards ahead to Dean's right.

Dean tightened his grip on the SIG and marched slowly toward the office, squinting as he made out a single light glowing through one of the fogged, barred-up windows.

He arrived at the door.

Took a step back.

Then he raised his foot, kicked the door in, and swiftly made his way inside.

61

The door to the office slammed against the wall.

Dean rushed inside.

His heart shot into his throat the moment he saw Jeremy, his eyes red and swollen as a robust man built like a bull held him close with a meaty arm wrapped around his chest.

"*Pally*," Dean said. "Are you okay?"

Jeremy nodded, tears streaming down his cheeks as he looked at his father with a pleading set of eyes.

"Drop the gun," the man holding Jeremy said as he pressed the compact Beretta in his hand flush against the boy's temple. "Right now."

Dean recognized the voice instantly.

It was the man he spoke to over the phone.

Aram fucking *Sarkissian*.

The mob boss clocked in at 6 foot 4 inches, 250 pounds. His fingers and wrists were peppered with gold jewelry. Cracks in his dark skin from years of chain-smoking also coated his menacing pair of blue eyes with a bile-like patina.

Aram flexed his grip on the Beretta. "Let's make a deal. You leave the office, and I take your boy outside. Once I get my hands on the money, I'll release him, and we both can walk away from this."

Dean adjusted his sweat-coated palm on the grip of his weapon. "No deal. The rollers are on their way over. You've got no say in how this plays out." He extended the SIG out further. "Now, let the kid go."

Aram shifted his massive weight.

Dean eased his finger across the trigger.

Jeremy looked at his father entreatingly as the sounds of emergency sirens gathered in the distance.

"You hear that?" Dean said. "That's the fucking cavalry. You're running out of time. You've got maybe two minutes before the SWAT team rolls in hot and cuts you to pieces."

Aram shot a look toward the windows.

The sirens grew louder.

"If I go down," he said, "I *will* take your son with me."

"*Dad*," Jeremy stifled his tears, "I'm scared."

"It's okay, buddy," his father assured him. "Everything's going to be okay."

"Don't make promises you can't keep, Blackwood," Aram said. "Don't be a fool like your father was."

Dean's eyes widened.

His stomach twisted into a knot.

The memory of Tommy's death played back at high speed.

"You gave the order to kill my brother," Dean said as he tightened his grip on the SIG. "You're the deranged fuck who gave the green light to kill him."

"Well, if your father had thought things through," Aram shrugged off Dean's comment, "your brother would still be alive. Take a lesson from that." He pressed the muzzle of the gun harder into Jeremy's temple. "Your son is about to follow in step with your brother if you don't put that gun down."

"Which one of you greaseball pieces of shit did it?" Dean asked. "Give me that much."

"You want to know who killed your brother?"

"I do." Dean answered. "And you're going to tell me."

Aram was silent.

He smirked.

Then he said, "I was planning on killing both you and your brother. You just moved out of the way of the car in time when I ran him over." Aram pouted his lip dismissively. "I guess that makes you lucky."

The newsflash made Dean feel like his legs were about to buckle.

His hand gripping the SIG trembled.

"You..." Dean batted his eyelids. "*You* killed him?"

"No, I ran him over," Aram clarified. "Technically the car killed him." He huffed. "That was the last time I ever had to get my hands dirty, actually. I don't relish killing a child, but it had to be done."

Dean, red-faced, had never felt a stronger urge to kill another human being in his life.

The sirens grew louder.

Red and blue lights flooded in through the windows.

Dean eased his finger tighter on the trigger of his SIG and glared at the man who murdered his brother.

He deserves to die, he thought.

The bastard who killed Tommy finally ran out of places to hide.

"*Kill him,*" the voice in Dean's head whispered. "You've been waiting for this your whole life. What are the chances, laddie? This is fate right here. Just end him and avenge Tommy's death once and for all."

Dean's nostrils flared.

The expressionless murderer caressed the trigger of his Beretta. "Your son is about to die, Blackwood," he said, his left arm hooked around Jeremy Blackwood's neck, his right hand pressing a Beretta against the boy's temple. "And I'm going to make you watch. I can live with being in a cell," his eyes glinted darkly, "but I know you can't live with *this*."

Dean clenched his teeth.

The man who killed his brother smirked.

A single tear rolled down Jeremy's cheek.

"Pally," Dean whispered to his child, "don't look."

His son closed his eyes.

Aram depressed his trigger.

Dean held his breath and did the same.

62

Two shots fired.

Dean's bullet struck Aram in the neck.

The mob boss's round merely clipped Dean in his left ear.

Dean rushed to Jeremy, blood flowing from the piece of flesh that had been ripped from his ear as he kicked Aram's Beretta away and scooped up his son in an embrace.

"*Pally*!" Dean ran his hands over every inch of Jeremy, his son crying hysterically and burying his face in his father's chest. "Are you hurt?" Dean said.

Jeremy shook his head, his response nonverbal and limited to gasps, hiccups, and a thousand-yard stare.

"I'm so sorry, son." Dean squeezed his eyelids shut. "I am *so* sorry."

Aram gurgled.

Dean snapped open his eyes and cut a glance toward the mob boss. Despite the fact that the brute had been clipped in the neck, he was still very much alive.

"End it," Aram groaned. "End it *now*."

Dean placed Jeremy down.

Pushed him to the side.

Dean stood up, raised his SIG, and trained the sights on Aram's head.

"Kill me," Aram pleaded. "Finish it."

Dean's finger slowly depressed the trigger. All his rage, torment, and pain of the past and present channeled into that moment.

"Do it," Woody beckoned. "You *want* this." He emitted a primal-like growl. "You *need* this. This is who you *are*."

Dean stared deep into Aram's eyes.

He looked at his son.

Then he stepped back, lowered his weapon, and secured it in his holster.

"*Why*?" Aram said with a dimwitted expression.

Dean scooped up his son.

Embraced him.

Then he told Aram, "That's not who I am anymore," as booted footsteps and radio chatter ascended toward the office.

The door flew open.

Dean angled his body around.

An FBI SWAT team rushed inside.

"*Freeze*!" the one in the lead yelled. "FBI!"

Dean held up his hands.

"Identify yourself," another agent chimed in. "*Now*!"

"Blackwood," Dean said as he held his son close. "*Special Agent* Blackwood."

63

Dean sat on the hood of the Civic as four FBI agents in windbreakers pulled the duffel bags of cash out from the back. Wilson was beside him. Jeremy was seated on the edge of an ambulance where an EMT gave him water and a blanket.

Jeremy waved at his father.

Dean winked in reply.

He's going to have nightmares from this.

Forever.

Dean closed his eyes.

Claire will never forgive me.

Jesus Christ.

What the hell did I do?

"You're lucky," Wilson said. "You know that, right?"

"Yeah," Dean replied. "I know." He turned his gaze up toward the helicopter circling overhead, the bird's spotlight sweeping across the Long Beach PD patrolmen, FBI agents, and emergency vehicles scattered along the docks.

"So what happens now?" Dean asked. "You guys hauling me away in cuffs or what?"

Wilson gestured to the cash. The bodies. Aram Sarkissian being loaded into the back of an ambulance. "This is a big get, D. Wouldn't have happened if you hadn't broken the rules."

"It's not over though."

"What do you mean?"

"Eldridge," Dean said. "He's still walking around. We know he was in league with Sarkissian who's gonna sing his heart out to try to cut a deal with the FBI. He'll turn on Eldridge. The only problem is that Eldridge is going to pull every string he can to make sure he dodges any blowback from this thing. Plus, we never figured out who was taking out the guys in his unit."

Wilson kicked at the ground. "I've been ruminating on that too."

Wait a second.

Dean squinted.

Wait, maybe there's a solution here.

"What is it?" Wilson said. "I can see you brewing up something in that little mind of yours."

"I am," Dean replied, a second wind hitting him as he pulled the SAC off to the side. "I think I have an idea."

64

The television inside Eldridge's living room was playing at a low volume. The images on the screen showcased the madness that had played out at the Port of Long Beach. Eldridge's gaze was fastened to the screen, a glass of top-shelf whiskey in his hand. He smirked approvingly as he took a long, generous sip.

"A disgraced FBI agent," the reporter on the TV said, "was at the center of a shootout tonight at the Port of Long Beach. The agent, Dean Blackwood, is currently on the run after shooting several high-ranking members of an Armenian Mob element."

The shot switched to a photograph of Dean.

Eldridge couldn't help but laugh.

"The FBI," the reporter continued, "and the Long Beach Police Department are asking for any information that will assist in the apprehension of Agent Blackwood. Authorities wish to stress that Blackwood, a decorated member of the United States Army Ranger unit, is a highly-skilled professional who should be considered armed and extremely dangerous."

Eldridge swirled his whiskey as he wandered out of the living room. "Solid work, kid," he mumbled under his breath. "You managed to dig your own grave, you dumb bastard."

He took another sip of his drink.

Placed the glass in the sink.

Prepared to move upstairs to pack his bags for Cabo.

Then a rustling noise from the backyard piqued his attention.

Eldridge spun around.

Took out his .38.

He cocked back the hammer, raised the weapon, and swept it from left to right, his eyes scanning his sprawling backyard through the pair of double doors that led onto the back porch.

"*Sweetheart*?" his wife called out from upstairs. "You need to pack *two pairs* of trunks this time, okay?"

"Sure thing," Eldridge replied. "Just give me a minute."

He waited.

Held the weapon steady.

Heard a breeze blow through and figured it must've been the wind kicking up a pile of leaves.

"You're good, Eldy," the SMASH captain whispered to himself as he lowered the .38. "Nothing to worry—"

A sharp metal *click* rang out behind him.

He turned around and came face to face with Dean Blackwood, the disgraced FBI agent whose SIG was trained at the center of his head.

"You're a sneaky son of a bitch," Eldridge said, "aren't you?"

"Gun down."

Eldridge tossed his .38.

"Heard your wife a second ago," Dean said as he pointed a finger with his free hand toward the ceiling. "Should we bring her downstairs for this?"

"You keep her out of this, you *fuck*," Eldridge grumbled as the vein in his forehead protruded. "She's got nothing to do with this. And if you're smart, which I seriously doubt you are, you're not going to do something as stupid as offing a high-ranking member of the LAPD."

"*Darling*," Eldridge's wife called out again. "Are you coming?"

Dean drew a breath.

Eldridge glared.

"Does she know about you?" Dean asked. "Does your wife know that you killed your own men? That you're in league with the mob?"

"Of course she doesn't. I'm not stupid, Blackwood," Eldridge snickered, "not like you and your family, that is."

"Keep talking to me like that, and your funeral is going to be closed casket."

"You're not going to shoot me, you spineless little *shit*. I've got you by the balls. The whole world is about to come crashing down around you. I've got the pull. I've got the juice. I worked too hard and too long to be in the position I'm in to not have it."

Dean pressed the end of the SIG into Eldridge's forehead. "You screwed up. Your little scheme to pin this on Haywood backfired on you *gloriously*."

"Keep telling yourself that, kid," Eldridge said. "There's only one of us who's going to walk out of this clean. To hell with you. To hell with the Sarkissians. By this time tomorrow, my face is going to be all over the news. You kill me, I'm a hero. No, you're the only one in deep shit here, kid. You *and* your old man. I've made sure this whole thing gets pegged on him if it goes south, which it has. I can make this look however I want it to, even if I'm dead."

"Well," Dean snapped back the SIG's hammer, "I guess we've got nothing else to talk about then, do we?"

"You're making a mistake," Eldridge said. "You've got every law enforcement element on the planet looking for you."

"I don't care."

"You won't shoot me."

"I've shot someone three times tonight already," Dean said. "I consider that a warmup."

Eldridge's nostrils flared.

Dean could see the fear welling up in the man's eyes. "Why did you take out the other members in your unit?" Dean asked. "Why did you kill Vendrell? Mohr? Harlow? Why did you push Adams down a flight of stairs, huh? Tell me that much."

"You should've played ball like your old man," Eldridge said. "You shouldn't have fought this. You should've let Haywood take the fall."

"You ordered Sarkissian to kill my brother."

"Because your father threatened to shut down the most lucrative operation I've had going for *years*. You're lucky it was your brother and not you. Hell, I had to talk Sarkissian out of wiping your entire family out."

Dean grabbed a fistful of Eldridge's shirt, swung him around, and pinned him to a wall. "I want the truth, you deranged son of a bitch," he grumbled. "Tell me."

"God damn you—"

"*Now.*"

"Oh, for crying out loud," Eldridge growled as he shot a look toward the staircase. "It's not a long walk, you asshole.

My boys in the SMASH unit were getting squirrely. We were on the cusp of cashing out our account with Sarkissian, and they wanted more than they agreed to."

"I don't get it." Dean winced. "You're saying you killed off your own people because they got *greedy*?"

"I didn't kill anybody," Eldridge said. "It was Mohr. I assigned him to take out Vendrell, Wyler, and Harlow. It was easy. The degenerate bastard was on the edge. Mohr just needed a little push, and I had enough blackmail on him to get him to comply."

"Who tried to kill me and Mohr?" Dean asked. "That night I approached him, someone tried to run us over."

"*That* was me," Eldridge said. "The second I knew Mohr was about to double back on our plan, I tried to take you both out." He rattled off a chuckle. "I tried to take you both out just like Sarkissian did to your brother."

"You're fucking *sick*."

"I cared about my boys, but I'm not about to let anyone get in the way of my retirement. It's about *my* bottom line at the end of the day, plain and simple." Eldridge's eyes lit up with a sinister glare. "It's *done*, you fucking cretin. Haywood took the fall just like I wanted him to. No matter what you do, I got away with this, and there's not a damn thing you can do about it."

"You can't get away with this." Dean eased the gun under the captain's chin. "You won't."

"I *will*," Eldridge said. "I *am*."

He shot a fist into Dean's gut.

Doubled him over.

Then he took possession of the SIG, hooked his leg behind Dean's and dropped him to the floor.

Dean groaned as he fell to the floor, cradling his stomach as Eldridge pressed the SIG to the back of his head.

"Age lends experience, son," Eldridge said. "And I've got a hell of a lot more of it than you do, little shit. You should have let this go." He waved the weapon around. "And now you're gonna die because you couldn't help yourself from sticking your nose where it shouldn't have been."

"*Lawrence*?" Eldridge's wife shouted from the top of the stairs. "What was—?"

"I broke a dish," The SMASH captain hollered back. "Just stay upstairs."

"Is everything—?"

"*Stay upstairs!*"

Eldridge rolled his eyes.

Dean did the same.

"You really fucked up my night here, kid," Eldridge said. "Thanks for that."

"Pull the trigger, Captain." Dean tapered his eyes. "End it."

"Will do." Eldridge took a step back. "Say hi to your brother for me."

Eldridge depressed the trigger.

The hammer snapped, but the gun didn't go off.

Dean stood up.

Eldridge tried to fire again.

Dean snatched the weapon away.

"Helps if the gun has bullets," Dean said as he ripped open his shirt to reveal the wire tap on his chest.

Eldridge's mouth dropped open.

Dean shrugged.

Then a trio of FBI SWAT members and SAC Kent Wilson trailing right behind them kicked open the front door.

"This is the part," Dean said as he secured a grip on the

back of Eldridge's neck, "where you put your hands up, motherfucker."

Eldridge did as instructed.

The SWAT team lowered him to the ground.

Then Dean took a pair of cuffs, secured Eldridge's wrists, and breathed the biggest sigh he had in days.

65

Two weeks had passed. Aram Sarkissian—handcuffed to a bed and tethered to machines—was still alive. Tyler Adams was still in his coma. Dean's father was in a daze. Larry Eldridge was in a cell, his wife was in hysterics over revelations that had been made, and Dean had been prohibited from seeing Jeremy until Claire could process the situation better, which were the exact words she spoke as they strolled down a sidewalk that offered a resplendent view of the ocean.

"I don't know what to say," Claire said, her face stricken with a mix of hate, sadness, and regret. "You put our son in harm's way. You've..." She clenched a fist. "You've seriously fucked him in ways we haven't even seen play out yet."

She's right.

Dean put his gaze on the ocean tides.

Don't say anything.

Regret washed over him in a cascading wave.

You'll just make it worse than it already is.

"You promised me," Claire said as she terminated her

stride. "You told me you had turned your back on your old life, on the way things used to be."

"Claire..." Dean struggled to find the words, his mind adrift in a current of uncertainty. "I'm sorry. I'm not sure what else I can say."

"There's nothing you can say."

"I know."

"Jeremy's a mess."

"I'm aware."

"We're *all* a mess, and you're responsible for it—for all of it." Deep red hues tinted Claire's complexion. "You son of a bitch." She crossed her arms defensively. "I should've known better." She wiped away the tear that slid down her cheek. "I should've known you could never change."

"That's not true."

"*Oh*, right," Claire laughed and rolled her eyes, "then I take it that the last few weeks and everything that happened was just a one-off." She stepped closer to her ex-husband. "You just don't get it, do you? You pride yourself with your sobriety. You wear it like a badge of fucking honor, but you've failed your entire life to see what your real addiction is. You're a fiend for *chaos*, Dean. You relish the action. It..." her eyes probed the sky for the words, "it wields a kind of high that you just can't turn your back on."

She's right.

You can't steer clear of it.

You can't turn away from it no matter how hard you try.

What's wrong with you, Dean?

Why can't you just be normal?

"The night Jeremy was taken," Claire said as her gaze drifted toward the beach, "the second I knew he was gone, my first thought wasn't panic. It wasn't fear or anger or any of the things a mother should feel when her child has been put in danger. The moment I knew he was taken, the first thought I had was, 'I knew this was coming.' Can you believe that?" She threw up her hands. "In the back of my mind, no matter how much distance you put between yourself and the past, I always knew that what happened was always going to happen."

Dean said nothing.

"I don't know where we go from here," Claire said as she brushed her hand through the air. "I can't have you at the house. I can't let you near Jeremy. Until the time comes—*if* the time comes—I need you as far away from us as possible."

"Don't take my son away from me." A light mist coated Dean's eyes. "*Please*. I can't live without him. I don't know what my life even *is* without him. I lost you. That was my fault, but I *cannot* lose him."

"He's still your son," Claire assured him. "You are still his father." She hung her head. "But you need to stay away, at least for a little while. You can call. You can still talk to him. But until I can find some peace of mind with you, with all of..." she gestured from Dean's toes to his temples, "*this*, I need you to respect my wishes."

Dean was quiet.

Processed the information.

Then he mumbled, "I understand," and said nothing more.

After that, Claire left, Dean gazing out to the ebb and flow of the tides. The dull roar of the ocean was the only thing that offered him some semblance of comfort.

"You know this was always bound to happen," Woody said. "You know that. Don't you, laddie?"

I avenged Tommy.

I shut down Eldridge.

I cleared Haywood.

I helped Kara's family find peace, but at the cost of this.

My son.

My life as I know it.

"This is your fault," Dean whispered. "I thought I had you under control."

"It's all an illusion, my friend," Woody replied. "Always has been, always will be. I'm with you for the long haul. I've got more say in this than you think I do."

Dean clenched a fist.

Angled his body around.

Saw a tattoo parlor a half-block away and smirked as a thought entered his mind.

"Don't do it, Deano," Woody protested. "*Don't.*"

"Fuck you, little man," Dean replied. "I'm the one calling the shots."

The lanky tattoo artist, ink covering his entire chest, pushed his rolling chair back and motioned to Dean's shoulder. "What do you think?"

Dean stood.

Approached the mirror.

Examined the silver-dollar-sized, disheveled leprechaun on his left shoulder with the red circle around it and the slash that ran across it.

"I like it," Dean said. "I like it a lot."

He waited for Woody to retort.

He didn't.

Dean paid.

Headed out.

Felt a bit of relief wash over him as he took another glance at the fresh ink before he slipped his jacket on.

Not a permanent solution.

Still a good start though.

66

"Aram Sarkissian gave up everything on Eldridge from his hospital room," Layla said to Dean, the two of them seated in chairs on the balcony of her apartment in downtown LA. "It's going to take a while for the dust to settle and all the charges to be leveled, but Sarkissian, Eldridge, and everyone else they were in league with are looking at sentences that'll probably stretch into the Rapture. Still a few details and confessions they need. This whole thing was a mess."

"Every case is," Dean said. "Nothing is black and white."

Layla shook her head and surveyed the towering structures that flanked her building. "It still amazes me that Eldridge did all this so he could cut his own people out of their share of the money. It's hard to fathom."

"Not for me," Dean said. "Men have killed for less. Honestly, Eldridge trying to pin this on Haywood and pull this elaborate scheme to hoard his money was the biggest mistake he made. If he had kept to his deal with Sarkissian and cashed out like he'd planned, he might've gotten away with it."

"What about Haywood?" Layla asked. "What's going to happen?"

"His name is getting cleared. The word I got is that the family is getting a good settlement out of it from the department too. I pushed Wilson to do a press conference to make it public. Should happen within the next few days."

"That's great."

"Make sure you make it a point to highlight that in your article."

"Trust me," Layla said, "I will." She settled back in her chair. "What about Tyler Adams? How's he doing?"

"He's recovering," Dean said. "But he's partially paralyzed in his left hand and left leg. He's still in the hospital. I feel bad for the kid. He's stuck in there watching movies all day and suffering for what Eldridge put everyone through, me included. I've stopped in a few times to see him. He's doing okay."

"What about your son?"

Dean averted his gaze. "His mother's pissed. I took about two steps forward and a hundred back with both of them after all this."

"You saved his life."

"I *endangered* it. I may have saved him but I just gave that kid a lifetime's worth of nightmares in the process." Dean stood up and braced the railing in front of him. "I agreed to do something I shouldn't have done. I found the guy who killed my brother. I learned some hard truths about my father, but part of me wishes I never got involved in all of this. If I hadn't stepped in—"

"More people would have died," Layla insisted. "Haywood would have been accused of something he didn't do, and Larry Eldridge would still be using his badge to commit crimes with impunity. And your son is going to live a full life now—he's alive. That counts for something." She stood up and joined Dean by the railing. "I don't want to shortchange the cost you've had to pay for all of this. I just want you to know that some good came of it."

"I hope so," Dean replied. "And it's going to take me a while to come to terms with that. Hell, after I get through this meeting with the brass this afternoon, I don't know what my future entails. I could be picking up litter off the highway until next spring in an orange jumpsuit for all I know." He waved his hand through the air. "But enough about that shit. I'll deal with it." He shot out his chin. "How's the article going?"

"I have to fine-tune a few details with the editor," Layla said. "He really enjoyed the last part of the article where you pulled that ruse on Eldridge with the news bit and got him to confess, by the way. He said it read like a Jason Bourne novel. He told me some guy he knows at Universal was talking about the film rights."

"No, thanks," Dean said. "I *lived* it. Don't need to see some third-rate action picture made about it."

"That guy from *Halo* could play you. You kind of look like him, you know."

"Yeah." Dean rolled his eyes. "I get that a lot."

The two shared the silence for a moment, a cool breeze licking at the back of Dean's neck.

"So what happens after this is done?" Layla said, her eyes brimming with anticipation. "Are you going back to your little cabin in the woods?"

"Just to get my stuff," Dean said. "I'm moving back here. I don't know what the immediate future with Claire and Jeremy looks like, but I still want to be closer to home. My dad took a bit of a turn after everything. Pretty sure the stress put some strain on his ticker. He needs me here."

"That's good to know. Might be nice having you closer to my home base. I mean," Layla shrugged, "I still might need to get a blurb or two from you for the article."

"For you, Layla," Dean picked up his leather jacket and slipped it on, "you can have as many as you need." He looked deep into her eyes, his admiration for Layla—and the fact that he felt like she was the only one still on his side —triggered a warm sensation to spread across his chest. "Thank you," he said. "For everything. I couldn't have done this without you."

"Likewise."

"Don't go too far."

"Same."

Dean stuck out his hand.

Layla shook it.

Then he made his way toward the door.

"*Dean*," Layla called out.

He turned around.

"What're your thoughts on pasta?"

"I'm a fan."

"Friday night," Layla said. "Here—8:00." She flexed her brow. "Unless you have any objections."

Dean shook his head. "Not in the slightest."

Layla reached out her hand.

Dean did the same.

The two interlocked their fingers and gave each other a reassuring squeeze.

67

Dean wasn't sure how long he had been seated at the conference room table. It might've been an hour, maybe even three, but to him, it felt like an entire day had passed as he told the story of his takedown of Eldridge and the Sarkissians over and over again.

"Agent Blackwood," the dark-skinned woman across from Dean said. "Is the information in your deposition here accurate?"

Dean turned up his bleary eyes and looked at the two members from the Office of Professional Responsibility seated across from him. "I have no reason to lie, ma'am."

"Then you understand," the mustached man beside the woman chimed in as he sifted through the files in front of him, "that your conduct in the past several weeks, your wanton disregard for both procedure and authority, has prompted a series of—"

Wilson, seated beside Dean, held up his hand. "With all due respect, Mr. Beam, this incessant lambasting of Agent Blackwood has been pretty consistent throughout the course of your line of questioning." He pivoted his gaze to the woman. "Same with you, Ms. Brandt."

"Underscoring the significant, well," Brandt shrugged, "*damage* that Agent Blackwood has done to the Bureau's reputation as well as the plenitude of insurance claims filed by this agency as well as the LA, Long Beach, and Glendale PDs as a result of Agent Blackwood's actions is a matter this department does not and *will* not take lightly."

"Your boy is in deep shit, Wilson," Beam said as he tapped his finger on the files. "We have good reason to lock Agent Blackwood up for a long stretch of time, all convictions of the guilty parties notwithstanding."

"You operated well out of your bounds, Agent Blackwood," Brandt added. "And I don't think you appreciate the severity of the situation you're in. You decided to take it upon yourself to use your badge and operate as a one-man army. You took it upon yourself—"

"So I'm the asshole," Dean cut in, throwing up his hands as he leaned back in his chair. "For crissakes, you fuckers really know how to redefine the whole broken record adage."

Brandt crossed her arms.

Beam shook his head.

"Dean," Wilson whispered, "cool it."

"The hell with that." Dean shook his head, straightened his posture, and flattened his palms on the table. "You guys wanna burn me—*burn me*. You wanna run in circles around the same story over and over again—*fine.* I did what I did. What happened, happened. Just quit wasting my time wagging your fingers at me and droning on about the OT that's gonna get pulled filing the paperwork."

A few seconds ticked by.

Beam and Brandt exchanged whispers.

Wilson glared at Dean for him speaking his mind.

"Agent Blackwood," Beam said. "There is a long road to travel down before there is anything in the way of a final statement being made on the matter of what will happen to you or your career. What I *can* say is that when all is said and done, I feel that formal charges against you will be filed."

Knuckles rapped on the door.

The heads in the room turned.

Dean's eyes widened when he recognized the Director of the FBI, Tim Wheelan, poking his head into the room.

68

N*o way.* Dean cocked his head to the side. *The director came down from Washington for* this?

"Pardon me," Wheelan said, flashing his million-dollar smile as he unfastened the top button of his coat. "I hope I'm not interrupting."

"Director Wheelan," Brandt said as she and Beam shot up from the table. "We were just—"

"I'd like to speak with the two of you outside." Wheelan squinted. "Privately."

Beam and Brandt exchanged glances.

They left the room.

Wilson leaned into Dean's ear as the director spoke with them outside. "This is odd," he said. "Really out of character."

"Yeah." Dean nodded. "I was thinking the same."

Five whole minutes went by, Dean watching through the window as Wheelan spoke with curt gestures to Brandt and Beam before they walked back into the room, took their files, left, and didn't so much as offer anything in the way of a furtive glance at Dean as they headed out.

Then Wheelan entered.

Took a chair.

Flashed his pearly-white grill and settled back. "Agent Blackwood. How are you holding up?"

"Good." Dean furrowed his brow. "I've, uh...I've never had the pleasure of meeting you in person before, sir."

"The pleasure is all mine." Wheelan chuckled. "It's good to meet the man who waged a one-man war against the LAPD *and* the Armenian Mob. I mean, good *God*, man." He waved his hand through the air amusedly. "I still don't know how you pulled that off."

Dean said nothing.

"Director Wheelan," Wilson said, "in regard to what happened with Agent Blackwood—"

"I'm well versed," Wheelan cut in, "with what has transpired, Agent Wilson. There's no need to continue to go through all the details. I am simply here to offer Agent Blackwood my gratitude for what he has done." His top-shelf bureaucratic grin was on full display. "You did this Bureau a *hell* of a service, my friend, and as far as anything in the way of, well, let's call it 'repercussions,' you have nothing to worry about. The matter, as of here and now, has ended. Agent Blackwood is, as the saying goes, 'in the clear.' The same applies to your father, by the way. As of today, all pending charges pertaining to his involvement with the Larry Eldridge money laundering operation have been dropped."

Dean was stunned.

Based on the pale look on Wilson's face, he figured he was as well.

"Sir, I..." Dean felt like he was out of breath. "I don't know what to say."

"There's nothing to say," Wheelan replied. "You are a

valued asset to the Bureau. Your tactics, your methods—however unorthodox they may be—are ones I hold in great regard. You should be commended, not put through an endless string of inquiries for having taken down a series of crooked and amoral individuals whose imminent testimonies have opened up many, *many* doors for us in terms of future investigations. If anything," he laughed, "I should be asking you what *you* want and what *I* can do to help in providing that."

Dean looked at Wilson.

The SAC said nothing.

"To be honest, Director Wheelan," Dean cleared his throat, "I want a clean slate. I..." His hand grazed the FBI shield clipped to his hip "I want to resign. I want to start fresh. I had a hell of a run with this thing, and I'm trying to," the fresh tattoo on his shoulder itched, "I need to switch gears here to something simpler, less chaotic, and I feel tendering my resignation is a good step in that direction."

The director's smile dissolved. "I see." He inched closer to the table. "Last I heard, you had a few years of this so-called 'simpler' living. You were living in a cozy little cabin owned by the Bureau somewhere up in Oregon, correct?"

"Yes, sir." Dean nodded. "That's correct."

"Chasing down bad checks, I believe."

"I was."

"So," Wheelan said, "you had your reprieve. You were well rested, and once we placed you back in the field," his smile returned, "look what happened. You took down, singlehandedly, both a corrupt faction of the LAPD as well as an element of the Armenian Mob. It would take hundreds of agents and years of field work to garner those kinds of results. You did it in weeks. I'm sorry, but," he wagged a finger, "a man of your talents is one we simply can't throw by the wayside. As my late grandmother said, 'Waste not, want not.'"

Dean squinted curiously.

Wilson furrowed his brow.

"Sir," Dean said, "I want to make it clear that I don't want to work for the Bureau anymore. I'm done." He unclipped his shield and slid it across the table. "I just want my pension and my life back to the way it was before all this happened."

Wheelan narrowed his eyes.

Tapped his finger.

Stood and then paced the room.

"Agent Blackwood," he said, his tone graver and more menacing, "you have worked for this Bureau for a long time. During the course of your career, you have taken down some of the most high-caliber suspects we have ever come across," he held up a pair of fingers, "two of whom were on our Most Wanted list." He approached the window and gazed out to the city. "If you think that someone with your faculties is going to just," he snapped his fingers, "up and quit, you're sorely mistaken."

"Sir..." Dean slowly rose from his chair. "I making it clear—"

"And *I'm* making it clear," Wheelan growled, the lines in his face tightening into a wicked grimace, "that you aren't going anywhere. You think that my clearing your name was easy? You think you've survived as long as you have in this game because you're *lucky*? The only reason you are still around is because my predecessors and I have shielded you from any fallout."

Dean's nostrils flared.

His complexion reddened.

Then his fingers slowly curled into a fist.

"You listen to me," Wheelan hissed. "And you listen well, Agent Blackwood. Unless you want to spend your life rotting in a cell, I'd suggest you take a seat, seal your mouth, and clue in to what I'm about to tell you."

Dean thought about charging, pummeling the director into oblivion, but then he thought about Jeremy.

The life he wanted.

The life he had to earn back even if it took him until his dying breath.

So he took a seat.

Stared straight ahead.

Tamped down his anger as Wilson clapped a hand on his shoulder and squeezed.

"I hate to dress you down, my friend," Wheelan said as he retook his seat at the table, "but in this case, it's warranted." He interlaced his fingers and rested them on the table. "I want to make something clear to you. After that job you had in El Paso years ago, we knew we had a rock star on our hands. The only problem was that we knew you were burned out. We knew we needed to give you some time to recharge and clean up before we put you back in the field."

"Director Wheelan," Wilson said, speaking slowly with his shoulders hunched slightly, "Agent Blackwood *chose* to take up this job, and it was—"

"Because you asked him to?" The director shook his head. "In many ways, Dean actually never had a choice in the matter. You see, we *knew* he would take on the job based on the circumstances that surrounded it. After all, we have an entire division of experts dedicated to predicting people's movements, so we knew once Dean learned that Aram Sarkissian had killed his brother—"

"*Wait*," Dean said, his eyes widening as his brain struggled to process the information, "you *knew* that Sarkissian killed my brother?"

"Yes." Wheelan nodded. "We knew for some time."

Dean gnashed his teeth. "You son of a—"

"*Watch it.*"

Dean took a break to calm his nerves. "You knew about Sarkissian," he finally said. "You knew more than you were divulging. You knew all along, and you kept it from me."

"Because we needed you to do," Wheelan said, "what you do best. We had it on good authority that Sarkissian was in league with Eldridge. We only had bits and pieces of the information, mind you, and though we tried all other avenues in an effort to bring them down, we were failing. Eldridge and Sarkissian were doing a damn good job of staying one step ahead of us for years, thanks in part to Sarkissian's connections he had in the federal government." He pinned his simmering gaze on Dean. "And then you came in, and we knew that once you'd piece together that Sarkissian killed your brother, you'd take him down without thinking twice."

Dean looked down.

Slumped down in his chair.

Blinked twice and started to wonder if it was all a bad dream.

"The orders that came from the top," Dean said. "When Wilson said that people at Hoover told me to look into this, it was you. You wanted to set me loose on Sarkissian and Eldridge this whole time because you knew you couldn't do it through the regular channels."

"And if you turned us down," Wheelan said with a palpable confidence, "we would have more than mildly insisted. You're an *asset*, Blackwood. We've spent millions of dollars training you into what you are today, and you will continue to do what I tell you to do until the day comes that you outlive your usefulness. This is the game, son," he chuckled, "and you play it pretty damn well. We need people like you—guys who will cross the line and do what needs to be done when all else fails. It's who you are. It's who you were meant to be."

Dean's body buzzed.

The room felt like it was spinning.

This is fucked.

This is wrong.

He fastened his gaze to the director.

These pieces of shit played me like a fiddle.

"Let me be clear here, Agent Blackwood," Wheelan went on. "As much of a valued commodity as you are, I'm not a complete asshole—you're not a dog, and I'm not holding you on a leash." He pouted his lip. "For the most part. You're back in the field now. You *will* be assigned to whatever high-stakes cases we throw your way, and after a certain point in time, we will cut you loose. When you're done, you're done, and you can ride out your pension until you're an old man puttering around in his bathrobe."

"When?" Dean said, amazed that he was still playing ball, though he knew he didn't have a choice. "When will you let me leave?"

Wheelan reached into his blazer.

Produced a sheet of paper.

Slid it across the table and tapped it with his finger that wore a West Point ring.

"Three years minimum," the director said. "Your pay will increase. We'll procure a residence here in LA so you can be closer to your family." He snickered. "Word has it that your relationship with your son is on the rocks, so I'm sure you'll appreciate being in close proximity to him and the rest of the family."

Dean held back a litany of colorful curses that lingered on the tip of his tongue.

"You sign this paper," Wheelan further explained, "and it's finished. Anything you do, anything done at the behest of us in the line of duty will never—and I repeat *never*—come back to harm you in any way. You'll be under our protection, and I'll see to it personally, as well as anyone who takes over my post, that you will forever be immune to whatever acts you carry out during your tenure."

"You mean anyone I *kill*," Dean clarified. "Anyone who gets hurt. Any damage I cause if shit goes south, right?"

"So to speak." Wheelan leaned across the table. "I have a flight in thirty minutes, Agent Blackwood, and *you* need to get out to Central California for an assignment I need you to tend to by the end of the day. I'd suggest you sign that paper." His eyelids tapered. "I don't think I need to go through a whole rigamarole explaining what will happen if you don't."

The director slid a gold pen across the table.

Dean ogled it.

Then he felt a nudge in his ribs from Wilson.

"It's the right thing to do," the SAC said before he turned and looked at the director, "as fucked of a deal as it might be."

"He's right," Wheelan said. "Do the right thing here. Make some money. Be happy in knowing that we got your back. Just be a team player here, Blackwood," he nudged the pen closer to Dean, "and sign the goddamn paper."

Dean closed his eyes.

You have no choice.

You can't fight this.

He looked at the pen.

Just sign it, do the job, and you'll get your life back.

It's only three years.

You can hack it.

You've handled worse before.

Dean picked up the pen.

Hovered his hand over the page.

Then he scribbled his John Hancock, breathed a sigh, and made a display of holding onto the pen permanently as a delighted Wheelan scooped up the paper.

"Welcome back, Agent Blackwood," the director said as he moved toward the door. "I look forward to hearing how things go in Bakersfield."

Wheelan left.

Dean stood.

He moved toward the window and stared longingly out at the city.

"I'm sorry, kid," Wilson said. "I never wanted it to go down like this."

"It's not your fault," Dean replied. "And there's no point in dwelling on it. Three years and then I'm out."

Dean picked up his badge.

Fastened it to his belt.

Fished out a nicotine toothpick and slipped it between his teeth.

"It's time to go to work."

AUTHOR'S NOTES

Thank you for reading *Drive To Kill,* book 1 of 5 in the Dean Blackwood series.

Be sure to check out Book 2, *Midnight Kill.* I've included a sneak peek on the next page.

As an independent author, reaching more readers can be challenging, and that's where I could really use your help. If you enjoyed the story, I'd be grateful if you could leave a brief review on Amazon. Your support makes all the difference.

To leave a review go to Amazon and search for "Drive To Kill".

SNEAK PEEK - MIDNIGHT KILL

Introduction

Wait until midnight, disable the alarm, and toy with the newlywed couple.

In San Francisco, a new breed of serial killer is on the loose —one who specializes in home invasions and crimes too dark to describe.

When the SFPD can't catch a psychopath, they call me.
     I've got a talent for tracking down sadistic jackasses like this.

But this time, it's personal.
     Threaten the ones I love, and the hunter becomes the hunted.

San Francisco's most wanted just made it to the top of my list.
     And I always keep my list clean.

PROLOGUE
San Francisco, California

The killer held up his knife to the moonlight. The way the light glinted off the blade mesmerized him. His chest tightened with anticipation.

He was jittery.

Excited.

Ready.

Tonight it starts, he thought. *The game.*

Then, checkmate.

He caressed the spine of the knife with his gloved index finger. His senses were alert—on fire. His skin prickled as he fought his urge to smile.

He told himself it was not the time to feel pleasure. Not yet.

Begin, the killer thought. He slipped the blade into its sheath, tucked it into the back of his waistband, and pulled the black wool mask over his face.

Go.

He scanned the neighborhood—empty, no one wandering around. Dark. The only illumination was the dull glow of the streetlamps, pockets of light here and there.

Quiet, the killer thought. *Peaceful.*

He loved the game. The killer pinned his gaze to the target, the backyard of a two-story house.

He took another look around.

He lowered into a crouch and moved.

Silently, he reached the side entrance of the home. He'd learned how to approach a target undetected years before.

You made me, the killer thought as he pulled out his lock-picking tools.

All of you.

His breathing was steady and controlled. He slipped the tension wrench and picked into the door knob, moving them with ease until the knob was unlocked.

He moved inside.

The house was dark and still. He took out his knife and slithered almost weightless down the hallway.

I am a wraith.

He had steered clear of the only camera the home-owners had installed in the front.

Dummies.

He stopped at the first door on his left.

The killer closed his eyes.

Flexed his fingers.

Kill.

He stepped into the room.

Watched as the sleeping couple's chests slowly rose and fell with each breath they took as they dozed peacefully.

You don't deserve this life, the killer thought as he narrowed his eyes.

I will take it all away.

The man in the bed groaned in his sleep.

Turned onto his side.

The killer stepped closer to the bed.

The man's eyelids fluttered.

The killer raised the knife.

Then the man snapped open his eyes, his mouth dropping open as he looked up and stared deep into the fiery eyes of the masked intruder beside him.

"Undeserving," the killer whispered as he brought down the blade. "Unjust."

The deed was done.

Finished.

Both of the targets were dead.

The killer had accomplished the feat in under 10 minutes—exactly as he planned it.

Sixty seconds after he finished with the woman, he had sneaked out of the neighborhood. Ten minutes after that, he was back at his safe house.

No one would catch him on any cameras. If the San Francisco PD stumbled across *any* footage, all they would see was a figure dressed in black—no face, no discernable features.

The killer didn't use a car.

It would take weeks for the cops to catch up with him.

He just needed a few days.

Perfect, the killer thought as he closed the front door to his safe house. *Every last piece.*

He allowed himself to enjoy the success of his mission as he stripped off his black clothing, bagged it, and stored it for disposal.

Then he sifted through his gear, took out a burner phone, and dialed the number for the SFPD's Homicide Division.

The phone rang.

The killer closed his eyes.

On the sixth ring, the call went to voicemail.

"Your move, Blackwood," the killer said before he terminated the call, snapped the burner phone in half, and focused on the surveillance photo of Dean Blackwood pinned to his wall, a drawn-on bullet hole in his forehead.

Made in United States
Orlando, FL
13 November 2024

53877090R00217